THE OLD CONTINENT

THE NORTH

THE UNCHARTED WILDS OF THE NORTH

THE BORDERLANDS

THE MALACHITE SEA

THE FEVER MOUNTAINS

SYBERA

THE EASTERN PASS

THE WESTERN PASS

EAGLE'S WATCH

THE EAGLE'S PASS

THE IRON SHADAR MOUNTAINS

THE WINTER PALACE

DREYHA

THE SYBERAN SEA

KILAMORE

FEATHERS OF SNOW

A GOOSE GIRL RETELLING

ALICE IVINYA

FEATHERS OF SNOW

Kingdom of Birds and Beasts: Book One

Published February 12th, 2021

Second edition July 2021

Third edition May 2022

Edited by Claire Staley

Cover design by Elena Lawson

Map design by Rachael Ward from Cartographi

❀ Created with Vellum

For Sarah Hill,
We have never met in person,
But you are the supporter everyone dreams of.
Thank you.
(And your books are awesome.)

PROLOGUE

*O*nce Upon a Time, the world was a wilder place than it is today.

The forests were ruled by the mighty wolf, Sal'hadar, the plains by the beautiful white horse, Tamunden, the air by the enormous eagle, Thrum'ban, and the water by the black whale, Bula. Everything was at peace and in balance. Humans were few and each lived in one of the four tribes, following the guidance of the land, and the law of the Beasts was in their blood.

But then a new race of humans came from across the sea. They were shorter lived and small in stature. They could not feel the power of the land, nor see the balance of nature.

The land collapsed into war as the new race wished to twist all to its purpose. Their numbers grew and grew. After decades of fighting, the Beasts and old humans were left with a choice; learn to live alongside the new race and teach them to curb their appetite, or upset the balance of power to make themselves strong enough to resist them.

The land was torn in two. In the south, man and Beast learned to live together and the power of the land dwindled beneath human rule. To the frozen north, the Beasts and old men resisted and fed off deep forbidden magic.

And so the power of nature dwindled and the age of the Beasts ended.

A DEVASTATING PROPOSAL

*G*overness Rosa pointed at her blackboard and the endless list of names scribbled across it. Beside me, Princess Elyanna was already looking out of the window with a vacant expression. She flicked her quill and scattered ink across a butterfly battering its wings at the glass. She repeated the motion until the wings were steeped in black.

"Lady Brianna," Governess Rosa said, already having given up on Elyanna. "Can you remember which of the nobility belong to the Old Blood, and which tribes their ancestors were in?"

Elyanna snorted. "Why does it matter? Nobody cares about the Old Blood. It doesn't mean anything anymore." Her eyes didn't leave the butterfly, now struggling under the unexpected weight of its wings. It brushed black smears over the glass.

The Governess ignored her, and I sighed, listing the nobles I knew in Sybera with the white hair and tall stature of Thrum'ban's tribe, myself and Elyanna

3

included, and those I knew with the blue-black hair of Bula.

"The Borderland nobility is mostly of Sal'hadar, and there are some of Tamunden's tribe there too, though they mostly rule Kilamore." I hoped the vague statement would pass, rather than trying to scan the names of people from distant countries that I would never meet, for any I recognized.

Governess Rosa seemed pleased enough and smiled at me. I wished she realized the more she favored me and ignored Elyanna, the more annoyed and embittered the Princess became. And Elyanna was in even more of a foul mood than normal, knowing the court were discussing her marriage prospects today. The Governess thought the kindness of reward would motivate both of us, but Elyanna hated anyone being praised over her. I gave the Governess a blank expression as an attempt to discourage her.

The Governess didn't seem to notice and bent to unfurl our essays from last week. Elyanna had given up on hers early and left me to finish it for her. Over the years I'd learnt a good impression of her handwriting. "I have finished going through your papers on the relationship between poverty and unrest in Gilava."

I sat up straighter. Gilava was the province owned by my family. Though I'd been sent here to the capital city of Hava when I was very young to be lady-in-waiting to Elyanna, I still wanted to learn as much as possible about my homeland. After severe flooding, Gilava was on the verge of another potato famine, and I wanted to understand how I might help the situation.

It was my hope that after Elyanna was wed in a few weeks, I would be released from service and able to return home. The thought sent a thrill of excitement through me. What would it be like to be surrounded by my own family and able to follow my own desires and interests rather than Elyanna's?

Governess Rosa continued to smile as she scanned my essay. "You made some very good points, Lady Brianna. Your reading is impressive. However, there are one or two areas I feel we can discuss further."

I nodded, picking up my quill. Elyanna hated reading and it was close to impossible to study in her company, meaning I had to snatch the moments I could. It would be much easier to learn from the Governess than it had been from books. I leant forward to show I was listening.

Governess Rosa pointed to a paragraph. "What you say here about the potato uprising of…"

Elyanna interrupted. "Who do you think they will choose for me to marry, Governess Rosa?" She tilted her chin up as she regarded our teacher.

My heart sank. Couldn't she hold on for just half an hour more before disrupting the lesson? This was about the people I would help govern one day, and they desperately needed help.

The Governess paled, recognizing the look in the Princess's eyes. "Well, er, it's hard for me to say. There are quite a few eligible young noblemen. I suspect the court will prioritize our relationship with Kilamore. As you know their new King is wanting to expand their borders and we don't, er, quite have the military they have."

I started to doodle galloping horses, imagining myself riding on Falada's back through the gardens. I drew his magnificent tail and mane streaming in the wind. I didn't want to be part of this discussion.

Elyanna narrowed her eyes at our teacher. "You think they'll marry me to the King of Kilamore?"

The Governess shifted and clenched her hands together. "Well, I wouldn't go that far. He is very powerful. I mean, I couldn't possibly presume to know what…"

"You don't know anything," she finished and stood up abruptly. "I need air."

The Governess bowed. "Of course, your Highness. I can continue the lesson with…"

"Brianna, attend me," she snapped.

I lay down my pen and gave an apologetic smile to the Governess. If she had praised Elyanna and ignored my work, she might have lasted longer. At the window, the butterfly gave a final limp flutter against the glass.

Elyanna was already striding from the study, and I trudged behind her, hoping I might be able to have the lesson another time. It was hard to predict what I would be able to do at the best of times, let alone today. My whole life dangled from Elyanna's whims, and I knew better than to upset her. Soon, so soon, she would be married, and I could ask to be freed from her service. I would have lessons in my own home in Gilava, with nobody to interrupt. I could train in the dueling ring as much as I wanted and ride all afternoon. But I wouldn't have Falada, not unless Elyanna gave him up, which would never happen. He was my happiness, and I wasn't sure how I would cope with losing him.

Elyanna stalked to her rooms, her face dark. She wasn't normally this quiet.

"What's wrong?" I asked, quickening my pace. She was probably waiting for me to ask.

She scowled at me. "Don't be ridiculous, Bria. You know what is wrong."

I chewed my lip, a flicker of fear sparking in my stomach. I'd said the wrong thing. It had been years since she had hit me or devised one of her 'punishments', but I could never shake the instinctive fear she had ingrained in me as a child.

"I'm sure your parents will consult you about it. Maybe you will have a few options?" I attempted a smile. "It might be fun. Imagine all the lords and princes who will come to Hava to compete for your hand?"

She made a disgusted noise in her throat. "Father will propose something stupid, I am sure. As if I would marry just anyone." She swished her trailing silk skirts angrily as she walked.

I laid a hand gently on her arm. "There's no use worrying about possibilities. Why not…"

She hit away my hand. "Oh, just stop talking. You're not helping."

I took a step back and fell silent, leaving her to her self-inflicted torment. I hoped she would dismiss me soon so I could rearrange a private lesson with the Governess, or, if I was too late to catch her, spar with the weapons master.

Truth was, I didn't care who she married if it meant I could leave here. Whatever man got her, I wished him luck.

We reached Elyanna's room, and she snapped at the maids who were still making her bed, so they scurried out. She collapsed onto her velvet couch and looked at the clock. "Is it lunchtime yet? I'm famished."

"I can ask the kitchens to bring something early?"

"Ask them for soup, but not as salty as last time. And that bread with the brown seeds. You know, the crusty one."

I nodded and left to find a maid. Why had she scared them off, rather than asking one herself? As I turned a corner in the corridor, I was faced with Queen Geraldina striding towards me in a blood-red gown, her face pale. Chiffon and silk wafted behind her like wings. I dropped into a curtsy.

She nodded. "Where's my daughter, Brianna?" Her tone was strained.

"In her room. I was just fetching her some food."

"Leave that. Follow me."

I sighed internally and followed the Queen. From her posture, she didn't have good news. She opened the Princess's door without knocking and sat down next to her daughter. Elyanna froze and her eyes went wide at her mother's expression. I slipped to the back of the room and hoped I would be ignored.

The Queen took her daughter's hands. "The court is proposing a match for you, darling. Prince Jian of the Borderlands."

I blinked as I processed the words. The Borderlands?

I wasn't expecting them to consider such a wild, dangerous place. The royal family there didn't have the best reputation either. They were known for violence, a people of war who kept to themselves.

"What?" Elyanna shook her head, her long white hair wiping the back of the couch. "You can't marry me to a crazed murderer! And so far from home. Mama, you must stop it at once."

The Queen patted her daughter's hands. "Your father hasn't approved it yet. The decision won't be finalized until tomorrow. I will oppose the council, and we'll try to come up with some more sensible suggestions."

"He's not even the eldest son. No, Mama, you must stop such talk at once. Why not marry me to the Kilamore King? I would be the most powerful woman on the continent."

She sighed and tilted her head. "Darling, Kilamore are traditionally our enemy, and they have such little honor, they might attack us anyway." She rose and smoothed out the gauzy layers of her overskirt. "I will stop the match and ask for one more suitable. Now try not to fret, dear. Brianna will look after you."

The Queen gave me a meaningful look and glided out of the room. Elyanna turned to me with a thunderous expression. "Did you tell them about my soup?"

"No, I…"

"Good, because I feel ill. Tell the maids no food is to be brought in here and I'm not to be disturbed." She collapsed back and lay with her arms folded, scowling at the ceiling.

I nodded, my mood rising at the thought of being dismissed. "As you wish."

"Then come back here and read to me." My heart sank again.

As always, I did as she asked. Ever since she had trapped me in that barrel when we were twelve, I didn't dare do otherwise.

I swallowed down the roughness in my throat, remembering the darkness and the cramps that still invaded my dreams.

❄

THE NEXT DAY, Princess Elyanna paced up and down her bedroom, biting her nails and letting out groans of frustration. Cushions were strewn across the floor and the contents of her jewelry box were scattered in glittering heaps in the thick carpet. She kicked a necklace at her floor-length mirror, and I winced as diamonds struck glass.

"Why is Mama not back yet? What could they possibly be talking about? They have had all of yesterday, and now it's almost midday."

I ignored my pounding headache and longed to leave and curl up quietly with a book. I was becoming snappy with exhaustion and hunger, but Elyanna was showing no signs of relenting. I took a step towards her, making a calming motion with my hands. "Please calm down, Elyanna. Even if they do marry you to that prince, he would have to treat you well for fear of angering your parents."

She glared at me, burying her fists in her blue skirts and swishing them in frustration. "It's all right for you, Bria. If I get sent off to a distant land to marry a monster, you can just stay here. You don't care." She collapsed onto the bed and hurled off the remaining cushion. "You have no idea how lucky you are being able to marry whoever you want."

I suppressed a sigh and stole a look out the window. It was a beautiful day and the garden was soaked in sunlight. The flowers were just coming into full bloom, and I longed to be surrounded by their heady scent in peace and calm along with a very large lunch. Elyanna hadn't let me leave all night and had continued to refuse food for both of us. Didn't she understand that this was always going to happen? There had always been a political marriage awaiting her. This was the price for her life of privilege and luxury. Our country badly needed the protection of an alliance now that Kilamore had its new restless ruler. The Borderlands had a strong military, valued familial loyalty, and were a sensible choice politically. Her marriage could save thousands of lives, and perhaps the kingdom itself. Not that I envied her.

Elyanna let out another groan and tugged out her hair pin, still lying down, then threw it at the wall where stones scattered from their settings. I took a deep breath and went to gather them up, before she could tell me off for losing any. "It's ridiculous," she hissed at the ceiling. "I wouldn't even become queen. Surely my station is above second sons? I don't want to languish on the edge of nowhere."

The rebellious part of me wanted to point out that

she was the third eldest on her part, but instead I made my voice as soothing as possible. "Come, Highness, let me sort out your hair."

I tugged her up from the bed and sat her in front of the mirror, where she pouted at her reflection. I pretended not to notice as she smudged the kohl under her green eyes to make it look like she'd been crying. If I managed to keep her calm for long enough, maybe she would decide she was exhausted and take a nap. Then I could finally leave for food and possibly even hide and read with Falada in the stables. He would be missing me, as much as he always denied it.

I was still brushing Elyanna's snow-white hair, the Princess blessedly silent, when Queen Geraldina flung open the doors, making us both jump. Her own pale hair was piled on top of her head in the intricate way she favored for state meetings, and she wore an authoritative midnight blue gown. Her bold makeup didn't hide the shadows under her eyes or the gauntness of her cheeks.

The Queen flung her hands into the air as she spoke. "Your father's gone mad. The whole council has gone mad."

Elyanna's skin grew so pale it was almost translucent, and her eyes rounded with horror. "Mama?" She didn't rise but held out a hand to the Queen, whose own eyes filled with tears. She hurried over to her daughter and buried her head into her breast. I took a step back towards the window, trying to give them privacy as my heart thudded in my ears. Elyanna was not going to cope well with this.

"You mean you're actually going to marry me to that man?" sobbed Elyanna into her mother's dress. There was an edge of shock to her voice that, for the first time in her life, her tantrum wasn't enough to get her own way. "Why haven't you stopped it? He will hurt me and kill me. You will never see me again, and it will be Papa's fault, and yours for not stopping him."

The Queen brushed her hand through Elyanna's hair and hushed her. "Now, now, it won't be as bad as all that. I didn't know your father well before I married him, and in some ways, it was quite exciting."

"Your husband wasn't a beast," she almost screamed. "They're of Sal'hadar, monsters that live to kill, Mama! The Crown Prince killed his wife in a fit of rage! Everyone knows that. His brother will now kill me, and you'll get nothing more than a delayed letter saying it was all a horrible accident."

The Queen sighed but couldn't hide the quiver from her voice. "Now, now, darling, that's nonsense. You are quite capable of defending yourself, but you won't need to. What if he's nothing like his brother? It may be nothing but rumors, and the Crown Prince's wife was just a Borderlander girl anyway. If he hurt *you* in any way, a foreign Princess, there would be war, and they can't risk that."

Elyanna rocked back from the Queen and flung herself away. "Father won't let us ride to war, even if they killed me, and you know it. We don't have enough men to match the Borderlands, and that's the whole reason you're marrying me off as a sacrifice. They're monsters, all of them. They're not even human."

"Darling, they're just as human as us, remember? He's as much a beast as you are a bird. The Old Blood means little these days. Besides it's good for royalty to have some of the Old Blood. He'll live for longer and so will your children." Her voice was soft, but her eyes were wide with panic. Her mouth sagged with hopelessness.

The Princess ignored her, sobs breaking up her words. "They say it is cold all the time, and you never see the sun. The land is nothing but ice and snow and mountains. The pass between our countries becomes impassable every winter. If they do hurt me, I'll be trapped with no way home."

"Oh, Elyanna." The Queen pulled her sobbing daughter into a fierce hug.

I pressed my hand against my throbbing temples and considered slipping out of the room and taking a break, leaving the Princess to her mother. A few minutes of quiet with a cup of tea, a sandwich, and some exercise would make the afternoon much easier to manage. The Princess wasn't going to calm down anytime soon. I lowered my hand and the Queen's eyes snapped to me at the movement. Her eyes narrowed and then widened, and her lips parted as she continued to stare at me. I took a step back at the intense expression and lowered my gaze.

"They'd never know," she breathed.

Elyanna raised her head and frowned at her mother before following her gaze to me. Her swollen features brightened. "Yes." She stood and clapped her hands together, a smile twisting her lips. "Oh, you're so clever,

Mama." Unease knotted my belly, and my heart started to pound, worsening my headache.

The Queen put a warning hand on her daughter's shoulder. "We need to think this through carefully, Elyanna, and not get carried away."

Both of them studied me again with hungry gazes, and I felt my unease shift to horror. My chest tightened, and I parted my lips to make it easier to breathe. "You can't seriously be thinking about sending me instead?"

Elyanna placed her hands on her hips. "Why not? We have the same hair color and you have enough of the Old Blood, if not quite of my pedigree. You're almost thin enough, you would just have to not eat for a while. No one from the Borderlands has seen me since I was little, so they won't know the difference. You could go in my place, marry that prince, save the kingdom, and we'll have peace. Meanwhile I'll stay here, and they'll be none the wiser."

I gaped at her, shaking my head slowly. I couldn't believe what I was hearing. "But the whole Court will know you're still here. The Borderlands would find out sooner rather than later, and they would kill me and declare war on you for tricking them."

The Queen glided over and took my hands in her ice-cold fingers. "Now, Brianna, I know this is a lot to think about, but if this plan was successful, you would be serving not only your mistress, but the whole kingdom. And just think about it, this is the marriage of your dreams. It would hugely benefit you. You would live the rest of your life as a princess. Wealthy, privileged. Most girls in your position could only dream of such advancement."

I pulled my hands from hers, my horror thickening at her words and the plan I could see forming behind her eyes. "They'll find out and kill me." I tried to sound as assertive as I dared.

The Queen narrowed her eyes and firmed her blood red lips. "Not if you play your part well. You have been with my daughter since before you can remember. You have attended every lesson with her, and I should hope you know as much as she about etiquette, politics, and the Borderlands. You have the white hair of the noble family, showing you have the Blood, and you look pretty enough. They know next to nothing about Elyanna, and people travel between the kingdoms infrequently. They are not a country for complicated politics and care more about honor and loyalty. They would not naturally suspect."

I sat down heavily on the bed, my head whirling. "But... but Elyanna will still be here. Everyone will know I'm a fake and word will reach them eventually."

The Queen tapped a finger against her lips. "Elyanna can disappear to the winter hunting palace." She turned to her daughter and reached out her hands. "You would have to give up your title, darling, and stay away from the capital, but I'm sure we can find you a marriage you approve of away from court. You could be one of my cousin's daughters. Nobody can keep track of her brood. I'll visit as often as I can."

"But I'll still be treated like a princess, of course?" Elyanna started to pace excitedly. "Does this mean I wouldn't have so many lessons? But I could take all my things, couldn't I? And all the servants. If I must disappear from court, I'd much rather it was to the hunting palace than a savage country days of travel away where I would never see you."

The Queen nodded. "Of course you could take your things. But you would have to give Brianna your ring with the royal seal."

The Princess pulled the ring from her finger with reluctance and watched the engraved opal sparkle in the light before shoving it into my hand.

"See if it fits," commanded the Queen. With a growing sense of hopeless inevitability, I slipped it onto my fourth finger where it nestled comfortably at the base. The Queen grinned in triumph as if this settled the whole affair.

I tugged the ring back off. "But what of me? What of my parents?"

Elyanna waved a hand in the air. "We'll just tell them you're dead. We could say it was an accident and send them some money in compensation. They barely see you anyway."

I took a step towards her, my panic reaching new heights. "What? No, that would break their hearts."

Queen Geraldina rested a calming hand on my shoulder. "We'll merely tell them you accompanied the Princess to the Borderlands to continue as her lady-in-waiting. You can still write to them. Your father is often at court and I'll keep an eye out for their welfare, if you cooperate. I will even add a few acres to their estate in Gilava. Maybe some soldiers to help clear the damage from the recent floods.

The last potato harvest was so poor due to the rains, the whole region is in desperate need of some financial support. I will provide that in return for your services."

My insides ran cold. "And what if I don't?"

The Queen's painted eyebrows slanted down. "Surely you can see this if for the good of everyone, dear Brianna? Of course, as you said, if you reveal your identity once you're in the Borderlands, they will kill you for pretending to be the Princess. In the meantime, well, I'll see to it that you are taken *straight* there with strict instructions to the guards. I'll send a letter to your parents asking them to join us in Hava with your brother where I can look after them. If you even *think* about running away, I will try them in court for not taking more precautions to protect their people from the floods. Many people lost lives and houses, I heard."

I paled and my voice sounded small. "You couldn't. The entire river flooded. They can't be responsible for that."

She raised her eyebrows. "Couldn't I? It would be very convenient for me to lay that mess at their feet." She reached out to stroke my arm. "But I won't, because I know what you are doing for our country and Elyanna. They will receive all the funding they need, and we will stop another potato famine. No more people need to die if you do as I say."

I opened my mouth to protest further, but no words came out. How could I reason with such madness? And the people of Gilava needed support so badly. And my parents... Part of me screamed against my silence. This was the one time I needed to draw a line and stand up against them. But I knew it was useless. It would only make things worse.

I remembered the darkness, the cramps, my screams. The sound of nails being hammered inches above my head. Elyanna's giggle.

The Queen prized the ring from my palm and slipped it back on my finger. The opal was engraved with the swan of the royal family, matched only by the ones worn by Elyanna's parents and two older brothers. I stared at it, wishing for it to vanish.

The Queen tapped her lips again and turned back to her daughter. "She'll also need Falada."

Elyanna frowned. "Really? Can't she have another horse?"

"Now, Elyanna, I know you love him, but half the world knows you own a Spirit-Horse. It would be odd if he didn't go with you."

"But what if he tells somebody that she's not the princess? There will be plenty of people with the Old Blood there who might learn to speak with him."

The Queen lay both her hands on Elyanna's shoulders. "He won't, darling. Nobody else will have the opportunity to form a bond," she flicked her eyes to me, and her voice hardened. "Will they, Brianna?"

"The King won't agree to this," I muttered, staring at the ring on my finger that declared I was the highest Syberan royalty.

The Queen shook her head. "He'll come around when he sees it's a way to keep his darling daughter close and safe, as well as keeping peace with the Borderlands."

I continued staring at the ring, a great crushing weight settling on my shoulders. I had thought I was about to finally be free of servitude. But now I was going to have to leave everyone and everything I knew to pretend to be Elyanna for the rest of my life. I was exchanging one cruel royal for another. I would marry a stranger in a distant, violent land, and nobody who cared about me would know. In return I would gain a husband who would kill me if he ever learnt the truth.

Elyanna seemed to be enjoying herself now, the corners of her lips curved up in that cruel smile she used when hunting as she brought down her prey slowly, arrow after arrow. "I've heard Prince Jian barely speaks and has a sour temper and keeps to himself and has few friends. He's so violent they keep him at the Border Forts as much as possible. I heard one rumor that he killed his own sister! Sometimes he locks himself away for days at a time."

I blocked out her words and tried to steady my breathing. I hadn't intended to marry for years yet; I was only eighteen. But if I refused, my parents could be executed. My chest constricted painfully as I thought of their faces. I might only see them twice a year if I was lucky, but I still loved them.

The Queen came and clasped both my shoulders again. "Brianna, it's time for you to stop being a girl and become a woman for the good of Sybera. You will achieve more in this one action than most do in a life-time, and you will live a life of luxury. Surely you can't object to such an advantageous marriage for one in your position?"

I opened and closed my mouth, but nothing came out. I felt like I was falling, falling, sinking into a sticky cobweb that wound tighter the more I struggled. Hadn't I long since learnt that struggling against Elyanna made her more cruel?

Queen Geraldina walked over to the dressing table and took a needle from the sewing box and stabbed her finger. She squeezed it over her snowy handkerchief embroidered with blue flowers. Three drops of blood bloomed vibrant on the white. She handed me the handkerchief and smiled. "This is my blessing and my protection on your life, Brianna. The Blood of the Swan still holds power."

I nodded automatically and took the blood-stained linen, trying to stop my hands from shaking. This action more than anything showed there was nothing I could do to stop this. The Queen wouldn't be wasting her Mother's Blessing if there was any chance I wasn't going.

Elyanna seemed to realize this too, and her eyes lingered on the handkerchief in surprise, a flash of jealousy clouding her eyes. The Queen clapped her hands. "You will both leave together in two days. Any later, and you risk getting caught in snow before you arrive. The Borderlands are much colder than here. Brianna, you will go north. Elyanna, you will go south with separate guards. You must swap mounts when you're beyond the city walls. Falada must go with Brianna or they will know something is amiss."

I was too numb to respond, still clutching the Queen's blessing between my fingers. It was hard to breathe. Hard to think. Queen Geraldina's fingers pushed my shoulder. "Go and rest now, girl. You need to pack and have some of Elyanna's dresses altered to fit. You will be a princess of Sybera from now on."

I nodded and walked out without seeing where I was going. I needed Falada. I didn't return to my rooms but broke into a run through the marble corridors, skidding around the giant ceramic pots of plants, and burst outside. I tore across the immaculate lawns and didn't stop until I reached the stables, sheltered by giant oak trees. The sweet, herbal scent of horses and hay engulfed me and helped the tears come. The stable boy studiously ignored me as I burst in with red eyes and stumbled into Falada's gold-painted stall.

The huge horse was lying in mountains of straw, his legs tucked beneath him. He lifted his head as I entered and his ears flicked forward. *'Brianna? What is wrong, child?'*

I collapsed into the straw and flung my arms around his neck. I sobbed into his white hair and tangled my hand in his mane. He nibbled on my hair, then rubbed his nose down my back. I lost myself in the dusty warmth of his coat.

'Brianna, tell me. Things are often not as bad as they first seem. You're making me all wet with your leaking human eyes.'

I sat back on my heels and rubbed my face on my sleeve, smearing dust. "I'm sorry, Falada."

22

The horse shifted and studied me with one eye. *'Tell me what happened.'*

When I was sure the stable boy wasn't in earshot, I whispered the truth in his swiveling ear. "Elyanna was meant to marry a Borderland Prince, but she's too scared to, so they're sending me instead. I have to pretend to be her and marry this man, who nobody says anything good about. I'll never be allowed home again." The sobs broke free again. "I'll never see Sybera or my family. I will never be Brianna again."

The horse snorted, scattering chaff from the straw. *'Nonsense. You'll always be Brianna, whatever people call you. I can see your soul, child, and it might be hidden, but it will not be extinguished.'*

"It's my own fault. I should have been able to persuade them out of it. I've never dared stand up against her, not since... not since I tried to save that kitten." I picked up a strand of straw and shredded it with my nails. "Maybe there isn't much 'Brianna' left to be taken away. I can never change anything."

Falada nuzzled my arm. *'We all become different as life goes on. Maybe you won't need to pretend much at all.'*

I sat back and leant against him. "You're coming too, with me, so they believe I'm Elyanna. They know she has a Spirit-Horse."

He snorted again, this time more sharply. *'Will they still have rolled oats?'*

I scratched between his ears. "I'll make sure they do." I flicked over the stray parts of mane that fell on the wrong side of his neck. The hair was silky and almost translucent. "I'm glad you're coming too."

"I don't believe they have asked me yet.' He bucked his head, which normally meant he was laughing. *'But I have grown rather fond of you over the years."*

I patted his neck, knowing that was as close as he would ever get to saying he loved me, but I knew that was what he meant.

'You'll be away from Elyanna. You always said you wanted that. You hate her. Don't be so sad.'

"You don't understand. I won't be away from her; I will *be* her. All my actions will be dictated by who she is." I wiped my nose on my sleeve. "I don't want to be Elyanna. I would prefer to be anyone but her, and I want to be me." I jabbed him in the shoulder. "Besides, don't speak ill of your owner or she might turn you into glue." I smiled to remove the sting of my words. "But yes, at least I won't be her lady-in-waiting anymore. Maybe I'll have one of my own. Though the Border-lands don't strike me as the sort of people to encourage people to be waited on hand and foot."

He shook his head, dislodging all the work I'd done to make his mane neat. *'You will have lots of time. Time for us to ride. And read. You will find happiness. They say the Land's Song can still be heard in the north. I'd like to see if that is true.'*

"But what if my husband is horrible? He's a prince. Maybe I'll just swap one cruel noble for another." A real fear clenched my stomach at the thought of what that would mean for me. It would be hard to escape him, and I would be expected to bear an heir. As a noble of Sybera, I was trained in self-defense and was much better with a sword than Elyanna, better than pretty much all of the nobles, but Prince Jian was an experienced warrior. He had Old Blood too. He would be stronger and still in his home, surrounded by friends and family. What if he was violent? I suspected nobody would help me.

'Just avoid him. Stay with me. He won't get past me if you don't want him to.' He lifted up his great head in pride.

I sighed and tilted my head back so it rested on his flank. "If only it was that simple. I can't live in the stables all the time. Not when I'm supposed to be a princess."

We sat in silence and the sway of Falada's chest started to lull me to sleep, but my brain kept turning the news over and over. I wished there was somebody else I could talk to, but the Queen would be furious if I breathed a word. I'd never felt so alone.

Tears warmed my eyes again and I took a shaking breath. "Falada, I really, really don't want to go. I'm scared."

He didn't reply but used his nose to push straw over my body before curling his neck around me. Finally, with his hot breath tickling my ear, I fell asleep.

THE POINT OF NO RETURN

*I*t was pitch black and hot. The barrel walls pressed in on all sides, shrinking closer and closer. On my lap was a drowned cat, its pale mouth gaping in agony.

Falada nudged me awake and I jolted up.

'You were whimpering in your sleep again. You have not done that in a while.'

I gasped in the dusty morning air, dragging in deep breaths until I had calmed down. The familiar sounds of horses stamping and chewing surrounded me, sharing their peace.

"Oh, Falada, it was that dream again. The same one. I thought it was gone."

He nuzzled my side. *'You are stressed and worried. It always returns when you're like this.'*

I leant forward and cradled my head in my hands. "It happened years ago. Why won't it leave me alone?"

Falada pushed me away and stood, shaking the straw from his back. *'We should ride. It will make you feel better.'*

I squinted through the window and saw the sun was already high in the sky. My stomach rumbled and I felt lightheaded. "I can't, Falada. I need to get ready and pack. We leave tomorrow. I haven't eaten in two days either. Elyanna will be cross if she can't find me after her breakfast."

The horse nudged me to the stable door. *'Food is important. You should eat. I will be here.'*

I kissed his soft nose and stumbled out into the gardens. The rear of the palace rose before me, white and spotless in the sun. The flowers on the creepers that draped from the turrets and flying buttresses were starting to wilt as summer died, and the leaves were turning scarlet. I tried to memorize every detail, for surely Hava was the most beautiful place in the world.

Two maids were waiting for me in my rooms and pounced their fussing hands on me, stressed by my late appearance and the state of my hair. One took my measurements so the tailor could alter Elyanna's dresses, while I begged the other one to find me a large breakfast.

They all must know about the planned deception, and I wondered what the Queen was bribing them with. More threats, no doubt, and far away placements. Maybe they would all end up at the Winter Palace.

I spent the day in a daze, my fate looming over me like a collapsing cliff, too high for me to outrun. I could only stand still and watch the rocks fall around me.

Elyanna called for me to take lunch with her, and I did my best to ignore her as she prattled on about all the horrible things she had heard about the Borderlands

27

and Prince Jian. The color was back in her cheeks, and her eyes gleamed at the outcome. A maid had curled her hair into ringlets. and she wore more makeup than usual. She was in a good mood.

"You will write to me, to let me know how you're doing, Bria?" She asked as she sipped her tea from the painted china.

"Of course," I mumbled. I kept my eyes on the plate of pastries, studying the intricacies of the icing to distract myself. I was in no mood for her games. Hopefully if I didn't react too much at her jibes, she would grow bored and leave me alone.

"I want to know every single detail, especially about Prince Jian. And what your room is like."

I nodded in reply. I'd eaten too much, and now I felt queasy.

"Make sure you pack lots of coats. I've heard it's cold and barren all year around. I wouldn't want illness to get in the way of your marital bliss. I suspect he'll want an heir quickly." She pursed her lips as she looked me up and down. "And don't forget to eat less and wear your corsets tighter. You'll need to wear more makeup too so you draw attention away from your nose. You don't want him to think you're ugly." She snorted.

I nodded out of habit, my mind becoming numb.

"Did you ever hear about what happened to Lady Hesta?"

I dutifully shook my head, and her red lips curled into a wide smile that dimpled her cheeks as she shook back her hair.

"Well, Lady Hesta was married off to some Dreyha

Lord after the Battle of Sedgehaven fifteen years ago. It was purely political in nature. Her husband didn't care about her at all." She lowered her voice. "He had a mistress, you see, and Lady Hesta failed to win him with her charms. He shut her away in part of his castle and almost forgot about her. She had no friends or allies there. Her only worth the alliance between our countries, and that only needed the wedding. She became a nobody. I heard he used to hit her if she displeased him." Elyanna smiled as she brought the delicate teacup to her lips. "She killed herself." Her eyes flicked to mine. "Let's hope you can win yours over with your *endless* charms. If he doesn't care about you, who will?"

My chest felt tight, and I struggled to breathe. I stood up abruptly, my knees hitting the table and making the china rattle. "Please excuse me, Highness."

For once Elyanna let me go, delighted by my reaction. She snuggled back into her padded chair.

I escaped into my room and took deep breaths, leaning against a wall. After all these years, why did I still let her get to me? Her comments were immature and uninventive, yet they still drifted through my mind to settle at the base. Each one a grain of sand making an endless riverbed that I would be sucked in and drowned under if I ventured there.

Distraction was the key. I found Governess Rosa and staff master John to give them my goodbyes. Sir John offered me one last spar, but I declined. He chuckled and said it was because I was afraid he would beat me and end my winning streak. In truth, as much as I loved to exercise with my sword when Elyanna wasn't here, I felt weak and nauseous. I was sure I would have plenty of chances to train in the Borderlands. Sir John had been a fantastic teacher, but I had learnt all I could from him. I hoped up north I would find somebody better to push me.

After dinner I took a book from the library and snuck back to Falada. I didn't want to spend the night alone. Especially if the nightmare returned. After they had found me inside the barrel, weak and terrified, the lid nailed shut, a servant had been blamed and punished, but many people had suspected Elyanna. Her mother had been furious with her. It was the only time I had seen Queen Geraldina shout at her daughter. She had said if she got a reputation for cruelty, it would damage her marriage prospects, and she would end up the wife of some fat old widower who just wanted a few extra heirs. Elyanna had only been twelve but had taken this to heart. She had stopped ordering that her maids be beaten and had stopped slapping me. But instead she had learned there are many other ways to be cruel.

Soon I would leave her behind forever, but still the nightmare had come back. My heart rate still increased when I saw the Princess smile. She had broken me that day, and though I had collected all the pieces of me, they didn't stick together anymore. I simply wasn't strong enough to face Prince Jian.

Falada didn't speak as I let myself in and curled up in the straw. He stood above me eating his hay as I opened my book and started to read about a world where princes were always charming and princesses were always good. It might not be true, but maybe tonight I could simply pretend and scare the nightmares away.

❄

FALADA NUDGED me awake and I sat up, frowning at distant shouts. Fresh sunlight streamed through the window and birds sang joyfully in the gardens. The shouts grew louder, and I heard my name.

"Falada," I gasped. "You should have woken me earlier. I wanted to sneak back into my rooms."

Falada snorted and walked to his water trough, taking a slow leisurely drink. *'You need your sleep for the journey.'*

The journey. Today I would be leaving forever.

I stood and brushed straw from my hair and dress. The forgotten book thudded from my skirt and I remembered I'd read late into the night. Myths and legends of the time when Spirit-Beasts ruled. If they had been anything like Falada, it must have been a better place. But Falada's blood was almost as diluted as mine. He was fast and intelligent and beautiful, but apart from the ability to bond and speak with a human of the Old Blood, there wasn't much remaining in him of those older noble races.

"She's in here!" That was the voice of the stable boy, I was sure of it. Why were they shouting? I rubbed my forehead. The headache that had started with Elyanna's tantrum still lingered days later. It was probably my fault for not eating and drinking well and sleeping in a dusty stable.

The boy appeared at the stable door and pointed at me in triumph. Behind him a page boy and a gardener hurried to his side. "See, I told ya."

I blinked at them in confusion and noticed the relief in the two newcomers' shoulders. The page boy stretched out his hand. Wasn't he Sir Hellard's servant? A sinking feeling made my legs leaden. Sir Hellard served the Queen, which probably meant I was in trouble.

"Please, my lady," said the page boy when I didn't step forward. He looked about eight years old. "They're all looking for you. You were meant to be in your rooms. The Queen fears you might have run away and is angry that you aren't preparing to accompany the Princess."

I sighed and pulled my book from the straw. "I don't see why it's so strange for me to be checking Princess Elyanna's horse today of all days."

The page shifted his feet back and forward, and the anxiety didn't fall from his face. He reached in and grabbed my hand, trying to pull me along, despite being two heads shorter than me. I shook my hand free. "I'm coming, I'm coming."

The page's urgency finally infused my body and I lifted my skirts so I could keep up with his jog across the lawns. Was Queen Geraldina really that angry? Surely she knew I would never be foolish enough to try to run. Not when she threatened my parents and the people of Gilava. Even if she was sending me far away to marry a stranger.

My racing heart had little to do with keeping up

with the page. I struggled to swallow and hoped I would have fresh water in my room, though the thought of breakfast made me feel sick. The boy led me through a servants' door and up spiraling stairs, not to my rooms, but to Elyanna's. My chest only tightened. I wasn't sure how well I could cope with her gloating today.

Sir Hellard stood guard outside her door in full plate armor, looking out of place. He had to be coming too to be so dressed up. He nodded to me as I approached and opened the door without a word. Inside Elyanna was arranging the white fur of her cloak around her neck and studying it from all angles in the mirror. The cloak was magnificent, but beneath it she wore a plain blue riding dress with divided skirts and high leather boots.

"There you are." The voice of the Queen made me jump and I turned to see Queen Geraldina directing two maids as they packed a pair of matching boxes with clothes and jewelry. "Where in the name of the Spirits were you? And what's happened with your hair?"

I resisted the urge to feel my messy plait for any remaining straw and curtsied. "Apologies, Your Majesty. I didn't sleep well, so rose early to go to the stable to make sure all was well with Falada." That was true if going there at midnight counted as 'early'.

She pursed her lips as if she didn't quite believe me, but then her eyes brightened as she dismissed the suspicion as unimportant. "Well you are to get ready in here, since you'll be wearing the Princess's clothes. We're going to have to bathe you first, though. You smell of horse."

I shrugged, nerves making me reckless. "The

Borderlands are days away. Surely I will smell of horse by then, whatever I smell like now?"

The Queen glared, warning she was not in the mood to be pushed. "My daughter would never wreck such a fine dress by putting it on smelling like *that*. You should be grateful for the outfit. Now bathe at once and be quick. We need to get you dressed and covered by a simple cloak before anyone wonders why the two of you are taking so long."

I bobbed my head and went into Elyanna's bedroom to bathe, barely feeling the warmth of the water or the tugs on my scalp as a maid combed my hair. A cold numbness penetrated everything until even my thoughts were frozen.

I was sprayed with perfume, squeezed into a corset, and then strapped into a silk gown entirely too grand for hard travel. The sleeves left the shoulders bare, as was the fashion, and it even had a small gauzy train. I hoped there was something more practical in the chests. Finally my hair was braided into a crown around my scalp, in the same style as the Princess.

The Queen inspected the work of her maids and nodded in approval. I was now an appropriate present to gift to a prince. My belly squeezed and roiled, and the corset felt bone-crushingly tight. The maids slammed the chests shut, and I wondered if they had packed any of the things I'd selected for myself and laid out in my rooms.

A horn blown outside the window made me jump and the Queen clapped her hands. "The procession is getting ready. Hurry, girls." She took Elyanna's forehead and kissed her on the brow. "I'll see you in the Winter Palace. I promise I will come soon."

The Princess smiled sweetly in return. "Thank you, Mama. I'll miss you."

I turned away from them to look out the window. A stained-glass pattern of roses bordered the glass and bathed the waiting crowd in scarlet. My parents weren't going to arrive in time from their estate to say goodbye to me. Not when they had only been given three days' notice that I was leaving. I hoped the letters would get through the pass reliably between our countries. Knowing that I might never see them again and couldn't say goodbye made me blink back tears.

Elyanna grabbed my hand, snapping me back into the present nightmare. "Come on Bria, we can't keep them waiting to say goodbye to their Princess. Mama says they're lining the streets for miles."

I followed her, my limbs heavy and clumsy, still lightheaded. As we entered the marble courtyard, a ceremonial guard stood to salute. The King kissed his daughter's hand as she climbed the mounting block onto Falada. He didn't even glance at me. I rode Elyanna's favorite palfrey, a skittish palomino called Fancy, and I arranged the cloak around myself so the grand dress was hidden. Two maids rode behind us, both belonging to the Queen, and behind them, Sir Hellard led a guard of ten soldiers, squires leading a few pack mules at the rear. I wondered if they knew what was truly going on.

The wide streets of Hava were a riot of color and waving flags as the whole population seemed to be lining the streets or hanging from second or third story windows. The noise was a leaden haze in my ears, and I kept my eyes fixed ahead, my grip on the reins tight. All eyes were on Elyanna anyway. I suspected most Havans had never heard of Lady Brianna, me being such a distant relation to the throne, that even Father normally explained it wrong. I had the white hair of the Old Blood, but when I was forever next to the Princess, it stopped being noteworthy.

Elyanna waved to the crowd and accepted silks and flowers from children. A few even offered blooms to me, and I accepted them with muttered thanks. People shouted well wishes for her wedding and others shouted about her bravery or beauty. By the time we reached Hava's silver gates, she was glowing with satisfaction.

I took one last look back at the palace. It was beautiful with its white flying buttresses, cascades of auburn creepers and marble statues on every level. Pale blue banners had been hung from every window to mark Elyanna's departure. It had been my home for over ten years, even if I had never felt comfortable there. I had little idea what Stonekeep, the capital of the Borderlands, would be like in comparison, other than cold. I turned my eyes forward with aching resolve.

Elyanna prattled to me about the Winter Palace until the party stopped at the crossroads. The Princess waved the guards off to give us some privacy and slid from Falada's back. She stretched and grinned at me. "You've been very quiet, Brianna. Didn't you enjoy the procession? When you enter Stonekeep, all eyes will be on *you*."

I didn't reply but slipped from Fancy, looking forward to Falada's larger, steadier back. I wasn't in the mood to talk, but Elyanna didn't notice. She flicked Falada's reins carelessly at me as she continued talking. "Make sure you're impressive in every way. They will think you're me after all. And you'll actually have to start paying more attention to how you look. No more simple plaits or smelling of horse. I can't have them think I am like that. You must maintain my reputation."

I frowned at her. "But *I* will be Princess Elyanna. They'll never know about you."

She shrugged. "I still care about my reputation, Bria. Now we should swap cloaks and be on our way. I want to reach my inn before nightfall."

I gave her my plain cloak and took her grand one. It sat heavily on my shoulders and the fur tickled my neck. Sir Hellard dismounted to help me onto Falada's back. I pulled myself up and towered over Elyanna, waiting for her to dismiss me. She walked to my foot and held up her hand. "I want my mother's handkerchief," she said, as if it were an afterthought.

It was tucked in my pocket and I touched the cloth subconsciously. "Why?"

Her eyes narrowed. "It's my Mother's Blessing. I am her daughter. I should have it, not you."

I hesitated. The Queen's Blessing probably held true power of protection and she had given it as the only reward for my journey. One look at the jealousy on Elyanna's face showed she wasn't going to relent, however, and I didn't have the energy to fight. I sighed and fished out the bloodstained linen, passing it to the Princess. She smiled sweetly and took it, then turned to mount Fancy.

"Mama said you were to take five guards," she announced.

I hid a sigh of frustration. "Five? The passes are dangerous and our road is longer. There is little danger between here and the Winter Palace."

Elyanna ignored my comment and rode to the party. She waved her hand in the air and the men divided themselves according to some prearranged plan, Sir Hellard staying with Elyanna. She pointed to the maids. "Both of you are to come with me, too." One of them hesitated, looking between us.

A stab of anger dug deep in my chest. I was giving up everything for her, why did she have to take even more from me? What was the point of this petty display of power? I tried to keep my voice reasonable as I spoke quietly so as not to be overheard. "I need a maid too, Elyanna. You will have plenty in the Winter Palace. You will be there by the end of tomorrow. I will be travelling for a week."

She raised an eyebrow and rode right up to me, her voice little more than a whisper. "I'm sure these gentlemen can give you a hand if you find yourself stuck in your corset. It will be good practice for your wedding night." She giggled and tucked stray hairs behind her ear, leaning back. "You have plenty of gold. Pick up some village girl on your way north. You'll be able to fool her."

I met her grin with a glare and barely suppressed my temper. I'd served and helped her for years. I was going to a foreign, dangerous land and marrying her betrothed so she didn't have to. How could she act like this? Why did she have to take every little thing?

Before I said something I regretted, I guided Falada around, and set off down the road at a canter. Whichever guards and horses were left from her clutches could follow me, but I'd had enough of Elyanna to last a lifetime.

The wind blew in my face and I concentrated on its cold kiss on my nose and cheeks, until everything else faded. After half an hour's hard riding, an older guard rode level and held out his hand. I recognized him vaguely. Sir Cuthbert? "My lady, the horses need to pace themselves, and the pack horses have fallen behind. This speed serves nobody."

Begrudgingly, I slowed and let the knight take the lead. I didn't speak, still frozen numb, yet hot with unvoiced anger. At least I would never have to see the Princess again.

'She's jealous of you, you know?' came Falada's voice invading my thoughts.

I snorted. "What could she possibly be jealous about? She has spent her entire life belittling me."

Falada shook his pale mane. *'She was jealous of many things, so she pretended none of them mattered. She wanted to be the best at everything. Don't hold this hate within yourself because of the hate she bears herself. Be free of it. It is no way to live. She only poisons herself.'*

I bit my lip and attempted to break free of the cycle

of thoughts analyzing every way she had ever wronged me, justifying and amplifying my anger. I turned my thoughts to Falada instead. "Are you going to miss her? You're bonded to her too after all."

The horse shook out his mane. *'I am happy to stay with you. I have been bonded to many people over the years. Some have souls that are vibrant. Some are weak. Often I miss them not. Elyanna always had a worrying tendency to take joy in other's pain. I fear it will only grow as she becomes older.'*

I leant forward over his neck. "How old are you, Falada?"

The horse stamped his front two feet. *'Older than you, child.'* The voice was accompanied by a sense of annoyance.

"Have you always been with the royal family?"

'Yes. Who else would want a Spirit-Horse? I can only bond with ones with the Old Blood.'

"I know, but... don't you ever just want to be free? Away from all humans?"

Falada snorted and shook his head, tugging the bridle. *'Away from humans? Then who would soak my oats or rub me down? I can demand whatever I wish, and it is brought to me.'* He angled his head to regard me with one big brown eye. *'The royal family have never owned me, Brianna. I choose to stay where I know people can afford to care for me and understand my demands. A wealthy royal family is the obvious choice.'*

I raised an eyebrow, suppressing a smile. "You give a lot of life lessons to pretend you only care about oats."

A young guard pulled up next to me with a friendly

smile. I sat up straight in the saddle and waited for him to speak.

"Can you really hear the horse speak, Highness?" he asked.

Highness. I was going to have to get used to that.

I raised my eyebrows. Of course I could. "We're bonded. I have the blood." I pointed automatically to my white hair as an explanation.

The young man looked ahead, still with a cheery smile. He had a head full of brown curls that bobbed up and down as he rode. "I wish I could talk to horses. Maybe I could encourage this one to move a bit faster when urged, rather than take every chance to swerve to the verge and eat grass." He leant forward and patted his horse's neck.

I frowned at him. "Only Spirit-Horses can talk," I snapped. The man shrugged and I regretted my tone. I was still seething from Elyanna and he was only trying to be friendly, after all. I needed friends. "What's your name, sir?"

"Oh, I'm not a sir. I'm still a squire. Jeremiah at your service." He gave a bow that was awkward from the top of a horse. "The Queen asked me to organize your new honor guard once we reach the capital of Stonekeep."

I hid my frown. He was far from the most senior of the men. He looked barely older than me, how could he head my honor guard? "It's nice to meet you. Don't you regret not being able to return home?"

He shook his head with a grimace. "My family is out of favor. My brother is Sir Yallen and he was caught in tax evasion relating to last year's harvest. I'm his third brother. The Queen said this could be a fresh start for me."

I nodded. "Hopefully we can both find our place in this new world." I looked around at the other guards. "Do you know these men well?"

He shook his head. "They are Sir Hellard's men. They serve the Queen mostly. They are returning home once we arrive. I'm the only one staying."

"Oh." Did the Queen not care to provide for me at all? Well at least I would have one Syberan with me in the castle. I doubted Falada would be allowed inside the actual building.

He shifted in his saddle. "I thought it very wise to have your lady-in-waiting to act as your double until we left the city. There might be those wishing to stop this alliance by harming you. Spies of Kilamore, you know? Though I did think she was quite arrogant."

It was all I could manage not to gape. He had to be the only one here who didn't understand what was going on. Clearly the Queen didn't even trust her own men to keep the secret in the Borderlands. Jeremiah couldn't be the brightest penny in the purse.

He frowned into the distance. "I must ask though, why did you let her take the maids? I thought that odd."

I fumbled for something to say. "Neither wanted to come. They didn't want to leave Sybera. I gave them the choice to stay with Lady Brianna."

The squire nodded. "I thought it must be something like that. You are very kind to them. It is my honor to serve you."

I tangled the reins around my fingers in thought. "If you're a squire, which knight do you serve?"

He sighed. "I did serve Sir Percy. I was doing well, but I wasn't expecting this promotion so quickly. To be the head of your guard is the highest honor, and before I've even become a knight. I'm hoping I can eventually be knighted in Stonekeep."

My stomach shrunk. If we were attacked, I didn't have much faith in this man's ability to protect me or organize a guard. I assumed the Queen had chosen him more for his lack of brains than any skill.

Dusk fell and Sir Cuthbert called a halt as the road became too dark for the horses to pick their way safely. I eased my aching muscles by the fire while they unpacked the tents and hauled my giant chest inside mine. I felt awkward as they worked except me, but I wasn't sure what needed to be done. I ate little of the stew for dinner and excused myself as early as I could. I didn't want to find myself in any more cheerful conversations with Jeremiah, and knew the other guards would feel more comfortable talking to each other when I was absent.

I hobbled into my tent, unrolled my furs and collapsed on top, sinking into the musty comfort. The lantern made strange shadows dance around the canvas flaps, and it was hard to tell which originated inside and which came from the fire. I gritted my teeth and pulled myself up to get undressed, hoping I wouldn't make a visible silhouette for the guards to laugh at. The tent was too low to stand, and it was hard to crouch in the rigid corset. I pulled off my dress, not caring that some of the fastenings tore. I couldn't reach the straps of my corset by myself. I cursed Elyanna's name under my breath for taking both maids. There was no way I was sleeping in this thing. I found my long knife and wedged it between my shoulder blades, sawing until the cords snapped. It took longer than I'd imagined, and my muscles burned in protest at the uncomfortable position. At last the ties snapped, and I managed to wiggle free. I took a few deep breaths and felt my rib cage relax. I tossed the corset aside; It was too ruined to wear it again. Hopefully I could get a new one before being presented to the Borderland King and Queen. Surely not even a princess could be expected to wear a corset the entire journey on horseback?

I shrugged out of my shift and realized with horror that I had started my monthly bleed. The material was stained and my thighs were a mess. The soreness of my muscles from the ride must have hidden the cramps. I hunted in the chest for my normal bag of rags, but nothing there was mine. It was all new or Elyanna's. Tears of exhaustion bubbled up, and I muffled my sobs from the guards. I couldn't do this. It was all too much. I buried my head in the furs.

But I couldn't stay like this, not while I was making such a mess. After a few shuddering breaths, I tried to clear my mind. I didn't need a maid. I just needed to find something to use as a rag and get to sleep. In the morning I would be less tired and emotional.

There were two other shifts in the chest. I tore one into strips and used water from my flask to clean myself as best as I could in the limited space and light. Then I bundled the soiled rags with the stained shift and hid them in the bottom of the chest. Once I'd wrapped myself securely, I dressed in the final shift to sleep. The fear of soiling this one remaining shift made tears press against my eyes again.

"Don't be silly, Brianna," I whispered. "If you stained it, it would be under your dress. Nobody would see. There's no maid to notice." I took a deep breath and blew out my lantern. The men's voices drifted in low swelling murmurs from the fireside. I drifted asleep thinking of giant wolves that ruled the forests and trapped little birds in their paws.

❋

AUTUMN WAS STARTING to paint the world with its jewel-tipped brush. The horses' hooves crunched the bronze leaves, and ruby and gold spiraled around us in the wind. The air was still mild, but the wind tugged at my cloak and pierced its way through my gloves. It was already colder here than it had been at Hava.

We rode through farmsteads and small woods, the road frequently busy with carts full of the harvest. Everywhere people were hustling and fretting about bringing in the crops before the weather changed. Whole villages were in the fields with sheaves of corn strapped to their backs, and children ran between them with water bottles and food and far too much energy.

I wondered if this was what it was like in Gilava and felt a pang of loss at never being able to join such a closely bonded community where each person was known and had their role to play. Instead I was a strange lady with a false name riding by without notice.

The land grew steeper as we neared the footholds of the Fever Mountains. The land no longer produced crops, but was speckled with sheep and cows and lone houses with threads of smoke coming from their chimneys all day long. The road became narrow and rocky and we were forced to ride single file. The wind picked up and flapped the sides of the tents at night making it hard to sleep.

On the third day we reached the mountains and made for Eagle's Pass. The Fever Mountain Range was high and the peaks were coated in snow, but the Pass remained clear. Huge boulders created a maze and we were forced to dismount so the horses could pick their own footing. The wind was loud enough to snatch words away, and I became used to hour after hour of silence.

Finally, we reached the far side and I found myself looking down at the Borderlands. I'd never left Sybera before and the thought of being somewhere completely new both excited and chilled me. Already the land looked different. At the foot of the pass was a squat tower of dark stone with men circling the ramparts. It was strange that they would have a fort here, when Syberans had never been a threat in the history of our two countries. I wondered if there would be trouble, but the soldiers let us pass without question. Beyond, as far as I could see, stretched a forest of dark pines, woven with roads. Here and there were cleared pockets around villages. To the east I thought I could make out farmland, and beyond, the distant sparkle of the sea. To the north-west were the infamous Sal'hadar Mountains, that kept the monsters of children's stories at bay; the Border. Their peaks were even taller than the Fever Mountains and made a jagged tear across the horizon. I wrapped my cloak around myself and hoped I would never have to travel to such a sinister place.

Jeremiah rode up with his normal cheery smile. "Straight ahead you can see Stonekeep, where we are heading." He pointed north. "See that dip and the tops of the spires over the trees?"

I nodded, though I wasn't convinced that they were spires and not just more trees.

"Two more days, Princess, and you'll be cozy and warm in your new home."

He didn't see that the thought of reaching Stonekeep made me colder than the bitter wind.

'You dislike him.' Falada turned his head to give me a long look with one eye. *'I like him. His soul is bright.'*

"Falada, you realize I don't know what you mean by that? I can't see 'souls'."

He snorted. *'You are prickly, Brianna, and not yourself. It's all these reflections on melancholy thoughts.'*

I sighed and scratched his neck. "I'm sorry. I'm just tired and scared." Voicing it out loud threatened to make me emotional again. "And it's that time of the month."

Falada shook out his mane. *'You are quick to excuse yourself. Quick to linger in self-pity. You should act to make things better. You should befriend the boy. You can trust him.'*

I glared at the horse. "Thanks for the empathy and support."

He snorted long and low so it sounded like a sigh. *'You're acting like a spooked filly and lashing out at those who feed you.'*

I slumped in the saddle, guilt and grief mixing in my heart. "Leave me alone, Falada."

He didn't reply. Above us the mournful cry of an eagle drifted.

❄

STONEKEEP LAY on the far side of a wide shallow river in the center of a valley. The water was full of waders and cranes and was speckled with boggy islands. The ground had been cleared of trees for several miles around to make way for rich farmland, and the crops were already harvested, leaving peaty soil bare for the crows and gulls. Even in the shelter of the valley, I could feel the wind worming its way into my clothes.

Stonekeep itself was not a city of beauty, and I could see little to admire as it grew before us. It was much smaller and more compact than the lazy sprawl of Hava, little more than a fortified town. The thick outer wall was dark grey stone with simple square towers, that hid the smaller buildings from view. Squatting in the middle like a giant toad, was the castle, though it looked more like a fort. It had neat towers and the central two bore spear-like spires that pierced the sky. There were no artistic touches or sweeping buttresses. No balcony gardens with hanging vines or statues on the eaves. This was a building of war.

It also looked like it would be an effective prison, and here I was simply letting myself be led inside.

I hadn't spoken to Falada since the morning before, and now I felt a desperate urge to make amends before we were separated in that dark squatting fortress.

I leant forward over his neck. "Falada, I am sorry. I shouldn't have spoken like I did. You're right, my circumstances don't justify me snapping at you."

The horse lifted his head higher. *'I forgive you, but make sure I get soaked oats tonight. And deep bedding. And I need a good brush.'*

I scratched him under his mane. "I'll make sure you have the best care in the whole stables."

We reached a long stone bridge that spanned the river on at least a hundred legs, and I resisted the urge to turn and gallop as the thick walls reared higher and higher. I was sure Falada would take me wherever I wished, for all his talk of oats. But that would leave the alliance in tatters and two countries searching for me.

Stonekeep was pure practicality, and I guessed so would its people be. I was used to the fussiness of Hava and the invisible role of lady-in-waiting. Everything was about to change. I wound my hands tightly into Falada's mane, and he didn't complain.

Jeremiah leveled his horse with mine on the bridge and gave me a grin. "So this is it, eh? Our new home. It's a bit dark, don't you think? They should paint the walls or plaster them or something to make it more inviting."

"That would be a lot of paint. I don't think they want

to look inviting. I think they're trying to scare off their enemies."

The squire nodded. "Well, it's effective. I wouldn't want to attack that."

I nodded in agreement, trying to conceive how big a siege engine would be needed to make a dent in walls so thick. The river was wide, and flowed on both sides, so it would be difficult to find a place for catapults in the boggy ground.

Jeremiah seemed to finally sense my mood, or maybe he had all along and simply been failing to cheer me up. "Don't worry, Princess, they will all love you. Your prince will see that he is a lucky man and all will be well."

I snorted, but a lump had formed in my throat that made it hard to reply.

Jeremiah raised his eyebrows in an earnest expression "Seriously, Highness. You have an ally in me. I will protect you."

I managed a small smile in thanks.

PRINCE OF THE BORDERLANDS

A guard had ridden ahead to announce us, and trumpets sounded as we clattered over the drawbridge. My heart started pounding as I grasped that this was finally happening. No more imagining or fretting. I was about to know for certain what the rest of my life was to be like. I was fully Elyanna now.

The city was overwhelmingly brown. Muddy roads weaving between two story houses insulated by clay and reeds over bricks. Even the people wore mostly brown leather or pale undyed wool. There was no parade or joyous welcome, and I hid my face under my hood and kept my eyes forward. I didn't want to feel their scrutiny.

The castle courtyard was a continuation of the mud, and animals were penned alongside the walls. A gaggle of geese batted their wings as they dived from the path of the horses. It was a far cry from the immaculate white paving slabs and gardens of Hava. Falada was whisked away and I only just managed to relay his command for oats to the stable boy when a man dressed in black bowed to me and whisked me towards the doors. He was armed with a sword, even though he appeared to be a servant. I was glad Jeremiah remained close on my heels as the other men were led to the barracks.

The castle was gloomy and a muddy narrow carpet lay down the center of the corridor. It was cold, even inside, and I wondered if it would be rude if I left my cloak on. The man in black bowed to me. "Your Highness. The King, Queen and Princes are waiting to receive you in the Grand Hall."

My mouth dried and I had to force my words so as not to stutter. "Can't I change first?"

The servant gave me a firm smile. "There is no need, Highness. They merely wish to welcome you before you are led to your rooms. They know you have been days on the road."

I bit my lip. I hadn't looked in a mirror since Hava and I wasn't even wearing a corset. This was not how I'd imagined meeting my future husband and his family. The first thing he would notice would be my attractiveness, surely? He would want to know whether he was to marry somebody pretty, and here I was looking like a mess. And if he disapproved of me, that would make me seem more disposable in his eyes. Easier to hurt. Elyanna had always been the cruelest to those she found distasteful.

I could hear my governess's voice in my head. *'The thing about first impressions is you can't make them twice. You must always be presented to impress.'* Elyanna wouldn't have found herself in this situation. At least she wasn't here to know.

The servant didn't wait for a reply and started to stride down the corridor. I turned to Jeremiah. "Do I look alright?"

He seemed taken aback and then grinned. "Beautiful, your Highness."

I felt myself blush, but his confidence helped. I turned and started after the servant.

Jeremiah came to my side. "Don't let them stand close enough to smell you, however."

I stumbled but let myself chuckle despite my thudding heart. "It's their choice to see me straight away. I can't help that you men didn't bother to transport a bath for me."

He didn't see through my false confidence and snorted in amusement.

The servant in black stopped at a tall pair of doors and waited for us to catch up. He rapped on the wood and they were flung inwards by unseen hands. A huge hall gaped in front of me lit from above by second story windows that did little to expel the gloom. Fires burned in every wall and in a great pit in the center. I blinked through the flames and smoke and made out four people on the far side. A man and a woman were seated on two thrones, and a pair of men stood beside them. My heart thundered in my ears and pins and needles shot down my legs. One of those men would be my husband.

I forced myself to move forward and circled the fire, keeping my eyes on the flagstones for courage.

The flames were hot and did little to steady my dizziness. I lifted my eyes and focused through the smoky air on the King and Queen. Both were draped in furs and neither had a crown on their heads. Their thick hair was as black as ebony, their eyes were elegantly tilted, and they had the tall stature of the Old Blood. The Queen stood and walked towards me, a warm smile on her lips. Her dress was in a wrap-around style I'd never seen before, lined with thick fur and sleeves that touched the floor. Behind her the King rose with a pensive expression, his outfit surprisingly simple.

I bowed into a deep curtsey, but the Queen grasped my hand and pulled me up. "There is no need for that amongst family." Her accent was strange, lilting. She smelt of smoke and pine and wore large golden disks as earrings that twinkled in the firelight. "You are very welcome, Princess Elyanna. You must be exhausted after your journey."

I returned her smile and tried to hide my nerves. "I am certainly eager for a bath. Thank you for the honor of your welcome."

She looked over my shoulder at Jeremiah and her eyebrows rose. "Is this all of your retinue?"

I nodded, resisting the urge to shift my feet. Jeremiah bowed low at the Queen's attention. The silence stretched and I stumbled to fill it. "My maid wished to remain in Sybera, Your Majesty. She turned back part way through our journey. I didn't wish to force her." I took a deep breath. "Besides, it might help my integration here if I have a Borderlander maid?"

The Queen's smile was wide and genuine. "Of course. I will arrange one immediately."

"The rest of my guard wish to return tomorrow before there is any risk of snow blocking the pass."

The King stood up, and I turned my attention to him as he swaggered towards me. I noticed he had a pronounced limp, though he still carried an enormous greatsword on his back. He didn't smile like his wife, but there was no hostility in his eyes. His hair was bound in a strange style that left half of it cascading around his shoulders. He nodded to me and I gave him a small bow.

"Your Majesty." I said, doing my best not to be intimidated by his height and build. It was not often that people were taller than me.

"Welcome. I hope you settle in quickly," he said gruffly. "There should be plenty of time for you to get acquainted with my sons." He angled his shoulders to gesture to the two silent men by the thrones. "Prince Kai Han and Prince Kai Jian, your betrothed."

I looked at Prince Jian as he stood behind his father. His arms were clasped in front of his crisp dark green uniform and his face was as blank as a guard on duty. His hair was short, unlike the rest of his family, and he wore no personal touches. He glanced at me and our eyes met, his cold gaze doing little to ease my nerves. He gave a small nod of acknowledgement and looked away again, seeming bored and uninterested. I felt my cheeks heat and looked at the floor. I felt small, as if I was nothing more than an unwanted, and possibly embarrassing, present. The story of Lady Hesta flickered through my mind. If I'd been the real Elyanna, would he have reacted the same way? She wouldn't have stood for it, but fought for attention tooth and nail until everyone did as she asked. I wasn't her, though, and had no wish to be. But I also didn't want to be weak.

I lifted my gaze to the Prince again and studied him while he focused on his father. He was tall, even for somebody with the Old Blood, easily the tallest man in the room, and slender, contrasting with the broad shoulders of his brother. His dark hair fell across his eyes with a long fringe as if to shut everyone out and his military uniform was immaculate, giving little away as to the person beneath. He stood still as if being inspected on parade.

Did he even have the slightest interest in me? The Queen followed my gaze and gave a worried frown to her son before stepping over to take my hands. "I know it must be strange, being so far from home and everything you know, but I'm sure you'll settle in quickly. Do let me know if there's anything you need."

I tore my gaze from my future husband and smiled at the Queen. "Thank you. I must confess, I'm very tired."

The Queen's voice warmed, and her eyes rounded in sympathy. "Of course, let me show you to your rooms. If anything is not to your taste, the housekeeper can rearrange it. The most important thing is that you feel comfortable."

For some reason her kindness made pressure build up behind my eyes, breaking through the determined shell I'd built around myself. The Queen took my arm to escort me from the room, and I glanced at the Prince who was still looking away. "When... when is the wedding?"

She glanced at her husband. "We were thinking about hosting it in two months to give you a chance to settle in and get to know Jian first."

My shoulders sagged as I sighed in relief. "Thank you. I was worried that it would be straight away."

The Queen waved my words away. "No, no, I remember what it's like meeting your betrothed for the first time and trying to find your way in a strange place where you don't know anyone. Besides, I'm sure you'll have some opinions on the celebrations?"

I hadn't even thought about the actual wedding, I'd been so preoccupied with what would come after.

The Queen must have seen the worry on my face. "Don't worry, my dear, we don't need to discuss that now. Come, let's get you to your rooms." She patted my hand which was laid on her arm and led me out of the hall. "Rest or explore as you wish for the rest of today. Tomorrow evening we have planned a banquet in your honor."

My heart sank but I gave her a smile. "That is very kind. Are there... any traditions I need to be aware of?"

She shook her head and her large golden earrings twinkled again. "It will be a simple feast with dancing. I will arrange for a seat for your new maid beside you so she can advise on anything you question."

I relaxed a little. "Thank you, Your Majesty."

She waved my words from the air. "Call me Fei."

❋

A MAID WAS ALREADY WAITING in my new rooms. Ruo was a motherly woman probably in her fifties with rounded cheeks and grey hair plaited around her scalp. She had a comforting air and I liked her immediately as she paused from stoking the fires to introduce herself. I hoped she would be a friend and ally in this strange place.

The rooms were very different from my ones back in Hava. The stone walls were unplastered and only adorned with a single faded tapestry of men fishing with long poles on a river. The receiving room contained only a simple desk, a dining table and four quilted chairs with no backs. Thankfully there was a woven rug on the floor to offer some warmth.

The second room was a bedroom. The four-poster bed was made of dark wood and was much lower to the ground than I was used to. There were no silk covers, only mounds of furs stitched together. A wooden barrel sat in the corner for washing, and Ruo was already busy filling it. Other than that, there was merely a large wardrobe and a vanity table. Elyanna would have passed out in horror. The thought made me smile.

Ruo bobbed her head. "I'll have the servants bring your chest in here, Your Highness. I know the Queen has already placed some dresses in your wardrobe as a gift. I would be happy to adjust any to fit you, as you wish. Is there anything else you need?"

"A new corset and some shifts, if I may. Mine got ruined on the journey."

The maid eyebrows twitched down for a second. "Of course."

"What is this?" I asked, pointing at two wide wooden pegs fastened to the wall beside my bed.

"That is for your sword. It is easy to access there if you need it during the night."

My mouth dropped open. "Am I likely to need a sword in the night here?"

She smiled and chuckled. "It's a tradition left from more dangerous times, Highness. The Border didn't used to be so effectively maintained."

I frowned. "But the Border is miles away."

Ruo's face saddened. "As I said, we used to live in much more dangerous times. Prince Jian has paid the Border Forts a lot of attention these last ten years and they are close to impenetrable, so don't fear. Most folk still believe, however, that not sleeping with your sword to hand is asking for trouble to come."

I looked back to the empty hooks and firmed my lips. My own sword was still in my chest, but this seemed an easy and sensible tradition to adopt. I would probably feel safer for it too. The wind made strange moans around the outside walls and the window shuddered.

Ruo poured the final bucket of warmed water into the barrel and left me to wash. It seemed they were more conscious of privacy here. The water was luke-warm and the tub slowly leaked water onto the floor. It felt wonderful to gradually become clean again. Ruo had left a plain linen dress and thick fur robe for me on the bed. When I was clean, I dried myself as fast as possible in the chill air before running for the clothes. The fur was soft and I hugged myself.

Ruo was not in my receiving room anymore, and I assumed she had gone to collect food. I brushed my hair as close to the fire as I could stand and watched the gentle waves return as the water evaporated. I studied the pure white of my hair and wondered what our children would look like when Jian's was pure black. Would they have one or the other, or a mixture of the two? My thoughts started to slide to less pleasant places, and I distracted myself by going to the window which was already dimming with dusk.

I leant on the windowsill and breathed on the glass to melt the gathering frost on the outside of the panes, before wiping away the condensation. A stray flurry of snow swirled past the window, and I pulled my cloak tight around me. If the weather was this bad in early autumn, what would winter be like?

My window didn't look over the town, but faced the endless slopes of dark pine, stark against the snow-dappled ground. Here and there I could make out the shining lines of waterfalls and rivers, the weather not yet cool enough to turn them to ice.

As I stood back, I froze, a tingle running down my spine. Something whispered, right on the edge of my hearing. A voice? I pressed my face back against the glass, sure I was imagining it, but not able to step away. The breeze blew around the catch and hinges of the window, kissing my cheeks with ice. '*Brianna.*' A child's voice, distant and faded.

I stepped back so fast my heel caught my skirt, and I

staggered to keep my balance. I shook my head. I had never been one for foolish imaginings. What was wrong with me?

I drew the curtains, even though it was still light. Just to keep the warmth of the fire in, of course. I took a deep breath and sat in the furthest chair from the window, where the crackle and pop of the fire drowned out the sound of the wind.

※

I HADN'T EXPECTED a banquet in my honor, and I wished they hadn't bothered. I wasn't as familiar with the etiquette of the Borderlands as I would have liked, and what if there were customs Elyanna knew that I didn't, revealing I was an imposter?

The first challenge was to decide what to wear. Did I wear a dress that I had brought with me, or would wearing one the Queen had gifted me be more gracious? I knew Elyanna would have chosen her gold gown. She loved how she looked in that and always complained she couldn't wear it more at court since everyone had seen her wear it twice already. But the neckline was lower than I wanted, and the whole thing was too dramatic. I wasn't comfortable in it, and just because I had taken Elyanna's name, didn't mean I had to take her personality as well.

I looked at the three dresses the Queen had given me and was touched that they were in the Havan style much more than Borderlander, with bare shoulders and gauzy, floaty material for trains. Maybe it would be acceptable for me to remain a Syberan for now. I chose one in a pale blue chiffon. It was elegant without being attention-seeking, and was in a cut I was used to wearing. I put it on and let Ruo fix pins around the bodice to bring it in to my size. After I'd slipped it back off, I automatically collected a needle and thread from my sewing box.

Ruo looked surprised. "No, no, my lady. I can do this for you. I will have it ready in time, don't you worry."

I smiled but took one end of the dress. It was strange to be the princess and not the lady-in-waiting. "I would like to alter it with you, if I may? I'm nervous about tonight and would like to keep busy."

Ruo's expression softened and she gave a small smile. "Of course. No need to be nervous, my lady."

We settled down in front of the built-up fire and started sewing the new lines Ruo had marked out. The fires were constantly lit in my room, even though it was just after midday, and I was grateful for the warmth. I listened to the cold wind echoing down the corridors of the castle as I sewed and sometimes jumped when it rattled my door. My lunch of bread and soup remained untouched on the table, despite Ruo glancing at it periodically as if to remind me it was there.

I snapped a piece of thread with my teeth and didn't look at Ruo as I dared to ask about Prince Jian. "What's he like?" It was so much easier to talk now we both had something to occupy ourselves. "My husband-to-be?"

Ruo tilted her head. "Well, he's very handsome, don't you think? A very good height. Especially since you are so tall yourself."

I jabbed the needle through the fabric harder than I needed. "But what's he *like*? Is he kind? Humorous? Studious? Athletic? Amorous?"

She bit her lip in concentration as she worked. "Well, he's quiet and reserved, but that's not a bad thing, dear. I've never seen him be deliberately unkind. He spends a lot of time training with the sword and drilling the soldiers. I'd say that is his passion. He's a general at the Border, you see, and spends almost half the year at one of the two forts. He leads his men well and is highly respected by them."

"Oh." I tried to envision our future married life. It sounded like he would be away most of the time fighting or training. I wasn't sure if I would be expected to go to the Border with him. It would be a strange marriage if we barely spent any time together, but who knew, maybe that would be better? The castle didn't seem too bad so far, just cold and a little depressing. I turned the bodice over to hem the other side. He was a man of war. Would that mean he had a taste for violence? Perhaps damaged by what he'd seen? Broken? I sighed and rubbed my forehead. The sooner I knew more about him, the easier this would all be.

Ruo patted my shoulder. "Now, now, my lady. I'm sure it will work out. Political marriages can be tricky, and I'm sure you must miss home, but there will be lots for you to do here to occupy yourself before the little ones come. There are many places to find happiness apart from marriage so you can find contentment and patience while your marriage takes time to grow."

Little ones. Those little heads of black and white hair

flashed back into my mind. But that would mean sleeping with the Prince. I suppressed a shudder at that vast gaping unknown. I couldn't think about that right now or I would never be able to look him in the eye tonight.

We finished the dress with time to spare and Ruo took her time filing my nails and weaving a blue topaz diadem into my hair. It felt nice to merely sit and feel the gentle tugs on my scalp. The room fell into peaceful silence, so different to when Elyanna got ready for a ball. But it was hard to ignore the nerves slithering around my stomach and constricting my chest. I had so much to learn and quickly. Ruo found two large silver earrings, not unlike the Queen's, and fitted them to my ears. Their weight was unfamiliar, but I liked the way they brushed my jaw when I turned my head.

A servant knocked at the door to summon us, and Ruo cupped my elbow to help me stand. She looped her arm through mine and guided me to the hallway behind the black-clad man. Jeremiah had been guarding my door and fell in behind without comment. Even he had dressed up for the occasion in a velvet doublet, and his cheeks were flushed.

"Do you think he'll like me?" I couldn't help but whisper to Ruo as we drew near to the hall, though I hated how weak it made me sound.

The woman squeezed my arm. "You look so beautiful, you could win the heart of the Frost King himself. Now try not to fret and enjoy yourself."

I heard the music long before I reached the Hall doors. The melody of pipes and fiddles was carried in the swirling smoke that clogged the corridors. Drumbeats vibrated through the flagstones and echoed my pounding heart.

Jian was going to be there, and I needed to make a good impression. In fact, the whole of Stonekeep was going to be there, ready to gape and gossip, and I wasn't even a real princess. I concentrated on the firm grip of Ruo and took deep breaths. I could do this. This was my home and family now.

The Hall was filled with trestle tables already laden with food. There had to be at least fifty people sat down in front of empty plates waiting to start. Was I late? As I entered, everyone fell silent and stood. I felt the heat rise to my cheeks and looked into the central fire, not knowing where else to look. Was I meant to say something? I glanced to Ruo, who had let go of my arm, but was standing tall. She gave me a reassuring smile and wink.

King Zihao's voice boomed through the flames. "Welcome, Princess Elyanna, to Stonekeep. From now on I see you as my daughter, and request that others see you in the same way. May you find prosperity and joy in these walls."

A great cheer and a clatter of knives pounding wood made me jump. I curtsied towards the high table and let Ruo lead me to my seat. The King and the Queen sat on their own table facing down the hall. The trestle tables had seats down the outside only, the middle side clear so servants could bring and take the food without leaning over us. This way every guest faced the central fire. My chair was on the end of the right table, the

closest position to the King and Queen. Directly opposite me, across the dance floor, sat Prince Jian next to
his brother. He briefly met my eye through the smoke,
and a cold shiver ran down my spine. He nodded, then
turned to Prince Han to converse. My mouth dried.
How could I be doing so badly at this already? He didn't
seem to notice my hair or dress or careful makeup. I felt
a fool for spending so much of today preparing.

Now I had been announced and seated, everyone
started piling their food onto their plates. I felt hot and
queasy, so I picked plain bread and vegetables, hoping
they would settle my stomach. After I had drunk half a
glass of wine, I dared steal a glance at my betrothed
again.

Prince Jian was dressed in a fancier version of the
dark green and silver military uniform and it fitted him
perfectly. Did he ever wear normal clothes? His brother
in contrast was dressed in velvets and furs with his shirt
ties loose around his neck. Prince Han caught me
looking at him and winked. I raised my eyebrows in
return to show I wasn't intimidated or willing to flirt,
and he chuckled.

I turned my attention back to Jian as he ate his food
efficiently with little emotion and tried to think about
how I could gain his attention. Some of the nobles and
servants had already finished eating and were gathering
in the middle of the hall to dance. They joined in a
circle around the fire and the music was much wilder
and louder than the dances in Hava. Servants linked
hands with lords and ladies and there seemed no order.
Jian gazed at the dancing blankly while one hand

swirled his wine around and around. His brother sat beside him and talked non-stop, not caring that Jian replied with little more than small motions of his head. As a second dance requiring partners started, Han left to ask one of the ladies to dance, but his brother didn't even glance at me. Surely he would ask me to dance soon?

I sat straight-backed in the chair and tried to look as regal and elegant as Elyanna did at these events. The dances were unfamiliar, and I concentrated on learning the steps, but as the evening wore on, I realized I was wasting my time as Prince Jian showed little interest in dancing. He drank glass after glass and slouched a little in his chair, looking bored and barely acknowledging me. As the dances ticked by, I felt myself color with shame. Surely everyone here would notice he wasn't interested in his new bride. I was being rejected in front of the world. I pushed my food around my plate and wondered if somebody else would ask me to dance to save my embarrassment. But of course, nobody could dance with the Prince's betrothed before he did.

I leant to Ruo who had blessedly not left my side, despite the way she tapped her fingers to the music. "Is it custom here for the guest of honor to just watch the dancing?"

Ruo looked awkwardly at Prince Jian. "Well, my lady, there is no obligation to dance or to abstain."

I leant closer to her. "I don't think he's going to ask me."

She pressed her lips into a firm line. "I'm afraid Prince Jian has never been much of a dancer. He can be quite… serious you see. And maybe he's concerned you wouldn't know the dances."

I frowned at the Prince and decided he was rude and uncaring. "I could ask him to dance?"

Ruo made a little lurch and then inclined her head. "You could, my dear, but it may appear… forward."

I bit my lip and stared at the brooding man staring at his wine. "Well he can't ignore me; we're supposed to be getting married."

Ruo lay her hand on my knee. "I should warn you, my dear. Prince Jian is not one to be forced into doing anything he did not intend to."

The dance changed to a wilder one, the pipes and fiddles speeding up in a frenzy. There was laughter as the dancers struggled to keep up with the pace, and one of the ladies fell over. She didn't appear at all embarrassed as her partner pulled her up. I used the distraction to my advantage and stood up to walk to the Prince.

His black eyes fixed on me immediately as I approached, but his face remained blank. My mouth dried as my courage evaporated and my pulses thudded in my ears. Was he trying to intimidate me? Or was he this cold to everyone?

I reached his chair and gave a small curtsy. He inclined his head, without dropping his gaze.

I tried to swallow but my mouth was too dry. "I was… er… wondering if you would like to dance?" I attempted a weak smile.

He dropped his gaze and leant forward to place his wine cup on the table. He stood and I took a step back, surprised again at his height. He looked at the wild dance. "You know this one?"

I shook my head.

The corner of his lips twitched, and he raised an eyebrow. "I suggest then that this is not the first one you attempt, my lady."

I tried not to fidget. "I had hoped you could teach me the next one?"

He gave a slight nod. "As you wish." He sat back down and picked up his wine again, looking at the dancers. I was left standing awkwardly on my own. I tried not to gape at his rudeness, or look pathetic to any onlookers, and stalked back to my seat. Now he would have to come to me at the start of the dance. I drummed my fingers on my armrest and slumped. How was I going to survive being married to a man like this?

The music finished and I looked over to the Prince. He sighed and stood up, straightening his jacket. I didn't miss the pointed look the Queen gave him, her lips a firm line.

Prince Jian strode towards me and gave a polite bow, extending his hand. "Would you honor me with this dance, Princess Elyanna."

"Of course." I stood and took his hand. I picked up one side of my skirts as I'd seen Elyanna do many times before and tried my best to glide beside him to the dance floor. As we took our place, I felt my cheeks heat, and I focused my eyes on the Prince's highly polished shoes. I had often danced in Sybera, but the attention had always been on people more important than me. Nobody cared who I danced with and whether I got the steps right. Now, it felt like every eye in the room was trained on me, the stranger. Their new Princess. I raised my eyes to the Prince. His face was smooth and expressionless; I couldn't read him at all, but his presence felt like a great unstable wave rearing over me.

The music started and I was grateful to hear a slow, steady rhythm with soaring pipes and gentle fiddles. I wondered if they'd done it on purpose when they had seen us take to the floor.

The Prince outstretched his hand, and I took it. Nerves made my mouth run dry. "Are you familiar with this piece?" His voice was casual.

"No, Your Highness."

"It's quite simple. Just follow my lead." His hand tightened around mine and a shiver ran up my arm. He took a step towards me, and again I was struck by his height. He tugged on my arm and I moved to the side, trying to copy the step the other ladies were taking. I looked around for an easy woman to follow.

"Ignore them," said Prince Jian. "Focus on me."

I looked up at his face and wasn't sure whether to meet that cold gaze or focus elsewhere. I tried to copy his emotionless expression to show he didn't intimidate me, but I doubted I was convincing. His hand touched my waist and he guided me into a walk of quick steps. He spun me and then his hands were on my back and he was dipping me low to the floor. I clung to his arms, caught off guard and certain he was going to drop me.

A smile flirted around his lips. "Don't worry, this dance is short, and you'll finish in one piece."

I was concentrating too hard to reply.

Slow steps followed, and I tried to feel the rhythm of the music to anticipate them. He performed the footwork exactly, almost ceremoniously, and I was clumsy in comparison. Well, at least I wasn't going to have a husband who stood on my toes. His hands cupped my waist again and he moved closer. My chest tightened as he surrounded me, and I felt trapped with a strange feeling of vertigo.

Then I was flung away, spinning, held together only by our fingertips. The music ended and I was breathing more heavily than required by the effort of the dance. He let go of my hand and gave a short bow, then strode back to his seat, leaving me standing alone on the dance floor.

A hand took mine as I stared after Prince Jian, and I turned to see who had saved me from complete humiliation. Prince Han was grinning and gave a bow. "May I have this dance?"

I curtsied in return and took his other hand. I sagged in relief at his kindness but couldn't shake the internal voice that reminded me of the rumors. Crown Prince Han had reputedly murdered his wife in a fit of rage. It was that rumor that had made Elyanna worried she would share the same fate.

The man before me now, however, didn't seem dangerous at all, beyond his stocky build. He had a broad smile and eyes that were creased with humor. He seemed like the sort of man who would laugh the loudest and longest when in his cups, yet listen to those around him. His long hair was fastened high on his head with a metal band studded with onyx, and strands fell free around his face. A thick silver chain circled his neck.

"Don't mind my brother. He's not used to spending time with ladies." He smirked.

"I wasn't aware we were that different to talk to. I don't believe he was overcome by my beauty or feminine wit."

Prince Han snorted. "He's not very good with change. Just give him time and he'll come around."

I glanced over to his younger brother who was finishing a sweet meat before carefully wiping his hands and leaving the Hall. I guessed that was the end of our introduction then.

"Elyanna?"

I jumped and looked back to Han.

He raised an eyebrow. "Are you wanting to dance or to block all the other dancers?" I realized the music had started.

I mumbled an apology and let his large hands guide me through the dance. He was much freer than Jian. His steps weren't precise, but I could tell he could feel the pull and passion of the music. I tried to smile and enjoy myself, but my thoughts kept turning to the coldness in my betrothed's eyes and the niggle of fear and fury that awoke in my stomach. If the real Elyanna had been here, she would have torn the place down at the slight. Maybe the only way I would be happy was to ignore him altogether.

"Why am I here?" I whispered, almost to myself as the music wound down. "If he doesn't have any interest in me."

Han sighed and led me back to the tables, taking a seat. "Don't be too harsh on him, he hadn't intended to marry either."

I gave him a questioning look as Han poured us both wine. "The Border has drained our resources, and that is partially his fault. He didn't have any choice but marriage, really, if he was to continue maintaining what he has started. It was Mother's decision for Jian to marry you in return for coin and trade. Women have always been far from his mind, but I'm sure he'll warm to the idea." He grinned with a childish gleam in his eyes and took a deep drink of wine.

I sipped my own wine and grimaced at its sourness before slumping back in my chair. Havan wine was always rich and sweet. I couldn't shake the feeling I would never belong here.

*

THAT NIGHT I tossed in bed and my chest ached with loneliness. I yearned for the familiar pale halls and faces of Hava and the warmth of the golden autumn sunshine there. I thought of Elyanna and attempted to suppress the wave of hatred that poured over me.

What had Falada said?

'Don't hold this hate within yourself because of the hate she bears herself. Be free of it. She only poisons herself.'

His words were true, and I knew I didn't want to live a bitter life, but I also couldn't forgive her or Queen Geraldina for doing this to me. But thinking about either of them wasn't going to help me now.

But Falada might.

I slipped out of bed and found the thick robe of furs. I tied up my leather boots and found some gloves buried in the bottom of my wardrobe. Jeremiah was leaning against the wall beside my door, his head sagging, and he jumped a full foot as I opened it, his hand going to his sword.

I giggled and looked around to see if he was alone. "Why aren't you in bed?" There were no fires in the corridor and my breath misted in the moonlight. "You must be frozen."

He straightened. "Well, you should have a guard at all times, Your Highness, and I haven't managed to form a trustworthy unit yet."

"When will you sleep?"

"At midday, Your Highness. I figured you would be less likely to be attacked when people were around."

I smiled at him. "Thank you, Jeremiah, but I doubt anyone is going to attack me."

He raised his eyebrows. "You don't know that, my lady, and the worst people always come at night."

I pulled my cloak tighter. "I will bring this up with the Queen tomorrow and ask her to put a guard under your control. You really should have time to rest." I headed down the corridor towards the courtyard.

His boots slapped against the flagstones as he caught up. "Where are we going, Highness?"

"I can't sleep. I wish to talk to Falada."

"Your horse? It's past midnight!"

"He's not just a horse, Jeremiah, he's my closest

friend. Besides, there will still be people awake from the banquet."

He didn't argue further but followed through the squares of moonlight thrown from the windows. I rounded a corner and found myself in an unexpected corridor. I must have taken a wrong turn in the dark. So much of this castle looked the same. I turned to ask Jeremiah which way we should go when I heard a voice. It was faint but firm. I crept forward and recognized the authoritative lilt of Queen Fei. I traced it to a closed door, treading carefully so as not to make a sound. When I heard Jian's solemn voice in reply, I couldn't resist the temptation any longer. I leant my ear as close to the door as I dared and hoped Jeremiah wouldn't judge me too harshly.

I jumped as a hand clamped down on my shoulder. I spun, but it was only the squire handing me a cup. I looked at it in confusion.

He grinned. "You have a lot to learn if you're going to do this," he whispered. "Place the rim to the door and you will hear better."

I did as he said and was amazed at how clear the voices became. I made a mental note never to say anything private in my rooms if Jeremiah was outside.

The Queen sounded exasperated. "What is wrong with you, Jian? Do you object to her in some way? Is she not pretty enough? Not got the right hair or eyes or something ridiculous like that?" Her voice was heavy with sarcasm, and I almost winced on the Prince's behalf.

"Mother, I simply don't have the time or patience for

this. I'm needed at the Border. There are people dying while we sit and drink wine and dance. I don't need a distraction, however pretty."

"You're needed *here*, right now. Don't you understand that marrying this girl and securing our alliance with Sybera will help at the Border? We need more money and trade to fund all the defense projects you have instigated. Sitting and drinking and particularly *dancing* is what will save lives."

"I've agreed to marry her, haven't I? That's the alliance sealed. I don't want to give her false expectations, and I don't understand why this has to take so long."

My heart sank. False expectations? A trickle of fear chilled my spine. Elyanna had never liked me and had made my life miserable. Surely getting Jian to like me would be the easiest way to protect myself from both him and others? But how would I be safe if I couldn't win him over? I had to make myself valuable in some way so I didn't end up like Lady Hesta.

"Because, Jian, she is going to be your *wife.* You will be wed to her for the rest of your life."

"Which may not be very long. I don't want to get her hopes up only to dash them."

"Jian! I'll have none of that nonsense from you. You need to put the poor girl at ease."

"Why? I'll barely be here anyway. She might as well spend time with you and Father and the Stonekeep ladies. She's a Syberan, she'll enjoy the softness of the castle. She's not part of my world."

I heard the Queen's heavy sigh. "Can you at least try

to court her? Speak to her? She's come a long way from home to get to know you."

"I both spoke and danced with her tonight."

"You know what I mean." Her voice softened. "She is going to bear your children, Jian. You should treat her with honor."

"I mean her no dishonor, Mother. It's just... I'm worried about my men. Tama'ha is restless. All the Spirit-Beasts are. I'm sure something is changing beyond the passes, and I don't know what that will mean for us. They may renew their attacks or try more dangerous tactics. Nameless, or worse."

"It's two months, Jian. Two months to ensure we maintain the finances we need to do whatever is necessary to repel them. You have used up generations of savings. This is the easiest way for your plans to become sustainable, especially your next proposed improvements to the Western Fort."

"I know, but in two weeks I must return. Just for a few days. Yes, I know your objections, but I need to keep their spirits up and hear the reports."

I moved away from the door, my spirit even heavier than before. He really couldn't care less about me. Worse, I was in the way of his work at the Border. It was easier to be cruel to somebody who was an inconvenience. He had his gold and his trade with Sybera and didn't feel I could offer him anything else.

At least I now understood how he viewed things. I stood, trying to see the positives. Maybe if he wanted next to nothing to do with me, I would have what I had always wanted: freedom. For the time he was at the

Border at least. Maybe being separate would be better than playing wife in a loveless marriage all the time. Especially if he was indeed violent.

But I was still too vulnerable, too disposable, and I couldn't shake the sting of abandonment. I felt ugly and broken, just like Elyanna always said. I wandered down the hallway haphazardly. I didn't care which direction I was heading anymore. After a few turns, I collected myself and turned to Jeremiah. He had always been loyal and friendly, and he had seemed the one person on my side apart from Falada. I had to make the best of what I'd been given. And to be fair, Elyanna was probably worse than Jian.

I forced my voice into an amicable mold. I needed Jeremiah to be my ally. "Thank you for accompanying me and guarding me so well. It can't be easy for you either, being so far from home."

Jeremiah gave a sharp nod. "Honestly, Highness? It's my honor. I never thought I would be given such a prestigious job. We'll settle in soon enough, and all this will become familiar."

I wrapped my cloak tighter around my shoulders. "I'm not sure I want freezing dark corridors to be familiar. Imagine what they are like in winter."

Jeremiah grinned. "I always loved snow. Don't tell me you don't enjoy a ride at dawn through unblemished white?"

I gave him a long sideways look, weighing him. "Who are your parents, Jeremiah?"

He straightened a little. "My father was Sir Ghert, killed in the Battle of Sedgehaven. He was one of the men Sybera sent to Dreyha to answer their call for aid when Kilamore invaded. My job now feels similar to what he was doing, just in a different way. Both of us are spending our lives protecting Sybera from Kilamore by helping the nations that cushion our borders. That is why I have so much respect for you, Your Highness. Sybera will be safe because now the Borderlands will always answer our call for aid, should Kilamore invade."

I nodded, but felt uncomfortable with his open faith. "And your mother?"

"Lady Sophia. She died giving birth to my sister. Tattia lives in Hava with our grandparents. My two elder brothers run the estate."

The sister in Hava must be reassuring for Queen Geraldina and Elyanna. If Jeremiah threatened to reveal my identity, they had an easy hostage. Though he would have to figure it out first, and he seemed far too trusting to be suspicious about me. I could see why the Queen had chosen him to be the one that stayed with me.

After a myriad of twists and turns, we made it to the courtyard. The frigid air of deep night clung to any exposed skin with icy hooks, but the vast expanse of the night sky was beautiful and tranquil. Far more stars than I had ever seen in Hava sparkled on the inky black, mirroring the frost on the cobblestones that glittered with moonlight. For the first time in Stonekeep, I felt peaceful.

Jeremiah led the way to the stables, and I felt guilty that he had already been there to check on his own mare, while I had waited this long to check on Falada. The stable door was bolted shut and the metal was webbed with ice. I was grateful when Jeremiah managed to force it open with his gloved hands. The sound echoed around the deserted walls.

Inside, the stables were lit by a single lantern. There was no fire, but the horses and prized cows radiated their own warmth and were bedded in deep straw. I found Falada's stable and unhooked the rope fastening the cubicle. He wasn't asleep but was pulling some hay from his hay net. A thick blanket covered his back and stopped at his shoulders. The swivel of his ear showed he'd heard my approach, but he didn't turn. He was in a bad mood with me. My heart sank further.

"Falada?" I touched his thigh and he stomped his hoof in response, though the effect was lessened by the thick straw. "How do you like your new stall?"

He didn't reply, so I studied it for myself. The straw was deep and his water was clear. It was only a little smaller than his one in Hava, though it lacked the carvings and gold leaf around the borders. There was an empty trough that still smelt herby and sweet from a recent meal.

I patted Falada again. When he continued to ignore me, I fetched a curry comb and started to rub his neck in gentle circles. He shifted his weight towards me. "I'm sorry I didn't come earlier, Falada. I was exhausted yesterday and then today I had to prepare for a horrible banquet they threw in my honor. I've met Prince Jian and he couldn't care less about me. He spoke to me as little as possible and *I* had to ask *him* to dance. He was the first one to leave tonight out of all the guests. I overheard him saying to the Queen that he wanted to be back at the Border Forts, and I was merely a necessary inconvenience. All he wants me for is Syberan coin. He is not going to look out for me. I don't know what to do." My throat tightened and I held my breath for the count of ten. I was *not* going to cry.

Falada's ears were both facing me, and his jaw chewed methodically. I breathed in the comforting scent of him and felt my fear melt away. I patted the horse blanket. "Do you want a warmer rug?"

'The stable hand didn't give me oats today. Only yesterday. I snorted meaningfully at him and he laughed at me. Said it would be bad for my health if he fed me treats while I'd had no exercise. Went on about laminitis as if I were some common pony. How am I to put up with this cold if I run out of energy? All my fat will burn away.'

I suppressed a smile and went to dig in the barrels for some oats. In the tack room I found a horse rug that was lined with thick fleece. I swapped it with the one he was wearing and tied the fastenings.

'It was a very boring day today. They didn't turn any of the horses out.'

"I'll talk to the stable hand tomorrow, I promise."

He snorted in response and used his thick lips to scoop up the oats as quickly as possible.

I giggled at him. "You're such a grumpy old man." I started to brush and braid his mane, knowing he would forgive me soon. "Now I know Jian is going to take no interest in me at all, I'll leave him to his self-important life and busy myself with other things. I need to find something valuable to do so I can earn my place here. Queen Fei seems nice and glad to have me, so hopefully

I can impress her. Jian said he won't even be here most of the time, but at the Border. Maybe I can find joy in other places."

Falada turned his head to study me. Finally, he nuzzled my arm. *'You're giving up?'*

I frowned. "Giving up on what? Jian will never be interested in me, and, as far as I know, that might be a good thing. I'll preserve my dignity by keeping my distance." I stood taller as if with pride, but the fear and sense of worthlessness weighed down my chest. The worry of how he would treat me during our times alone together if he didn't like me dug cold figures into my stomach. I had nothing in my favor.

Falada blinked slowly and swished his tail, though I could see no flies. *'Brianna. You have known him for one day and have judged him very harshly for one who cannot see souls. I thought you wanted a happy marriage? You often spoke about how your marriage would be your escape back in Hava.'*

I frowned and tied off the plait. "I did. I expected to marry somebody I fell in love with back in Gilava. That's why I'm so upset Elyanna has made me come here and marry this icy, self-important… dismissive…" I fumbled for the right word and grunted instead. I didn't want Falada to see my fear and anger was an easy mask.

'But he is still going to be your husband? Just because you can't choose who to marry, doesn't mean you can't fight for happiness. Don't choose to be miserable to justify making your anger towards Elyanna burn brighter. You don't know him yet. Maybe you could learn to love each other if only you tried? Don't lose that chance.'

I gaped at him. "But I have nothing to win him over with. And no idea if he is a person I even want to be close to. *He* is the one who won't have anything to do with me. What do you expect me to do? I have little to recommend me."

He snorted again and bucked his head. *'Calm yourself, child. Don't fear the worst. Waive your verdict and try to get to know him. Choose to fight for the marriage you want. If you give up now, it will be impossible. If he is as horrible and violent as you say, once you confirm this, stay away from him.'*

I snorted. "You don't understand human marriages. You can't choose to fall in love. And you haven't met him. He's horrible. I'm not even sure he has friends."

He turned a bright eye to me. *'You said you'd barely spoken to him.'*

I put the curry comb back on the shelf and dropped my forehead into Falada's side. I did want him to like me. If I pleased him, he would treat me better, and I would have leverage in our relationship. "Fine, I'll try to get to know him better, but I suspect it will just make everything worse when he rejects me again and again and again."

Falada pushed me roughly with his head. *'Remember who you are, Brianna, and don't let Elyanna's mask change you.'*

I hesitated, trying to work out his meaning. The last person I wanted to become was Elyanna. Falada chewed the end of my braid to soften his words, and I pulled it free before it became too wet with green slobber.

Jeremiah stumbled to a halt outside the stall, making

far more noise than necessary on the floorboards. "Princess? There are men looking for you."

My stomach tightened in the same guilty way it had as a child when our governess caught me stealing honey cakes from the kitchen for Elyanna. I shoved the emotion down. I hadn't done anything wrong in coming to see Falada at this hour.

I gave him one last pat on the neck and tied my cloak tighter to brace for the cold. Outside I could hear men's voices and the sharp crack of heeled boots on frozen stone. The sound of geese honking rose from the barn built against the rear of the stables as they reacted to the commotion. I hoped this incident hadn't woken the entire town.

Jeremiah opened the stable door, and I stood in the pool of yellow light made by the torches of the men. "I'm here. What is wrong?"

Ruo wore a worried expression and hurried over to me. Her long grey hair fell unbound to her waist and her skin was pale with cold. The other men looked like soldiers with Prince Jian at their head. I met his eyes and thought I caught a glimmer of fear before cold annoyance twisted his lips. For once his uniform was not immaculate. His shirt was undone at the neck, revealing his collarbones and the breadth of his shoulders, with a fur coat thrown hastily over the top. I turned to Ruo before my face could consider blushing. "Really, I am fine. What has happened?"

She attempted a smile and rested a hand on my arm. "The night is cold and so I went to your rooms to restock the fires while you slept. But I found you and

Jeremiah gone. I couldn't find you anywhere, so I alerted the guard, and they alerted Prince Jian. Forgive the commotion, Highness, but you shouldn't be wandering alone outside in the dark."

I rubbed my arms. "What are you talking about? I've not left the castle and I'm not alone. I have been with Jeremiah and Falada."

"Your Syberan boy doesn't count." Jian's voice was clipped with suppressed anger. "And I doubt your horse could defend you."

I took a step forward, angry now for both myself and Jeremiah at such a slight. My trepidation grew that he was so willing to humiliate us publicly. "Jeremiah is the head of my guard, and if you haven't noticed, you have provided me with none other. Falada is a Spirit-Horse."

The Prince scoffed. "His Old Blood is dilute. He wouldn't stand a chance by himself."

I stepped right up to him and raised my eyebrows, exasperated. "A chance against what? Explain this to me. What are you afraid of within your own castle?"

His brows lowered. "Borderlanders do not go out alone at night. That is how we live. You're not in Sybera anymore. You'll have a proper guard assembled in the morning." He spun on his heel and strode back into the castle.

I gaped after him. I hoped Falada had heard the slight and realized what an insufferable man he was. I clenched my fists into my skirts.

Ruo prized my arm away from my side and hooked her own through it. "Come now, my dear. It is long past the time we should be in bed. What possessed you to visit your horse on such a cold night?"

I let her pull me back into the dark corridors, and the men dispersed. I didn't meet any of their eyes, still embarrassed at being publicly chastised by my betrothed and that they had all been disturbed at such an hour for my sake. If I needed to get him to like me, I was doing a poor job indeed.

"Ruo, what is going on? Why does nobody go out alone in the dark? Surely your courtyard is safe."

The middle-aged woman sighed and patted my arm where it was linked with hers. "The Borderlanders have many traditions that have been handed down over the years. They are very important to us and are adhered to because they keep people safe and save lives. Yes, you were most likely safe tonight." She hesitated for a moment as if choosing her words carefully. "But there might be a night where you wouldn't be safe alone out there. Our people have a dark and bloody past. We do all we can not to welcome trouble."

I swallowed but kept my voice light. "So all that panic was because I broke one of your traditions?"

She chuckled softly. "In truth, I feared you had fled. The night is cold and the land around here is harsh. I was worried for you."

I covered her hand with mine. "I'm not going anywhere, Ruo. I understand this is my home now."

She smiled and ushered me into my room where she piled the fire with logs. "Don't be too harsh on Prince Jian for his words tonight. He has lost friends and people close to him to the darkness up at the Border. The world he is used to is a dangerous one."

I climbed into bed and warmed my feet on the warming pan which was thankfully still hot. My eyes flickered to my sword which I had dutifully hung on the hooks in the wall. Maybe everyone would calm down if I started carrying it around with me. I remembered the flicker of fear in Jian's eyes before it had been replaced by annoyance. Yes, it was probably best if I kept it close.

VOICES ON THE WIND

*R*uo woke me up far too early by dragging open the heavy curtains with a flourish. "Up, up, my dear. The King and Queen are going out to ride this morning and have invited you to join them."

I stared at the bare stone ceiling and kept the covers pulled up to my chin against the chilly air. It was strange the beds here had no canopies. Maybe it was another one of their excessive traditions, so nobody could be concealed by them. "Will *he* be there," I muttered.

She snorted as she threw a riding habit onto my bed. "He will if the Queen has anything to do with it. Especially when you confirm you are going. She'll drag him out by his ears if she has to."

I laughed at the image and blinked my grainy eyes. I shouldn't have gone to bed so late. I wished I could sleep in, but Falada was right. I should at least try to get to know him and understand why he was so unfriendly, even if it merely confirmed my opinion.

I let Ruo choose all of my outfit, the leather dyed dark blues and reds to contrast with my pale skin and hair, and a fur hat to keep the cold at bay. I actually preferred the simple, practical cuts of the Borderlands over the fussiness of Hava. The clothes had an almost military smartness to them, which I found strange considering how most of the time the sharp lines were covered in furs.

Jeremiah bade his leave as I left the room. His eyes were shadowed and his skin pale. I reminded myself to ensure Jian provided me with an adequate guard so Jeremiah could rest. He might be naive, but I couldn't question his loyalty.

The party was assembling in the courtyard. I was engulfed by noise: the ring of hooves on stone, the excited yaps of dogs, and the snorts of horses forcing people to raise their voices to talk.

Falada had already been taken out and bridled. A bright blue saddle blanket, embroidered with silver, stood out smartly against his white fur. He rocked his head up when he saw me and pranced a few steps in excitement. I giggled and reached to his soft nose in greeting.

As I mounted, I took in my companions. Ruo was unfortunately not joining us, but I felt stronger in Falada's company. Jian was already mounted and was still wearing his military uniform. I wondered if it was partly to annoy his mother by giving a constant message of where he felt he ought to be. He struck me as the sort of man who could never turn off and relax. Prince Han, however, was dressed in white fur with a bright red tunic beneath. He was laughing with an open face towards a young man whose hair was in multiple thin braids that fell to his waist.

Behind him, three women were gossiping with coy glances towards the elder Prince. All of them had hair styles that were far too elaborate for a simple hunt, with long hair pins that glistened in black hair that shone like silk, and two had painted eyes and lips. I wondered if this was another reason Jian preferred to be less notice-able. He didn't seem the sort to want a gaggle of girls hassling him for attention.

The King and Queen sat regally on their mounts and were the closest riders to the gate. A ring of space had formed naturally around them, and they chatted amicably together. The way Queen Fei looked up at her husband with a mischievous twist to her lips, suggested they were still in love. I tightened Falada's reins and shifted in the saddle. I needed to make a good impres-sion today. There would be many eyes on me.

The low drone of horns sounded and Falada pranced sideways before pushing forward, eager to be at the front.

"Falada," I hissed. "Stop showing off."

He pulled the reins sharply forward in reply. Jian had already fallen to the back, I guessed so he didn't have to speak with me. I couldn't remember ever meeting a noble in Hava who was as reclusive as the Prince.

The ground had thawed from the chill of the night, but the air still held a bite and I was glad of the warm fur of my hat. We trotted across the plains to the dark stands of pine trees that spread on and on into the distance. When we entered the shadows of the woodland path, the sharp scent of pines filled my nostrils and the soft ground cushioned the horses' hooves. The party slowed to a walk, and the hounds went tearing off into the trees. The pine branches were so dense, they didn't leave much light for undergrowth, and I wondered how much prey we would find here.

I rode Falada with a straight back, trying to look as regal as possible and stole furtive glances at Prince Jian. He stared ahead or into the woods and looked disengaged from the rest of the party. Was he going to interact with me at all? We were going to be married in two months, he could at least talk to me. Ignoring me wasn't going to get him back to the Border any quicker. I wanted to know what he was like, even if it was just a glimpse. Was he a thoughtless brute or a private philosopher?

The Queen pulled up beside me, a large bow already strung on her back, and she asked shallow questions about the quality of hunting in Sybera and the breeding of the horses. Though I loved to ride, I'd never enjoyed hunting. Elyanna did though; murdering innocent animals was almost a passion for her, so I answered the questions as best as I could. My thoughts kept turning to the butterfly she had sprayed with ink until its wings became too heavy to fly. Those kittens she had drowned in the water trough. Maybe it *was* an escape to come here.

After a few miles we paused to let the horses rest and drink from a stream. The dogs yapped happily around the hound master and the atmosphere was relaxed. A servant passed me a wineskin and a heel of bread.

Worried that the alcohol would go straight to my head, I dismounted to fill up my water bottle from the stream and gasped as the icy water flowed over my hand. It was so bitterly cold, my bottle slipped from my fingers, and I cried out as it was taken by the current and bounced back and forth between the rocks as it flowed away. I took a few steps after it, but then a gloved hand snatched it from the water. I looked up and saw Prince Jian pressing in the stopper and handing it to me. My heart started to thud in my chest. This was my chance to start a conversation.

"Thank you," I said, my voice sounding strained. I took the bottle and clutched it to my chest, trying to think of something to say.

The Prince nodded and headed back to the horses and I cursed under my breath. I needed to think of an interesting conversation topic, but it would help if he put in some effort too. He could at least pretend to be interested in me as his future bride.

I rushed to catch up over the icy rocks before the opportunity went, but he spoke first, making me jump. "Do you know how to use that?"

I frowned and reached his side. "I'm sorry?"

He gestured to where my sword was strapped to Falada's saddle. "Your sword. Can you use it?"

I raised an eyebrow. "Of course."

He tilted his head with a disbelieving twist to his lips. "You used to train in Sybera?"

I gave a firm nod. "Most days. Most nobles do."

"Against other women I presume?"

I frowned and folded my arms. This was an area I could prove my worth in. "And men. Is that quite so unbelievable? I could beat all the other nobles."

He shrugged and looked me up and down with a quick sweep of his eyes. "You're just so... skinny."

I swallowed down my annoyance at his tone and almost said I was better than Princess Elyanna, before remembering I was supposed to be her. I dried my hands on my skirts and strapped my water bottle to the saddle, turning my back to him. I asked lightly, "Do you want a match?"

He barked a laugh. "I wouldn't just let you win, you realize."

I pulled myself into Falada's saddle so I could look down at him. "Likewise. I understand if you don't want to; you might get hurt."

He shook his head slowly, a small smile twitching his lips. "Fine, we'll spar tomorrow." He mounted his own horse in one swift, elegant motion.

"Is it not normal for you to fight women?" I focused on pulling on my gloves and gathering the reins rather than looking at him. It was easier to be confident without seeing his dismissive eyes.

"Yes, but they're Borderlanders, not southerners. Everyone here has to be prepared in case there is a breakthrough at the Passes."

His words caught my interest and I turned to look at him. I knew little about the Border which this kingdom defended. The books said that beyond it lay a wasteland of monsters. Beasts and men purely of the Old Blood but twisted by their search for power. My nanny had scared me with stories of the Beasts when I'd refused to go to bed or come in from playing in the garden. It was of little concern to Sybera, however, so we hadn't studied it further than how the threat had militarized Borderland governance.

"Does that ever happen?"

He looked off into the forest, his expression turning vacant. "Not in the last ten years."

I leant closer towards him. "What happened ten years ago?"

His eyes met mine and they were colder than ever before. "A lot of people died." He kicked his horse and trotted off to the front of the group, leaving me wondering if I'd touched a forbidden subject. Maybe this was why nobody went out alone in the dark.

The rest of the group was starting to move, and I nudged Falada to join them.

'He's not very talkative, is he?' The horse shook out his mane and chomped on the bit.

"No, he's not," I replied. "And not very friendly either. I told you so. What am I going to do?"

A deep voice from behind me made me jump. "Oh, don't worry too much. You get used to him. It's the way he talks to everyone." I turned to see Prince Han riding up to us on his huge chestnut warhorse. I felt my cheeks heat at being overheard. The Crown Prince gave me a wide smile. "As I said before, he takes a while to adjust to new people."

I smiled at him, but my insides recoiled at being so

close to a man who had probably killed his wife. "Any advice for conversation starters?"

He thought for a moment, scratching his short beard. "Eh, no not really. His passion is the Border, the defense of the Forts and the loyalty of his men, but they can also be touchy subjects for him at the moment, so I wouldn't recommend them."

Great. "Does he have any hobbies?"

"Eh," he pulled his hand through his hair. "He likes to spar and read military books."

I sank down into my saddle. He sounded so boring. At least the sparing was an area I could join him in.

Prince Han cleared his throat and seemed uneasy as if not sure he should keep talking. "Jian has lost people very dear to him in the past. It makes him... cautious about his attachments and protective. Some might say overprotective. Just... give him time. He is a good brother to me and a fine general to his men."

The sharp blow of a horn made me jump and the horses leapt forward, ending our conversation. Falada launched into a gallop in excitement, and Han's words were torn from my mind. Some poor animal must have been sighted. I tried to merely focus on the joy of the ride, but Falada wanted to *win*.

He leapt a log with a high-pitched whinny and flared his nostrils, his head nodding faster and faster. I gripped hard with my knees as he wove tightly between the trees.

"Falada," I warned, but he didn't respond. I could feel the excitement quivering down his flanks and his joy at the reckless abandon of the chase. I held on tight and trusted his judgement.

There were no Spirit-Horses in Stonekeep, meaning Falada stood a full two hands taller than even the Crown Prince's horse, and had the longest legs. He was the fastest, and he wanted to be recognized as such. He sped between pines, and leaped streams and rocks. He caught up with the hounds and the other riders fell behind.

I caught sight of our quarry through the trees; the grey bushy tail of a wolf, its ears flattened with panic. I wanted to pull Falada away and not take part in this, but I knew it was too late. The dogs growled and attacked the snarling wolf, leaping onto its back. I rode past the rolling mass of fur and teeth before I eased Falada to a walk, not wanting to see the wolf ripped apart. I knew their numbers had to be kept down or they would take too much of the livestock, or worse, prey on children, but it didn't make the act any less distasteful.

The zip of an arrow whizzed overhead, and a bundle of white fell to the pine needles in front of me. I edged closer and saw a dove beating its wings against the snow-speckled floor. It was pierced clean through by an arrow.

'Help, help.' The voice was quiet, thin.

I froze in shock. Surely this was a trick of my imagination? It should be impossible for me to hear this bird speak. It wasn't of the Old Blood and we weren't bonded. It made no sense.

"Falada?" I asked.

The horse snorted in return. His breaths were still labored from the chase, misting the air around us.

"Can you hear the dove speak?"

He shook out his mane and swiveled his ears forward. *'Perhaps. Faint on the wind. I'm surprised you can hear it.'*

Cold shot through me as I watched its helpless fluttering, the arrow holding fast. Crimson seeped into white feathers. I felt sick. "Do... do all animals talk?"

'In their own way, yes. But only those of the Old Blood can use words that humans understand. This bird must have the faintest of bloodlines. There is no outward sign at all. But the magic in these woods is strong. I have never run that well before.'

"What does that mean? How can I hear it?"

The hiss of leather sliding against leather made me jump as Prince Han dismounted beside me and thudded to the ground. He strode to the dove in long strides and snapped its neck. He met my eyes and grinned. "Too squeamish to do the deed?"

My nausea only grew, and I turned away before I disgraced myself.

I heard a woman's voice behind me, bright and flirtatious, as I steered Falada to the main party. "What did you expect from a Syberan? They're all so fragile. She wouldn't survive a day on the Border."

Han's reply was low and soft and lost in the whisperings of the pines.

SIXTH LEVEL SWORDSMAN

I woke up feeling energized and was dressed in tunic and leggings before Ruo had reached the room. I stretched my muscles and did a warm-up routine with my sword. It was frustrating that I hadn't sparred in almost two weeks, and already I could feel the stiffness in my thighs and arms, but I was still going to wipe that dismissive smile right off Jian's arrogant face. This was one thing I had truly excelled at back in Hava. Not even Elyanna had managed to hold me back.

I ate a light breakfast of fruit and drank only water. This close to the mountains, it was safer than the water in Hava and I was grateful to be able to keep my head clear. I was looking forward to finding an activity to do with Jian that wasn't awkward and wouldn't involve the embarrassment of an onlooking crowd.

Jeremiah already knew where the training grounds were and looked better than he had in days. The Queen had provided me with a guard of two extra men, so two could guard me at night if Jeremiah wished. It was good to see the squire looking fresh and alert, his boots shined and his cheeks shaven. He led the way down busy halls with a bounce to his step.

I had hoped to reach the training square before Jian so I could familiarize myself with the weight of the training swords, but he was already there sparring with an important looking soldier. Despite the cold of early morning, sweat gleamed on their brows, and I guessed they had been fighting a while. I shaded my eyes to take in his footwork, the side he favored, his strengths and weaknesses. But their swords *flew* so fast I became lost in the beauty of it, and it took all my willpower not to gape. Borderlander swords were thinner in general than the ones in Sybera, and the fighting style was faster, more graceful. I'd only fought against Syberans before. My confidence faltered.

Jian saw me and called a halt, bowing sharply to his opponent and then nodding towards me. The stocky soldier returned his practice sword to the staff master, stripped down to his uniform, and left without acknowledging me. From the brocade on his chest, I guessed he was a commander, maybe a captain. I pulled on a padded tunic that stank and strapped on the knee and elbow guards. There were leather braces for both my arms, decorated with tide marks of dried sweat and warped out of shape with age and use.

The staff master handed me a wooden sword, weighed down with an iron rod through its center. Its balance was different to what I was used to, and it felt awkward in my hand. I performed a few practice swipes and adjusted my footwork to stop me overreaching myself. I wished Jian hadn't been here early; this was already unfair.

I looked over my shoulder to where the Prince stood at the edge of the ring drinking water, his expression was blank, but his eyes were analyzing me. I looked away as my skin prickled, and I walked to the center of the ring, not checking to see if he would follow.

I picked a spot and checked the ground for rocks before picking a stance. Jian strolled in front of me with his sword resting casually on his shoulder, and his lips pressed together in amusement.

He looked at the dirt as he swung his sword down. His fringe fell forward, dripping. "You do know I am a sixth level swordsman and General of the Guard at the Eastern Pass, right?"

I shrugged. I had no idea what 'sixth level' meant anyway.

He shrugged back. "I am merely letting you know. It's completely acceptable for you not to do well."

I grimaced. "Are all Borderlanders so arrogant?"

His eyes met mine and there was no playful boasting in his gaze. "It's not arrogance, it's the truth." His voice was flat.

I felt a shiver ripple down my spine. Sure, I had been good in the ring at Sybera, but we were a country at peace. This man slew monsters. I shrugged again.

He raised an eyebrow. "I'm not the one with an inflated view of my talents."

I opened my mouth to object, then thought better of it. I couldn't let him goad me into anger; it was the oldest trick in the book. I rolled my shoulder and held my wooden sword up in a defensive position. He swung his up casually and then sprung forward, testing my guard. I parried and stepped back into neutral. He lunged again, this time testing the other side of my guard, and again I parried, but only just. He was quick and nerve-wracking in his precision. I tried to give nothing away with my expression, but I felt like every move I made was stripped bare under his prying eyes. He lunged a third time, and this time he caught me off balance. My sword merely skimmed his as he broke through and landed a blow to my side. I grunted, but could tell he was softening the blow. I tried to retaliate by bringing my elbow down on his outstretched arm, disarming him. But he was too quick and spun, landing a blow on my other side.

He took a few steps back and cocked his head. "You need to work on your left side. It's a glaringly obvious weakness."

I felt a stab of annoyance at his tone, but it was soon suppressed by a bubble of excitement. This man could fight, *really* fight, far better than any of my instructors back home. And now I didn't have Elyanna cutting our training sessions short, or complaining when I did well, or making me fan her when she got hot. And finally, I had the elusive Prince's full attention.

"Again," I said, rotating my toes into the dirt.

He attacked, this time high, and I shoved his sword away, only for it to spin and come at me in a diagonal thrust. I barely got my blade down in time. His face was now close to my hilt, and I tried to ram it towards his nose. He leapt back, faster than I'd have thought possible, and I staggered forward a step before catching my balance.

He raised an eyebrow. "You're fighting dirty for the training ring." His breathing was as steady as before.

I shrugged. "I thought you were a *sixth level swordsman*. I'm sure you can cope."

He gave me a patronizing smile. "Of course. Especially when it makes you wobble like a toddler." He pushed his fringe back. "Now, I want to see your attack."

We must have fought for a good hour before my arms were on fire, my back aching and I could barely lift the sword anymore. I bent over, leaning on my knees, panting.

Jian spun his wooden sword in his hand. The sweat in his hair made it stick up at strange angles and curve over one eye. It should have made him look foolish, but I begrudgingly admitted, the look suited him. He was much less sweaty now than he had been with the soldier earlier. "Well, you were better than I was expecting."

I straightened, letting my sword rest on the ground and wiped the sweat from my eyes. "If you're sixth level, what am I?"

He picked up my sword for me and walked back to the rack, where the staff master was oiling chainmail. "Third level, possibly fourth," he called over his shoulder.

"Third or fourth?" I said, my voice laden with disappointment. "But I've been training my whole life. I beat my staff master in Hava. I could beat everyone."

"That's not a bad level. You have the slight advantage

of the Old Blood but were coddled, that's all. That's not an option for people here. Still, I expected you to be a two at best." He placed the swords on the rack, pulled off his padded jerkin and strode back to the palace without a glance or a farewell.

As soon as he was out of sight I hobbled to a bench and groaned at all my bruises. I was going to need a long bath after that session, and I hadn't managed to touch him once. Still, I supposed, if there were people defending us against monsters, I wanted them to be good.

Jeremiah came to the bench with a big grin on his face. "That was very impressive, Your Highness." He sat down beside me and stretched out his legs.

"Was it? I feel like I was thoroughly beaten." I groaned as I tried to lift my arm to take off the disgusting gauntlet.

My guard's eyes were focused on the place Jian had disappeared. "I've never seen somebody fight like that. You stood well against him."

I wasn't sure I liked his gaze of admiration as he stared after the Prince. "Well, hopefully I will be able to improve here."

It felt strange having this bit of my identity torn away. If I was no longer exceptional at sword fighting, there was nothing left of note about me. Well apart from being a Princess, but that was Elyanna, not me. I expected to feel despair and frustration, but I still loved swordplay and always would. Maybe here, the challenge would make me love it even more. Maybe I could become a sixth level swordsman too and gain the respect of these people. Maybe working hard would gain Jian's affections. If I had been able to win Elyanna over, my life would have been so different.

Jeremiah nodded, his smile wistful. "I'm jealous that you trained with him. Most soldiers would give an arm and a leg for a session like that."

I massaged my legs and felt them stiffening already. I hurried to take off the rest of the protective padding. "Well before you consider trading yours, help me get back to my rooms, will you? I think I may need both your arms as all my muscles are starting to die a horrible death."

He chuckled and held out his elbow as I hobbled to my feet.

❄

I WAS INCAPACITATED for the rest of the day, but I welcomed the painful ache of my muscles. This was what unhindered learning felt like. Ruo ran me a bath and rubbed stinking lotions into my muscles that flinched at her touch, then left me lying on my front in bed, with nothing but a blanket over my back while they absorbed into my skin.

I asked her to read to me, any book which would help me understand the Borderlands better. To my surprise she picked a book of children's stories. I frowned at the cover from my half-buried position. "I was thinking more of politics and history, Ruo."

The older woman shook her head, her large bronze earrings tapping against her neck. "You can't understand history or politics or indeed anything, until you understand the stories of a place. Stories are of the heart and of the blood. Every thought is governed by them. The people of the Borderlands are raised on stories and so you must read them."

She opened the cover with a loving caress, and I grinned as I wondered if this was merely a case of self-indulgence.

She read the tales and they all spoke of the Beasts and men of the Old Blood. They spoke of half-crazed talking animals and deep magic and bravery against the odds. Men and women fighting alongside each other, but wit and cunning being praised above strength. Girls rode wolves and babies suckled from foxes. Bears loved one moment and killed the next.

The stories were so embellished, I couldn't tell what was fact and what was fancy. But in all of them, a strong message ran: Whether rich or poor, strong or weak, the cautious and careful survived. The hasty and ill-prepared perished.

When she had finished, I eased myself into sitting, grimacing at the pain that rippled through my back. "What happened at the breakthrough ten years ago, Ruo? Were you here in Stonekeep?"

Her eyes tightened, and I almost regretted asking the question, but it clearly still impacted them, and I wanted to understand.

"I was. The Eastern Fort was attacked and some of the enemy got past and melted away into our forests. The casualties were highest at the Fort, but it took months to track down every Spirit-Beast. There were deaths across the entirety of the Borderlands. Princess Feng fell. She was only thirteen and such a bright flame." She stopped to shake her head, then gave me a pained look "My husband died too, but not in vain. Not one Spirit-Beast made it to Sybera or any other country. We kept the south safe."

I rested my hand on hers. "I'm so sorry for your loss."

She gave me a broken smile. "Thank you, dear. It was a long time ago now, but my son, Chen, and I both miss him still."

"And Prince Jian?" I breathed.

"He was at the Eastern Fort when it was attacked. He was only fourteen but received a reward for bravery."

I hugged my knees into my chest, a shiver refusing to leave my blood. "It sounds awful."

She nodded and gave a gentle smile. "The Forts have held since then, but we always take care. It is not inconceivable that one or two Spirit-Beasts have entered our realm undetected over the Sal'hadar Mountains."

I looked at my sword hung on the wall and nodded. She patted my knee. "Don't fret, dear. You are very well protected in Stonekeep. Now I recommend we take a stroll in the garden to loosen those muscles. Maybe we could think about what color drapes you would like at your wedding?"

I nodded and got dressed but couldn't shake the image of a fourteen-year-old boy facing intelligent, giant Beasts as the Fort was overrun. No wonder he hadn't been impressed by my little show of sword play. I suspected he would never be impressed by me at all.

✳

THE NEXT DAY I did my exercise routine in my room, then decided to take a walk around the castle to familiarize myself with its echoing halls.

I opened the door and was surprised to see Jeremiah was absent and the two new guards were standing to either side. They turned and nodded at me, bringing their fists to their chests in salute. Both were dressed in chainmail with scaled armor over their shoulders and chests. One had short black hair, shorter even than Jian's, and rings in his ears. He had a short beard that framed his mouth, yet left his cheeks bare. The other was clean-shaven and had his hair tied in a neat topknot with a red linen tie hanging from it.

I shifted on my feet. "Oh. Where is Jeremiah?"

The first one replied with an amused smile. "Resting, Highness. He is not well. We are guarding you today." I guessed he thought Jeremiah weak for needing some time to sleep. A niggle of guilt settled in my stomach for not taking more care of him. He spent hours standing in this cold, bare corridor day and night with little to do.

I focused on the guards and lifted my chin to hide my disappointment. Jeremiah was easy to relax around and talk to. These men looked intimidating, even if they were both shorter than me. I forced myself to remember I was Princess Elyanna now. "Thank you. What are your names?"

"Cai Hong and Hai Rong, Highness." The short haired one indicated that the first name belonged to his companion, who gave a sharp bow. "We've been assigned to guard you as long as you require. We are both of the fourth level."

"Fourth level swordsmen?" Why were the Borderlanders always announcing their levels?

He bowed his head again. "Yes, Highness."

I took a step forward. "I am going to take a walk around the castle. I assume at least one of you should accompany me?" So I don't get shouted at by Jian again.

Hai Rong's lip twitched. "We are both assigned to protect you, Highness."

I started walking down the corridor, choosing directions on a whim. "I can imagine this is a rather boring assignment for you?"

Hai Rong chuckled. "Not at all. Neither of us have been in Stonekeep for most of the year. It will be a welcome break to spend time with our families, and we both asked to be stationed here. Cai Hong has just become a father."

I turned to him. "Congratulations."

The solemn man nodded. "Thank you, Highness." His voice was deep and rich.

"Boy or girl?"

"Boy. We've called him Jian."

I raised my eyebrows in surprise. "After Prince Jian?"

"Yes, Highness. In his honor. Prince Jian saved my life at the Border. Little Jian wouldn't be here without him. It is our prayer that he grows up to have the same strength and loyalty as the Prince."

I looked away from the guard and frowned. "I am sure he's very touched by the gesture."

It seemed that even though he had few friends in

Stonekeep, Jian was deeply loved by the soldiers at the Border. I supposed they got all his attention after all. I couldn't help but feel a quiet burn of jealousy. How could I compete with them?

I rounded a corner into a cloister. The covered path surrounded a courtyard with a leafless tree in the center, shading an empty fountain. It was mostly paved in stone and looked as dreary as the rest of this place. I missed the autumn fire of Hava and the way the gardeners changed the plants in the garden so there was color at every time of the year. A gentle scattering of snow fell from the clouds and drifted around the cloister before melting. I hugged my thick fur cloak.

As we turned onto the far side of the cloister my heart dropped as I saw Prince Jian talking with a soldier. I recognized him as the commander Jian had been sparring with before me. They were deep in conversation and didn't turn at our footsteps.

I quickened my pace up to the Prince and cleared my throat. "Prince Jian, good morning." Behind me I heard the slap of leather as both my guards saluted, hands to chests.

There was no emotion in Jian's face as he regarded me and gave a stiff nod. "Princess Elyanna."

I didn't let his lack of enthusiasm deter me. "Will you spar with me again?"

He turned his face to the side, and I was sure I saw a flicker of annoyance in his eyes. "I'm sorry, Princess, but I am needed to train our soldiers who will be rotating to the Border next month. There are plenty of other people available for you to spar with." He started to walk away, leaving me to follow a pace behind.

I tried to not let my disappointment show in my voice. "How far away is the Border?"

The captain responded this time. His hair was short like Jian's and their uniforms were similar, but that was where the similarities ended. Whereas Jian was tall and slender, the captain was broad and stocky, and his cheek bore a twisted scar. If he had any of the Old Blood, it was only a trace; I was taller than him by at least a finger. "Two days' ride to the Western Pass. Three to the Eastern Pass, Your Highness."

I kept my attention on the Prince's back. "Can I go and see it?"

Jian stopped and turned. "Absolutely not. It's too dangerous and the Fort is not a hospitable place."

I took a step back at his tone. Han had said he was overprotective after all. "It can't be that dangerous. Won't I be surrounded by *Borderlanders* and *sixth level* swordsmen?" I placed my hands on my hips. "I thought the monsters haven't broken through for ten years."

He frowned at my guards as if they had somehow put the idea into my head, then focused back on me. "No, but there is still fighting. There are other dangers too, rockslides, avalanches, unsavory men and women, the cold."

His gaze was too intense, and I looked down at his chest and the double row of buttons. "I won't truly understand this place and this way of life until I see the Border."

He turned and walked away. "Sometimes it's better

when you don't see the dark side of things. Understanding only the light is not a bad way to live." He disappeared around the corner and the captain bowed to me while hopping to catch up. I tugged my cloak in frustration. Why did he have to be so hard to talk to?

I would never understand him if he hid away everything that was important to him. How could I find my place here and protect myself if he so clearly labeled me as worthless?

"He's very preoccupied, Highness," said Hai Rong from behind my shoulder.

"He's very rude," I corrected.

"He might not be charming like Prince Han, but he cares deeply about what he does and that's not a bad thing," added Cai Hong in his softer voice. "He has thrown all his energy into the Border defenses. He's not one to pretend. You'll always know where you stand with him."

I sighed internally. Clearly these men would always be on his side and those words didn't help. I wondered what had happened in Jian's past to make him like this. Was it simply the trauma of the breakthrough ten years ago? Or was there more of a reason his brother and men were so quick to defend him? I didn't think they would tell me. "Who is the other man? Are they close friends? He should have introduced him."

"Captain Cheng Jun. Jun has known Prince Jian since they were children. He's the man ultimately responsible for the training of our soldiers," Hai Rong replied.

I pointed to him. "Will you spar with me? It looks

like I'm going to have to settle for a *fourth level swordsman*."

He looked a little surprised. "If you wish, Highness."

I gave him a bright smile. "Good. I'll go back and get changed." It would be nice to hit something hard and pretend that I was strong and unafraid.

PATIENCE

Stonekeep didn't have a library as such, but it did have a tower where the children were taught, and each of the round rooms was rimmed with books, maps, and drawings. It was a quiet space where I could browse and learn at my leisure unlike in Hava where Elyanna would get bored in the library and drag me away. People came here when they didn't want to be disturbed.

I was looking for information on the Border while Jeremiah played a strange game with Cai Hong in one corner with small figures shaped like wolves, horses, whales and eagles. They could each only move on certain squares and Jeremiah was enraptured by it. He more than made up for Cai Hong's silence by talking at length about every possible move he could do. He didn't seem to grasp that keeping his plans to himself would be far more prudent.

The only information I had found on this floor were drawings of the Forts from twenty years ago contrasting with five years ago. In the older drawings they looked half deserted and crumbling. The more recent ones showed new walls and ever-expanding defenses. It looked like the Borderlands were better protected against the Spirit-Beasts than ever before. As for information on the Spirit-Beasts themselves, I was surprised by how little information there was apart from old myths and legends.

I left the guards to their game and spiraled up the stairs to the floor above. I stumbled around a stack of unbound pages and jumped when two heads looked up at me from another game board. It was the two Princes, wine in their hands and an apple and cheese platter scattered across a pile of books.

Prince Jian regarded me without interest, though Prince Han gave a wide grin, slapping his thighs. "Elyanna!"

I took a step back towards the stairs. I wasn't in the mood for Jian today. "Sorry, I didn't mean to disturb your game."

Han stood up. "Nonsense. Come, come." He beckoned me over. "I am about to thrash Jian and I want to have a witness, or he'll pretend it never happened." He grinned at his brother who raised an unamused eyebrow in return and sipped his wine.

"It's only because you cheated."

Han sighed theatrically. "It was one move, ages ago. You're just holding a grudge."

The corners of Jian's lips twitched up. "I am planning my revenge."

Han sniggered. "Need to impress your woman now

she's in the room?"

I shifted. I was definitely not comfortable being referred to as Jian's woman, which I supposed was ridiculous since we would be married in seven weeks. But I didn't want him to own me. I wanted to be treasured and safe.

Jian sighed and moved a black wolf onto a green square. "No, you're the one who feels the need to impress the women, Han. Though why you like them all fawning over you, I have no idea."

I shifted again, feeling like they had forgotten I was here. I took a step back towards the stairs, wondering if I could slip away, but Han's head shot back around to me. "Elyanna, come and join us. It's my last day in Stonekeep, so it would be rude to refuse." He grinned, showing all his teeth.

My heart sank, and I chose a stack of books to balance on top of by the board. "I'm afraid I don't know this game."

Han shrugged. "I'm sure Jian can teach you sometime." He grinned at his brother as if sharing a secret joke.

I ignored Jian and stayed focused on Han. "Where are you going?"

"North-west on patrol. We visit all the small villages in the west every year before winter to make sure they have what they need and to gather reports of the area. Keep track of the numbers of wolves and such." He moved a horse away from the wolf. Jian quickly moved a whale into a blue square, blocking it from the rest of its herd.

"How long will you be gone?" I studied the board trying to work out which pieces belonged to whom.

He shrugged. "About three weeks most likely. But don't you fear. I'll be back with plenty of time before the wedding." He moved an eagle next to Jian's wolf and grinned at his brother. "Somebody's got to embarrass him on his wedding day."

Jian's eyes were on the board and he moved three pieces at once. Everything about him was careful and measured apart from his fringe, as if he wanted something to hide his face behind. "You mean you will embarrass yourself, and I will have to think up an excuse to extract you?"

Han snorted. "I might as well have fun while being a general embarrassment. You'll be more embarrassed than me, I assure you."

Jian raised his eyebrows. "You can't move."

Han frowned. "Now, hang on a minute. You're almost dead. I must be able to move."

Jian cocked his head. "It doesn't take many pieces to beat you when you're not paying attention."

Han studied the board and swore. "I really thought I had you."

Jian spread out his hands. "You never beat me. Even when you cheat."

"Maybe I was paying attention to something more important?" Han raised an eyebrow meaningfully at his brother, who glared at him in return.

"I am here, you know." I folded my arms.

Han stood. "Well, I'll leave it to you, Elyanna, to beat him on my behalf in my absence." He pulled on his fur cloak and wiped the pieces from the board. "Forgive my departure. I've got a hoard of ladies to say goodbye to."

Jian gave him an exasperated expression. "Of course you do."

Han hesitated and squeezed his brother's shoulder. He spoke so softly, I wasn't sure I heard the words correctly. "You can let her in, brother. It won't happen again. You deserve to be happy."

Then the heaviness was gone from his face, and he winked at me and headed for the stairs as if he'd never spoken. What had that been about?

I looked at the board and edged into the elder Prince's seat. "I've never learnt to play board games." Elyanna had never had the patience. I lifted my eyes to Jian, but he was focused on assembling the pieces that Han had scattered into a mess. "I'm surprised you have time. You're so busy."

Jian arranged the pieces deftly across the four colors of squares. "Han enjoys them and he's leaving tomorrow. Despite his habit of cheating, I enjoy his company. Besides, they keep the mind sharp. I have time for one more quick game." He finally met my eyes, and I suppressed the urge to fidget. Something about being so close to him made me nervous enough that I couldn't quite catch my breath.

"I'm honored." My nerves made the comment sound less sarcastic than I'd intended.

He ignored my response and started to point at pieces on the board. "You can be wolves and horses, they're the strongest pieces for beginners. I'll be whales and eagles. The blue squares represent water, the green represent grass, the brown is forest and mountains, the white is air." He ran through the moves each type could make on the different colored squares, but I was only half listening. I studied the features of his face, trying to figure him out: his straight nose and high cheekbones. This jaw that swept to a pointed chin with its arrogant, self-assured tilt. Those dark eyes that bordered on black and looked at everything with such intensity, yet easily seemed bored. Together his features were striking more than handsome, as if designed to put you off-balance. I still couldn't figure out what he was really like beneath.

Jian indicated that I should make a move, so I did one of the few moves I was sure was allowed. "Falada keeps saying that the Old Magic is stronger here. What does that mean?"

Jian straightened a little at the question. "The further north you go, the stronger it gets. It's why Spirit-Beasts with pure Old Blood live there." He moved an eagle onto a white square.

"But what does that mean? What is the Old Magic?"

He hesitated. "Your move."

I moved a horse two forward, keeping on the green squares where I knew it was allowed. "Well?"

He tilted his head. "Why do you ask?" He moved two eagles to kill my horse and his eyes flicked up to mine.

My mouth dried, and I hurriedly frowned down at the board. "How can two eagles kill a horse?"

He shrugged. "These represent the Spirit-Beasts of old. If you see a full-blooded one, you will understand. Your Falada is a pale shadow." He placed my horse neatly by the board. "Your move."

"You've not answered my question." I tried to keep my voice light and unintimidated. I moved a piece at random.

"And you haven't answered mine. Why do you ask? Did something strange happen?" The intensity of his gaze heightened and the skin on my arms prickled. It felt like he was the center of a whirlpool, and I was a leaf spinning uselessly around him.

"I… I thought I heard the voice of one of the birds killed in the hunt. It looked normal, not like a Spirit-Bird. How is that possible?"

He sighed and relaxed, pushing his fringe back from his eyes. "Many animals here have traces of the Old Blood, and many of the people. The Old Magic is part of the land. We walk on it, eat it, drink it, breathe it. It amplifies that blood unpredictably, as well as giving general strength. Sometimes strange things happen." He moved his whales down a column of blue I assumed was a river dividing the grassland from the woods.

"What sort of strange things?" I moved my closest wolf away from the water.

"For fleeting moments, individuals sometimes do things of the Old Blood they shouldn't be able to with their diluted blood. Han, for example, heard Falada yesterday, even though they're not bonded. Sometimes both individuals having some of the Old Blood is enough."

I leant forward. "He did?" A surprising flash of jealousy squeezed my chest.

He snickered at my horror, and I felt some of the tension leave my back. "Only the once. Like I said, sometimes these things happen. Spirit talks to Spirit. It's not within anyone's control." He gentled his voice. "I know the voices can be disconcerting, but the easiest thing to do is ignore them."

He moved his eagles a ridiculous number of squares and surrounded my horses.

I lowered my hands flat on the board in surprise. "You can do that?"

He nodded, impatience tightening his shoulders. "I did explain the eagles can fly as far as they wish if no other pieces are in their way and can move in a unit."

I moved my wolves further from the water, and Jian reached out to block my hand. His skin was surprisingly warm compared to mine. "There's no point doing that. You've lost."

I gaped at him, withdrawing my hand. "But we just started, and I still have all but one of my pieces."

He shrugged. "Look at the board. You can't regroup, you can barely move. My eagles will pick you off one by one while the whales hold you in place, and that is simply boring."

I sat back and folded my arms. In frustration "You're a bad teacher. You didn't explain any of what you just did."

"I can be a good teacher, but only to those who wish to learn. Right now, you don't." He stood and straightened the uniform of his coat. It was as smart and clean as always. "Ignore the voices, Princess, and don't think on what they say."

I straightened, regretting my childish response. "Where are you going?"

"I must approve the supplies for the Fort of the Western Pass and organize a guard for their transport. It's not long now before the snows come, so this time of year is always busy." He gave a stiff bow. "Excuse me, Princess."

I opened my mouth, but I wasn't quick enough to think of something to say before he disappeared after his brother. I groaned and flicked the pieces over one by one, not caring if they skidded off the table. Elyanna deserved to marry such an indifferent, insufferable man. Why hadn't she let me go home to Gilava?

I wasn't meant to be here. I wasn't the one who could win his affection. I could hear Falada's voice, telling me to be patient, kind and gracious, until I knew what he was like. But I wasn't sure how long I could go on like this.

*

RUO PULLED out one of my finer dresses with fox fur lining its sleeves and laid it on my bed. She turned and dug around for a matching coat.

I raised my eyebrow while I chewed on bread dipped in golden egg yolk. I was still dressed in my shift and the fur coat I used as a bedrobe, my feet bare. Ruo had barely spoken to me, perhaps picking up on my bad mood left over from yesterday.

"What's the occasion?" I asked, covering my mouth as I spoke so I didn't spray crumbs. Elyanna would have never talked with her mouth full.

"The Queen has asked for your company this morning. Her mood is always a little low the day one of her sons leaves. She is probably wanting you to distract her as well as give you both the chance to get to know each other."

My stomach twisted with nerves. "When are we meeting?"

Ruo glanced out at the weak beams of the sun peeping through the fractures in the clouds. "You have enough time for a bath and to do your hair. I think she wants to show you the town." She saw my expression and chuckled. "Don't you worry, dear. Queen Fei *wants* to like you. You will see enough around the town to find topics of conversation."

I nodded and finished my eggs and toasted bread with more vigor. Whatever Ruo said, this meeting felt like a test to see if I was suitable to marry Jian. I didn't know what she would expect from me. I thought back to the stories Ruo had been reading to me. Fables and myths designed to shape children's moral compasses. Wit, cunning, perseverance and caution had been praised. Was this what Ruo expected me to take from them? Were these the values the Borderlanders all held, spread by the medium of stories?

Well, it was a place to start.

Ruo fastened the last tie on the back of my dress and I thanked her, making for the door. She caught my arm and pointed to my sword. "I would take that, if I were you."

I gave her a thankful smile and strapped it to my waist. "I should wear this, not because I'm in danger, but because it makes me look cautious and prepared, correct?"

Ruo snorted. "You're in the Borderlands, my dear. You should be cautious and prepared all the time because you *could* be in danger."

I sighed. My maid smiled and softened her voice. "But yes. It will make the right impression. This will be the first time most of the townsfolk have seen you."

She handed me some rabbit fur gloves, squeezed my hand for support, and opened the door. Jeremiah was there by himself, and he appeared to have been informed about our meeting with the Queen. His uniform was spotless, and his boots shone. He'd even given himself a close shave.

"You're looking very smart, Jeremiah."

He grinned and gave a bow. "Don't want to let you down, Princess."

I patted him on the arm. "Of course you won't." I looked down and took a deep breath. "Let's just hope she likes me."

He snorted. "Nobody could not like you."

I gave an uncomfortable laugh and started heading down the corridor so I didn't have to reply to such a comment. There was one man who made it very clear he didn't like me, and he was the man I most needed to win over to secure my place here.

The Queen was waiting for me in a corridor, gazing out of a window at the frost in the willow trees. Every elegant branch glittered with shards of ice. She wore a thick coat of black bear fur with a blade hanging from her waist. Her skin was pale as she faced the frigid air, and her lips were painted blood-red. She had always been kind and gentle to me, but as she stared out, lost in thought, she cast an imposing aura.

She turned at the sound of my boots and her features relaxed. I wondered for the first time if she wore a mask as a persona to shut people out, just like Jian. Only she had several theatrical masks that she could change at will. With me she was kind and mother-like. With the next person she could be a merciless judge or an all-powerful ruler. She was meant to be politically astute, after all. I wondered how long I would have to get to know her before I could tell what she really felt.

"Elyanna." She held out her hand and looped it through my arm before I could curtsy. "Thank you for joining me this morning. Will you walk with me? I'm told you have not yet explored the town."

"No," I admitted. "I have not left the walls of the castle since arriving." And even then, Jian had told me off. "I am very grateful that you can spare the time."

We reached a doorless archway that led to the open cloisters. No wonder it was always so cold when there weren't even doors. We passed the tree and the fountain and entered an arch which led to icy steps down to the large courtyard outside the castle where the stables and armory were. I was glad of Queen Fei's hold on my arm as the cobbles were treacherous.

"How are things going between you and Jian?" The Queen kept her eyes forward as she asked the question as if giving me space to think.

"He played a board game with me yesterday. He

taught it to me."

The Queen looked pleased and a little relieved. "Good. I hope he was gracious with you."

I tried to keep my tone neutral. "He killed me very fast."

The Queen raised an eyebrow at me. "And how will you respond to your defeat?"

I considered my answer. Something about the Queen's expression suggested I was being tested. "Well, I don't think Jian will be the best person to teach me, since he is so busy. But if I can learn from another, maybe next time I can entertain him with more of a match. I know my guards can all play it."

Queen Fei pursed her lips in amusement. "You never know, you might come to enjoy it."

We were standing in the center of the courtyard, and the Queen stopped abruptly, steadying me. The doors of the lean-to barn that was joined to the stables crashed open, and dozens of geese burst out making a tremendous racket. Two adolescents wrapped up in furs and layer upon layer of faded material tried to herd them with long sticks out into the town. It was chaos, but somehow the geese all eventually sped down the main road to the South Gate.

The Queen looked at the sun. "They are late. The geese go out later this time of year so the ground has a chance to thaw, but I would still have expected them to leave by tenth bell. Soon the snows will come, and they won't be able to leave their barn at all. From my rooms, I can always hear the racket they make when they come and go. Sometimes I think it's the only thing that gets Han up when he's hungover."

I chuckled. "Well, there certainly are a lot of them." I squinted into the bright sun to see if any ran away into the maze of houses.

The Queen led us forward again. "They are an easy animal to keep here as they find food on the floodplains and swampier areas. The sheep and cows must travel further from the walls to graze."

We followed the trail of the geese, and I had to concentrate even more on my footing, as now droppings littered the cobbles. Such loud and dirty animals would have never been allowed near the palace in Hava.

"How are the wedding preparations coming along?" The Queen's voice was bright with excitement.

I licked my lips. "Ruo is helping me design the dress. I don't have many opinions on the menu or decorations. I find myself anxious about misunderstanding the traditions here."

The Queen patted my arm. "Well there is an army of servants at your disposal. Anything you are not sure about, they will take care of. Though you should feel free to bring in your own traditions as well."

I nodded. When I thought about the wedding day, I felt numb and slightly sick. I couldn't picture any of it, so how was I going to make decisions as trivial as the color of the drapes?

"Elyanna, I understand this is a nerve-wracking time. I remember it myself, and it gets better as strange worlds become familiar." She lay both hands on my shoulders and fixed me with her large, dark eyes. "Be strong and determined, show no fear, but also be willing to bend. The most rigid reed is the first to break in a storm. You will find your place, I am sure."

I nodded to her, still feeling numb, and she removed her hands. "Thank you for your advice, Your Majesty."

"It's Fei, remember? Now let me show you the market. It won't be anything like what they have in Hava, but they normally sell roast grouse, and I don't know what Li Ping flavors them with, but they beat anything we have in the palace." She smiled warmly and I realized her probing questions were over for today.

I lost myself in the busy bustle of the narrow streets, trudging through the sticky mud, listening to ferocious bartering at the market, and weaving around rickety carts and stubborn mules. The city was caught in the excitement of preparing for the snow. Everywhere I could see animals being sold, houses being insulated with fresh water reeds and clay, queues for new boots, and groups of older men and women sitting in circles around open fires sewing and knitting as they gossiped. Child after child ran through the gates with bundles of firewood strapped to their backs. Apart from a few dark-skinned families originating from Kilamore, everyone had the features and tan skin of the Border-lands. My own pale hair and skin got more than one curious look, before people bowed their heads when I met their eyes.

I was amazed at how comfortable the townsfolk were with their Queen walking through their midst and decided I liked the lack of fuss over royalty here compared to Hava. There was a freedom in being able to wander around like everyone else and eat fried grouse straight off a stick. I felt the tension in my shoulders unwind. There might be giant ferocious beasts outside the walls here, but I was starting to feel safer within.

※

I BIT through the thread to snap it as I finished hemming the cloak for Jian, and I hoped he would like it. At least there would be something to remind him I existed when he escaped up to the Border. Horses galloped around the hem and birds flew above their heads. On the back was a giant wolf head, the symbol of his house, and a reminder that he had the Old Blood in his veins. On the left breast I had sewn a small swan over his heart. A reminder he couldn't get rid of me, and that I was of the Old Blood too. I was stronger than he thought. Or at least I hoped I was. I glanced down at the same swan embossed on my royal signet ring and sighed. The bird that represented Gilava was a heron, but I supposed I would never be able to use that again. It would be nice to sew it on something, though, maybe disguised amongst other birds. It would be my reminder of why I was here. My family and the people they governed were being kept safe and were being given the money they needed to rebuild. I let the thought fill me with strength.

Ruo was stitching a pair of large boots and I watched her quick fingers dart in the firelight. There was a question I had wanted to ask for so long, and I felt like I could only ask her.

"How did Han's wife die?" I asked and she jumped.

"What brought that question on?" I didn't reply and Ruo grimaced and shook her head sadly. "It was a terrible accident. Xiaoxiao fell down a flight of stairs. She had been drinking and didn't break her fall as she should have done."

I stabbed the needle into fabric, even though I had no thread attached. I didn't dare look Ruo in the eye as I asked, "Was it Han's fault?"

Ruo set down the boots and faced me so I was forced to meet her gaze. "Is that what you heard?"

I didn't reply, unable to find the right words.

"Han, Xiaoxiao and all the royal family have the Old Blood of Sal'hadar's tribe, the ancient wolf. It is diluted, yes, but still they bear certain traits. They can be quick to anger, strong, proud, stubborn." She smiled as if seeing memories pour out before her. Whereas I heard the words whispered in Hava; 'violent', 'dangerous'.

Ruo sighed. "Han's temper is the most unbridled. He is not the most disciplined of men. But he also loved fiercely, and not a person on earth could doubt he loved his wife." Her smile dropped and she folded her hands in her lap. "There was an argument in their rooms. They fought often and loudly, so it was no cause for alarm. They had both been drinking, and Han ended up hurling a chair into the wall over something she said. She ran from the room, still shouting back in anger. Their guards saw her trip as she tried to run down the stairs. She was killed instantly."

Cold squeezed my heart and constricted my throat. "Oh," I managed. "That's awful."

Ruo took up her boots again. "To this day I don't believe he laid a finger on her in anger, though I'm pretty sure she threw more than one item at him over the three years they were wed. They were a couple who argued but loved each other fiercely. I don't think he will ever get over her. He knows he will need a wife if he is to be king, but he gives excuse after excuse to his mother."

"I'm sorry that he lost her." I wound my finger in my skirts. "Do you think Jian would be like that? When I'm angry or annoyed I tend to draw into myself and go silent or snappish. I don't think I would do well being shouted at. Or… anything else."

Ruo tilted her head. "I've seen him in fits of rage, don't get me wrong, but to Jian, discipline is everything. He sees full Spirit-Beasts and humans with undiluted Old Blood, warped by the deep magic at the Border, and chooses to be as different from that as he can. He fights against the very blood in his veins."

I frowned and Ruo gave me a knowing look. "As far as I can tell, you in Sybera ignore your Old Blood completely."

I shrugged and chewed my bottom lip, still thinking about Jian.

Ruo lowered her voice and looked down at the boots. "You don't have anything to fear from him, child. Well, other than thoughtlessness that comes from being preoccupied by the Border and his men. He would never intentionally harm you, verbally or otherwise."

Ruo's words brought me more comfort than I had anticipated. She knew the royal family well, and I trusted her judgement of character, though it was always hard to know what went on behind closed doors. At least it was one less thing to fear, but I was still far from feeling secure in my position here.

I looked out of the window at the gentle flurries of snow in the wind. "Everything about him relates back to the Border. I want to go there, to the Forts in the Sal'hadar Mountains, and see for myself so I can understand how he views the world."

Ruo reached over and patted my knee. "It is not a pleasant place, my dear, but in some sense you're right. You will never understand Prince Jian if you don't understand the Border."

She stared down at the boots and there was a shadow of sadness in her eyes. She blinked and picked them up to start stitching again.

"Who are the boots for?" I asked.

She smiled as she caressed the leather. "My son, Chen. He is posted at the Eastern Pass of the Border, and I thought I would send him some warmer boots for winter. They say it can get cold enough for your toes and fingers to fall off in those forts, so I thought I would line these with lambswool. I send blankets up there every few months, so I thought I would send these too."

"Do you make the blankets too?"

She nodded. "There is a group of us in the town who meet up once a week to gossip and knit for the soldiers. Most of us are mothers or grandmothers of men there."

I sat up straighter. "Can I come?"

Ruo shifted. "To tell you straight, I'm not sure how comfortable they would be with a princess."

"I could go in disguise."

Ruo burst out laughing. "What, with your white hair and height? Your Syberan features? Everyone in Stonekeep knows who you are, dear. It's just a knitting circle for women past their prime. Nothing exciting."

I sagged and looked at the embroidered cloak, wondering if Jian would ever even wear it. "It sounds like you are genuinely helping others. I would like to be useful too, especially if it involves company. Let me at least help fund you?" I had to be worth something to somebody here.

Ruo reached out and gave my knee a quick pat. "Thank you, my dear, I'll pass your offer to the circle." She raised an eyebrow with a knowing smile. "Perhaps you're already being more useful than you know. You've sacrificed a lot to be here, I can see that. You'll find your place in time."

I swallowed and shrugged. She sounded a bit like the Queen, and I wondered if I appeared to be moping around in self-pity or desperately eager to please. Neither was the picture I wanted to paint. "I hope so."

✳

THE FIRST PROPER snowfall had dusted the forests outside my window, and for once the sun shone. I dressed warmly and asked Ruo to accompany me in the gardens. Jeremiah and Cai Hong trailed behind talking about that board game I still hadn't got my head around.

Jeremiah seemed to be getting enthusiastic about it. Then again, standing around watching my door all day, or trailing me around gardens had to be pretty boring. It was good they could occupy themselves with something.

Ruo was talking about design ideas for my wedding dress and describing what brides had worn at all the recent weddings in Stonekeep. I was amazed by her eye for detail. I didn't have any strong opinions on the matter and was happy for her to get carried away designing mine however she liked. Though the dress she had been most impressed with had been Xiaoxiao's, and I didn't want to echo her unfortunate fate. Maybe I would add a Havan twist to the traditional flowing Borderlander shapes.

My mind started to drift as we trudged down yet another path between bare bushes. Through the crunch of snow, I heard a child's whisper. '*Briaaaanna.*'

I looked sharply at Ruo. "Did you hear that?"

She blinked as she looked up at me, the sun glaring into her face. "Hear what, my dear?"

I frowned. I had to be imagining it. Nobody here apart from Falada knew my real name. I shook my head. The guards weren't reacting either.

I brushed the snow off a white marble bench and sat down to enjoy the view of the unblemished garden. The pond was frozen, and a family of ducks waddled across the surface.

A whisper came from right behind my ear. This time I could hear two children's voices speaking in time, male and female together. '*Welcome, Brianna.*'

I started and leapt from the bench, my hand flying to my sword. My guards were at my side in an instant, their own blades drawn as they scanned my surroundings. Jeremiah leaned over the bench to examine the snow on the other side. "Are you alright, Highness?"

I looked around wildly. There had definitely been a voice immediately behind me, but there was nothing there. The snow bore no footprints and there were no leaves on the trees or bushes to hide behind. I didn't take my hand from my sword hilt.

I cleared my throat. "We should go back into the castle."

Ruo and the two men looked at me with questions in their eyes but didn't voice them out loud. I was glad when they all stayed alert. If I could hear something they couldn't, did that mean it was something of the Old Blood? But the voice hadn't sounded like the weak cry of the bird, or the human sounding voice of Falada. Jian had said that strange things happened here to those with the Old Blood and to bear them no heed.

But the voice or voices knew my name.

If the Borderlanders found out I wasn't Elyanna, they would be within their rights to kill me. None of them cared about me enough to want to protect me. And back in Hava, I dreaded what Queen Geraldina would do to my parents and brother if I ruined the alliance. I couldn't ignore this voice, and there was only one person who I could talk to who knew the truth: Falada.

I dismissed a bewildered Ruo and asked Jeremiah and Cai Hong to wait at the stable doors. As I rushed to

Falada's stall, the commotion unsettled the gaggle of geese present in the neighboring sheds, and I saw the tip of their wings flap above the gate. They had to be shut in permanently now due to the snow, and I wondered if their honking would be another thing for Falada to complain about.

'What's wrong, little one?' Falada's soft voice filled my head before I could even see him over the stable door.

I hurried into his cubicle and threw my arms around his neck, breathing in his dusty, herbal scent. "I wish you could be with me inside the castle."

He nuzzled my arm, then reached up to continue eating from his soaked hay net.

"I heard a voice, Falada. One that nobody else could. It said my name. My real name. A whisper behind me."

There was silence apart from the sound of teeth grinding hay.

'If nobody else could hear it, why are you worried?'

"Because it means that somebody or something knows who I really am and could give me away."

He snorted and hit me gently with the tip of his tail. *'You humans worry about so many possibilities. There is nobody else here with the blood of the great eagle Thrum'ban. It is likely the voices you hear are silent to everyone else.'*

I stepped back and frowned at him. "How can you not be worried? How does it know what I am? Nobody else does apart from us."

Falada turned away from the hay net and tilted his head towards me. *'Peace, Brianna. If it could and wanted to give you away, it would have done so already. I suspect it is*

135

nothing to fear. A whisper in the wind means little in these lands.'

I found a comb to brush his mane. "Do you think it was a Spirit-Bird? It sounded different."

'There are many voices and many types of bird.' He swung his head to look at me with one eye through long, pale lashes. *'Just don't follow where it calls.'*

A shiver ran up my spine, and I forced a smile. "Don't worry, I've already got one annoying Spirit-Beast in my life. I'm not tempted to find another."

He flicked his tail and stomped a hoof, bucking his head. *'I'm not annoying.'*

I laughed and nestled my forehead into the hollow between his neck and his shoulder.

"Princess Elyanna?" came Jeremiah's voice from the stable corridor.

I sighed and poked my head out, reluctantly leaving Falada's comforting warmth. "Yes?"

"I think we should go inside. Word is that Prince Han's men didn't reach their next village. Hai Rong says everyone is on edge."

I undid the stable door and shook the dust from my gloves. "Why has Prince Han not made the next village? Is it the snow? I assume it's deeper further north."

Jeremiah shrugged, a helpless look on his face. "I don't know, but Hai Rong is worried about you being outside. Maybe your betrothed is going to get protective again." He gave me a wry smile.

I elbowed him for his cheekiness. "Come on then, we don't want to cause a fuss. Knowing Prince Han, he probably got distracted by a tavern."

Jeremiah nodded but looked uneasy.

"What is it?"

"What spooked you earlier, Princess?"

I searched his eyes in alarm that he might have heard it too, but there was only concern there. "It was nothing. I thought I heard something in the wind. I'm still not used to the sounds it makes up here."

Jeremiah nodded, but still looked uncomfortable. "You know I would protect you against anything?" he said slowly. "You don't need to keep things from me. I would never betray a secret or judge you."

My heart twisted a little at the earnestness in his eyes and I wondered where his words were coming from. "Thank you, Jeremiah. You are the best guard I could have hoped for."

He smiled and stood a little taller as he led the way back to my rooms.

❄

I WAS FINISHING my exercise routine after a light breakfast when Hai Rong opened my door mere seconds after knocking. I was about to scold him but stopped when I saw his alarmed expression. I leapt for my sword before he could speak. "Your Highness, you should come."

I strapped the sword to my waist. "What has happened?" I hurried to his side.

"Prince Han's men have been found. And the Prince himself." His face was pale and the normal private amusement was missing from his features.

"Are… are they alright?"

He met my eyes with a flat expression. "They're dead, Princess."

My insides turned cold and the world dropped around me. I forced my lips to shape words. "Dead? How?"

He shook his head. "The scouts have brought Prince Han's body back with them. The royal family are gathering. You should be there to show your respects."

I nodded and followed him down the corridor, snow battering against the windowpanes. The news tried to seep through my numbness, but it didn't make sense. How could a man so vibrant and full of life be dead in an instant? And what had killed all his men? They had not been to the Border, and Kilamore troops didn't scout the Borderlands like they did in Sybera, creating small skirmishes.

My mind and body became detached as Hai Rong led me down several flights of stairs to a room I had never been to before. It was in the very foundations of the castle and was so cold, my breath misted in great clouds around my head.

The room was dark and had a low, stone-vaulted ceiling, and I halted in panic. I was back in the barrel, the lid mere fingers above my head, the darkness pressing in. My fingers bleeding from scrabbling against rough wood for hours. Hours and hours with no way to escape.

"Princess?" Hai Rong held out his hand to help me down the last step. "Are you alright? Have you… have you never seen a dead body before?"

My heart hammered and my brain screamed for me to run. Escape. Protect myself. I took deep breaths and focused on the guard's calm face, gripping his hand hard enough to hurt. Gradually my terror lessened, and I forced trembling words out, hating how weak they made me sound. "This place brings back unpleasant memories."

Hai Rong nodded and tilted his head. He didn't let go of my hand and I was surprised by his understanding. "We can wait upstairs?"

I took deep breaths until the room came into focus before me. Just a room with plenty of space. I could do this. I shook my head and motioned for Hai Rong to lead on. He let go of my hand, but I stayed close to his back. We ducked under the stone vaults of the ceiling and neared a pool of pale light with a vigil of silent people. I dug my nails into my palms, helping me stay grounded, even if my hands refused to stop shaking. The body of a man lay on a slab. Above him was a wide chimney that bore high windows and mirrors, reflecting daylight down and onto the remains of Prince Han. The rest of the room lingered in darkness.

"Are you alright?" whispered my guard in my ear.

I nodded. "Thank you." *Just breathe, Brianna.*

I found a place to stand at the back of the crowd and waited for my eyes to adjust to the odd lighting. As more of the room became visible, and I could see how wide it was, my heart calmed. The King and Queen stood to either side of their son, their heads held high in pride, but silently weeping. Men and women stood around them, stances stiff and upright in respect.

Behind them, seemingly cut off from the rest, was Prince Jian, a pocket of darkness surrounding him.

I waited in silence as the memories leached away and felt the cold eat into my bones. I began to feel truly present in the room. It had to be part of the family tomb, the natural cold used to preserve the bodies until burial. I wondered how funerals were performed here and what rituals I might be expected to perform. Those thoughts were easier to concentrate on than the dead Prince in front of me. I hadn't known him long, but Han had been kind to me.

There were fragmented mutterings, and one by one the people left. The block of reflected sunlight tracked across the floor. Prince Jian didn't move. He stood completely still as if on parade, and my heart broke. Did he really have nobody to comfort him at this time?

As the people left, the view in front of me cleared, showing pale light streaming in slanted pillars onto the man lying on the table, covered in an embroidered cloak. His sword and bow had been laid to either side and the skin of a wolf lay at his feet.

I dismissed Hai Rong, so Jian and I were the only ones left. The guard hesitated, but I gave him a smile to show I was truly alright, and he bowed and left. Jian remained staring at the shrouded body of his brother, and he had to be freezing. I trod softly toward him so as not to disturb him, despite my legs being frozen and clumsy. I could no longer move my toes and my fingers were cold, even though I kept them under my armpits. Now that everyone had left, Jian looked so alone, almost forlorn. I bit my lip. If I was to be his wife, wasn't my role to support him in everything? Just as he was meant to do for me? I crept forward, the air heavy with grief, and stopped beside him. He didn't acknowledge me, but kept his eyes on his brother, his face a frozen mask. I could almost physically feel his pain.

I stood only a few centimeters from him and joined him in his vigil, keeping as still as I could and resisting my body's need to shiver. Softly, I let a song drift from my lips, the same song I had sung at my grandmother's pyre. It was an ancient song of Thrum'ban, but I suspected it would serve a son of Sal'hadar just as well. Jian didn't stop me, so I let the notes take on more power and volume, the song of mourning and happy memories and future hope. Of winter stealing life, but not forever. Of kings long sleeping in stone tombs, but never forgotten, until their barrows shaped the land.

I glanced at Jian and he was still unmoving, but a tear bled from the corner of his eye. He refused to blink it away or let his mask fall. Why did he hide everything away? I finished the last line of the song, the eerie notes echoing from the bare stone walls. I held my breath and slowly took his hand with numb fingers, ready to pull it back if he reacted badly. His fingers twitched, and then he interlocked his icy fingers with mine. His hand moved easily despite the chill of the room, and his palm was rough. Nerves tingled down my arm to my heart and I stared forward, struggling to keep my breathing steady. I was acutely aware of his closeness and the way his presence swamped mine.

I fished around my head for something to say, but nothing seemed right. I squeezed his hand instead, hoping it wouldn't come across as foolish. Already it felt warmer in his grasp and easier to move my fingers. His breath shuddered as more tears broke free and streamed down his face. He didn't seem like the aloof, cold prince anymore, merely a man grieving for the second sibling he had lost. I hoped my presence was a comfort, even if it was a small one. At last he let go of my hand and wiped his face with a handkerchief.

"Thank you," he murmured. "For the song."

He turned and left me standing alone in the cold, my heart still thundering in my ears, and my hand still warm from his touch.

❄

I RETURNED to my rooms and bit back tears. Prince Jian's pain had been obvious, but I didn't feel like I could intrude anymore. He most likely wished to be alone.

Ruo handed me a cup of hot mulled wine to warm my fingers and stoked up the fires.

I studied the small cuts in my palm where I had dug in my nails. "Do we know how they died yet?" I asked, my throat raw.

"No, dear. Though I heard there were signs of a fight. There will be an investigation." She came over and patted my hand. "Don't worry about that for now. You have much to concentrate on yourself. This will be a big change for you and Prince Jian."

I blinked at her without comprehension and then it hit me. If Crown Prince Han was dead, Prince Jian would be the new heir to the throne. If we married, I would become queen of the Borderlands. My heart pounded with shock mixed with terror. This was not the life I had been prepared to live. Would they still want me to marry him? They didn't seem like the sort of people who would change their minds. Gone were all hopes of living a life of freedom whilst Jian spent months at the Border. I would have to rule alone when he was absent, and Jian would have to base his life around Stonekeep and leave his forts behind. His life was here now, and I had the feeling he was as ill-prepared for this role as I was. But maybe this was the purpose and role I was looking for.

I looked at my maid with wide eyes. "I can't be queen, Ruo. I don't know what to do."

She smiled at me and placed another book in my hands. "Yes you do. You are the daughter of a queen and have the Old Blood in your veins. You know what to do. Start with the stories."

So I curled up in front of the fire and read.

When my eyes were heavy and Ruo had left for the night, I wrote to Queen Geraldina. She would want to know this news as soon as possible and would be angry if I didn't inform her. Her supposed daughter was about to become joint heir to the Borderland throne. The Borderlanders would be surprised if I didn't tell her and may have already noticed my lack of letters. I signed it Elyanna, just in case it was intercepted, but hoped nobody else would read it. I gave it to Jeremiah to find a rider and hoped the snows wouldn't hinder its path.

THE BORDER

I was stretching my back after finishing embroidering Jian's cloak when there was a sharp knock on the door. I frowned at Ruo who opened it and dropped into a curtsy. Prince Jian entered and I stood up in shock, knocking the drinks table and causing the cups to rattle. I hid the cloak behind me.

He bowed, and I returned with a shallow dip. "Princess Elyanna, I came to tell you I am leaving for the Border. I must speak to those who may know what happened to Han and his men. I should go now before the trail becomes cold. My father is leaving with men to search the area of the attack, but my mother will remain here, and you will have enough men to keep you safe." He didn't meet my eyes. His grief was carefully contained within emotionless efficiency, but a darkness weighed over him.

I took a step towards him. "Take me with you. Let me help."

He shook his head, his brows lowering. "It is too dangerous. I wouldn't be able to vouch for your safety."

I took another step closer until I was merely a foot away from him. "I am not afraid."

His eyes flashed, meeting mine for the first time and my stomach dropped. "You have never been faced with death."

I wet my lips, my heart pounding. "I need to see, Prince Jian. I need to understand if... if I am to be... to be queen. How can I help you rule if I haven't seen what we protect the world against? I will have nobody's respect."

I saw the battle in his eyes, the twitch in his jaw. I saw I had a chance and leapt for it.

"You can't keep yourself at a distance from me if we are going to learn to work together. Our country will suffer if we can't be united as king and queen."

His eyes traced my face for a moment and I held his stare. "Fine. But you must never leave my side unless you are in your room. You will be cold and uncomfortable; the food is stale and many of the men and women are uncouth. The ride will be hard, and we won't have time to slow for you."

A thrill of excitement shot through me. "I won't get in the way, I promise."

"Ruo will have to remain here. Your bodyguard may come but will be under my command."

I bit my tongue at the way he ordered me around like a child. Now was not the time to argue.

He stared at my face for a moment longer, and I feared he was going to change his mind. There was a vulnerable tilt to his lips and a heavy weight seemed to lie on his shoulders. The weight of a kingdom and thousands of lives. I wanted to help him and feel useful, but I wasn't sure how.

"When do we leave?"

He dropped his gaze. "One hour. Bring no luxuries, just your sword and warm clothes. We must travel light."

I nodded but he was already leaving the room. I turned to Ruo and clapped my hands. "He said yes! I'm going to the Border."

Her face was grim. "That you are, my dear, and it is a hard life there. We must get you prepared." She hurried to our pile of embroidery in one corner. "You can take the blankets and boots with you. I'll write a letter for Chen."

❄

MY HEART POUNDED SO HARD, it felt like it was bruising my ribs. I took Falada's reins from the stable boy who was lunging him in a trot around the ring as a warm-up. Apparently, Jian had meant it when he had said we would ride hard. We would canter from the start.

Jeremiah grabbed my hand as I led Falada towards the rest of the group. I raised my eyebrows at him in surprise. He leaned close so his words wouldn't be overheard. "You realize you don't have to go to the Border? This won't be a pleasant ride."

I freed my hand before anyone could see. "Yes. It's

146

my choice. I want to understand why this place is so important to Jian, and so many others."

"I just…" He looked down to the floor.

I tried to catch his eyes. "Jeremiah, what's wrong? If you don't want to come, you can stay here if you wish."

His face came up and his eyes flashed. "No. No, I would follow you anywhere as your guard. I just wanted to check you were comfortable doing this. You're doing a lot for a man who is so rude to you. You've never been to a war front before."

I gave him a quizzical look. "This is my own wish, Jeremiah. Now hurry for your horse or you'll be left behind."

He gave a vague nod and hurried away. I watched him for a moment then shook my head to clear it. I supposed riding to a cold dangerous border wasn't exactly something Elyanna would have done. Maybe he was worried Jian had forced me into this.

I tied the blankets and my own belongings to the saddle. I had more than the soldiers around me, but Falada was stronger than the other horses, so I didn't fear falling behind. I saw Captain Cheng Jun checking the bags on two pack horses and felt a little jealous he was coming too. Jian always seemed to choose talking to him over me. The previously clean-shaven man had allowed stubble to grow on his cheeks, and I wondered if it was to protect his face from the cold.

"We're going to the Border, Falada." I pulled myself into the saddle.

'I hear it's cold up there, and the stables are small.'

Despite his words I could feel the bound-up excitement tensing his muscles, yearning for release.

"It won't be for long. Maybe we will see some true Spirit-Beasts."

Falada gave an insulted snort.

Jeremiah was still retrieving his horse, but Hai Rong and Cai Hong rode up to either side of me. There was a grimness to both of them, but Hai Rong still managed a smile.

"Ready to see the delights of the north, Princess?"

I studied them both. They wore their armor beneath layers of furs and had small packs on their saddles. "I'm sorry that I'm taking you away from your families after all."

Hai Rong shrugged. "It won't be for long. Cai Hong might actually sleep better in the Fort than he does at home with his baby."

The second guard snorted, the red strand that tied his hair drifting in the cold wind. "That would be something. I can't deny I'd travel past the Border itself right now, alone and horseless, if I could get some sleep."

Hai Rong laughed, but it sounded forced and discordant. I wondered if they had both lost friends in the group that had ridden with Prince Han. It seemed everyone knew everybody here.

Prince Jian rode up to our group, surprising me. He looked me up and down and the bundle tied to Falada. I felt like a new soldier being inspected by their officer. "Are you ready?"

I gave him a confident look. "Yes."

He nodded and his gaze lingered on my face, his

expression unreadable. My lips parted and I was about to question what he was staring at, when he looked away and raised his fist. The gates of the castle wall opened, and the horses streamed out. Falada sprang forward, and I had to tug on the reins to slow him before he could race ahead. I turned and saw Jeremiah already behind, spurring his horse on to catch up.

We clattered through the town and over the bridge into the endless pine forest.

❄

THE SNOW THICKENED the further north we went, and Jeremiah and I stood out more than I had expected. Not only was it our hair color, Jeremiah's curls and our accents, but also how obvious it was that everyone else had traveled fast and camped in freezing cold conditions before. I had wanted to seem tough and capable but realized I was going to need help with many things. Thankfully Cai Hong and Hai Rong seemed to be expecting this and were quick to stop Jeremiah from trying to drive tent pegs into the frozen ground and point out that camping beneath a skeletal tree, which we had both thought sensible for shelter, was not the best idea since the windblown snow was accumulating along that side. They showed us how to lay pegs horizontally and pack snow over them, or stuff bags with snow to anchor points, and build a little wall of snow around the edges of the tent.

It was a three-day ride to the Eastern Pass and every night Jian inspected my tent before I slept. I wasn't sure if it was a test or out of duty to protect me, but it made me feel a little safer before I crawled into the narrow space and shivered the night away.

The scenery, however, became more and more dramatic the further north we went. I had never seen mountains as tall as the ones before us, and their white slopes reflected every color of the sun. Our own path became steeper, resulting in stunning views down hidden valleys and frozen lakes. Rolling hills of snow, each a different shade of white depending on how well they caught the sun, and how many clouds dragged their shadows over the trees.

After our first day on the road, houses and villagers became scarce, and I guessed nobody wished to live close to the Border. The only buildings were fortified supply points which could provide food and fresh horses. We didn't stop, however, Jian preferring to camp outside in sheltered dips where there were already built up fire pits left to be uncovered, and cooking pots under wooden trap doors in the ground. How they managed to find them under the snow, I couldn't fathom.

Even though Falada coped easily with trotting through the snow, every one of my muscles ached. I couldn't remember the last time I had felt my fingers or my toes, even when sitting by the fire. The castle of Stonekeep was warm and luxurious compared to this. Still, my excitement to see the Border was undimmed, and the growing horizon of majestic mountains only amplified it. I was sure this must be the most beautiful place in the world.

On the third day of travel, I noticed that all the men were on edge, and I adjusted my sword in its sheath periodically as we rode so they wouldn't freeze together. The tracks of animals crossed our path, and it was clear, even to me, that they were far bigger than normal.

I pointed to a track of bear paw prints, that were half again as big as any I had ever seen, and turned to Hai Rong. The hood of his fur coat was pulled so far forward, I could barely make out his face. "Does this mean Spirit-Beasts have broken through the Border."

He grinned at me, his teeth white in the shadows of his hood. "No, Highness. The ones who are pure Old Blood are bigger. Much bigger. Many of the animals here have traces of the Blood, and are larger this close to the Border. But they are mostly dumb animals. When you meet a pure Old Blood for yourself, you'll see the difference."

Falada snorted and shook his mane. *'The man underestimates them. No animal that large could be called dumb. Their souls are too strong. Besides you can hear the Land's Song here. It is beautiful and will bless all who honor the earth. Animals will thrive even without the Old Blood.'*

His words were cold comfort, and I scanned the trees constantly for giant animals that might be as intelligent as Falada. I couldn't stop imagining how things had ended for Han and his men. Had giant Beasts stalked and killed them? Wild men? They were still out there, somewhere. My eagerness to reach the Fort was stronger than ever.

"What is the Land's Song?" I asked to distract myself.

'It is the Song the Old Magic sings around us. It shows the land is in balance here. It is healthy.'

I nodded and breathed in the fresh air. There was a primordial peace and rightness about this place, and I wondered if that was what he meant. But I could also feel the danger within this wilderness.

I was testing the movement in my fingers, frustrated with how badly they gripped my sword hilt, when Jian pulled up beside me. I looked at him in surprise. He hadn't talked to me for the entire ride. He was taller than me, but his horse was small enough that our eyes were level. I liked that he couldn't loom over me when I was on Falada. That bubble of sadness and responsibility still encompassed him and made it hard to know what to say. I wasn't sure if I would ever feel at ease with him.

"The Fort is just ahead, Princess. Stay close to me, and we'll find you some suitable rooms. None of them are big. You may need to leave some of your saddle pack in the stables." He nodded to the rolled-up blankets attached to my saddle.

I patted the roll. "Oh, don't worry about this. It isn't for me. It's the blankets that Ruo's friends made for the men for winter, and boots for her son. I was going to hand them out. There are some gloves too and I brought letters." And the cloak I'd made for him, but now was not a good time to untangle that from the rest.

Jian tilted his head in surprise. "They will welcome those. It was a good idea to bring them."

I grinned at the first compliment he'd ever given me, then felt foolish for letting it affect me so much. "I thought maybe I could help repair clothes while I was here too?"

He nodded, and I noticed ice crystals had formed on the ends of his fringe, swinging in the breeze. "Every man knows how to repair his belongings, but some may need more help than others."

His posture seemed relieved, and I guessed it was because it sounded like I was going to keep out of trouble. I hoped I would be allowed to explore a little.

His attention returned to my saddle. "So if that bundle is for the men, where are your belongings?"

I patted a leather bag behind me.

He raised his eyebrows. "That's it?"

I frowned. If I was under-prepared it was his fault. "You said to travel light."

The corner of his lip twitched. "I did." His eyes creased with amusement. "I just hope you realize how hard it is going to be to wash your clothes."

I shrugged. "I wasn't aware I was expected to impress. You'll have to cope with me looking like the rest of you. You have female soldiers up here, do you not?"

He gave me one of his long probing looks that I couldn't interpret and seemed to see more than it should, then held up a hand. "One more thing. Tama'ha is coming tomorrow. She leads Sal'hadar's old tribe. The creatures of the forest." He gave me a warning look and slowed his words. "Don't let her scare you. If she smells fear, she will seek to control you with her words. Hopefully she won't notice you at all."

I swallowed and nodded, not sure if I was more excited or nervous. At least Jian was talking to me now.

Jian tightened his lips in what could have been intended to be a smile and spurred his horse forward, kicking up snow. I stared after his dark graceful figure, stark against the snow, and wondered if he ever felt moments of true happiness, or if he was always too caught up in grief and responsibility. As we rounded a stand of pines, the Fort finally materialized, looming dark lines half-buried in the snowy slopes ahead. It was much bigger than I was expecting, and its height was exaggerated by the fact its base was part way up a mountain slope. It filled the pass completely in a block formation with squat towers and thick walls that somehow managed to be beautiful in a brutal way. Wooden pulleys jutted out between levels and flags stood frozen on the towers. From down here, the Fort filled half the sky.

Hai Rong snorted, and I realized I was gaping with my mouth open. I sat straighter in the saddle and lifted my chin. "It's very impressive."

"I remember thinking that too, until I saw what we were holding back. Then I wished it was twice as tall." He was smirking as if at some private joke, and he flicked one of the rings in his ear.

I frowned. "It's not been breached for ten years, and I've seen how it's grown in that time. The drawings from twenty years ago made it look like it was about to collapse. Seems like it's plenty big enough now."

He nodded. "It keeps them back well enough. But only because of Prince Jian. He was the one who secured the funding and the training. He doubled the watch." He lowered his voice. "I liked Prince Han a lot, and would never speak ill of the dead, but I'm glad Jian will be king. He has a way of seeing things as they really are. He will always see us defended."

I shifted in my saddle, still uncomfortable with the topic. I had so far to go before these men would respect me as their queen.

As we neared the Fort, the road had been cleared of snow, and Jian picked up the pace. I could feel the eagerness of the men to arrive and escape the wind.

The doors to the Fort were huge, easily four times the size of a man, and I wondered why. Surely their size made them less defensible? Jian didn't call for them to be opened, however, instead leading us up a slippery flagstone walkway to a smaller door buried in the rocky slope of the mountain. This door was low, and we had to dismount to enter, Falada needing to dip his head.

Instead of the tunnel leading to a courtyard, I was surprised to find the stables were indoors, to one side of a wide hall. A mass of corridors branched off at every angle, many of them no taller than me, but some large enough for a man standing on horseback. The effect was confusing and disorienting. From what I knew of Jian, I had expected him to design this place using neat patterns and order. This seemed like it had been designed by a child.

There was no stable boy and we each rubbed down and picked the hooves of our own horses. At least Falada would be out of the wind, and a fire burned in an alcove in the opposite wall. He busied himself with his hay net then commanded me to soak it since it was too dusty.

When he was in a new rug and the clumps of ice removed from his hooves, I left his stall and found Jian waiting for me, leaning against the wall, his arms folded. Despite the cold and the darkness, he seemed more relaxed here, less on edge and impatient. He was talking amicably with Cai Hong, and even chuckled with a genuine smile. Jealousy niggled my stomach again. I had rarely seen him smile, and he had seemed so withdrawn since Han's death. Now he would laugh with a guard when he wouldn't even talk properly to me? Jian stopped his reply as I approached, though his expression remained light. "Ready, Princess?"

I pulled off my gloves and started to blow on my fingers. "Sorry it took me so long. Falada wants things certain ways, and my fingers feel like blocks of ice."

He glanced at them. "You should check them regularly. If they turn black or green, tell me."

I looked down at my fingers in alarm. "What do you mean?"

"Sometimes people lose their fingers or toes to frostbite here."

I stared at him. "Really?"

He snorted at my expression. "Just keep an eye on them."

I opened and closed my mouth but couldn't think of a reply. Jian set off down the halls carrying a torch, and I followed, hearing Jeremiah's boots stomp behind me as he hurried to catch up. The corridor was not wide, and for a moment of panic, I expected to suddenly feel like I was in the barrel again. But the light from the torch and Jian's quick pace, kept the attack at bay. I breathed a sigh of relief. It was probably helped by the fact the Fort didn't feel like a building at all, more like an endless animal warren. The corridors were poorly lit tunnels with unmarked intersections and dead ends. There were thick wooden doors at many of the junctions and heavy beams resting on the walls to bar them. Some walkways were only wide enough for a man to squeeze through sideways, and I kept my eyes away from them as horror twisted my stomach. I would never be strong enough to enter one of those.

I peered down a large pitch-black corridor as we passed it. "Why is this place so confusing?" My voice echoed in reply.

Jian glanced over his shoulder. "It's designed to funnel enemies down certain paths, and to give ways our men can escape without being followed. It separates different types of Spirit-Beasts according to their size, and also separates the men of the Old Blood from those they are bonded to."

I shivered, imagining being chased by monsters through these dark tunnels. "If the Beasts are as big as you say, I can't see them getting very far down here."

Hai Rong snorted. "Most are very big, but not all of them are bears, wolves and eagles. A snake would fit down here easily."

I stared at him. "There are Spirit-Snakes?"

Jian frowned back at us. "That is speculation on Hai Rong's part."

My guard shrugged. "Makes sense to me if there are. These corridors always reminded me of snake tunnels."

Jeremiah shuddered. "I hate snakes."

I raised an eyebrow at Hai Rong. "Snakes like the heat. Why would they be here in the snow?"

The guard grinned as he clapped Jeremiah on the back. The Syberan was looking a little pale. "Snow snakes."

Jian shook his head with a smile. I tried to put the image out of my mind.

After a confusing labyrinth of turns I would never remember, we reached a line of doors leading to dormitories.

Jian pointed to a door. "Princess, this is yours. Your men will sleep in the two rooms on either side." He met my eyes. "Don't go wandering. Rest and I will collect you in the morning before Tama'ha is due. I'll make sure you're all brought breakfast." His face grew heavier as he mentioned the Spirit-Beast's name as if he had remembered why he was here.

I nodded and longed to collapse onto a bed. I also longed for a bath but suspected that wouldn't be an option. How did the men bathe when it was so cold, anyway?

My room felt like a cave lit by a single oil lamp, but thankfully the ceiling was high. The walls consisted of rough rock and the only furniture was a small table and a low pallet bed. I dumped my bundle of clothes and lay the extra blanket I had packed on the bed. There was no fireplace, and the room was already cold. The wall pegs for my sword were by my bed in the same position as in the castle. I balanced my sword across them. I would be fine in here, as long as the lamp didn't go out.

The room was depressing, but it did little to dampen my excitement. Finally, I had made it to the Border. The place of legends.

TAMA'HA

*I*t felt like every soldier in the Fort had come to the main hall to see Tama'ha, and the cavernous room swallowed us all easily. There were giant doors on either side, one facing the Borderlands, the other the wilderness to the north, showing that the Fort was far wider than it was deep.

The towering doors facing the land of the Spirit-Beasts flung open on creaking hinges, and I automatically stood on tiptoes to crane over the guard in front of me. I realized I was acting like a little child, not the Borderland Queen I needed to be, and flattened my feet. I was taller than most of the men, anyway, I just wished Jian had let me stand closer to the front. It took most of my concentration to keep the nervous excitement from my face. I would see a full Old Blood and fill the blank in my mind. No more would I be the butt of jokes and knowing looks from the guards. I would understand Jian and this way of life. My first monster.

Cold rushed in through the doors, and a wave of

snow tumbled across the dark stone. A long, large snout appeared a full foot above my head. My mouth dried, and I stepped back despite myself. The surrounding soldiers were silent and unmoving as an enormous wolf padded into the room, its black lips pulled into a strange, unnatural grin. My eyes were level with the rippling muscle of its shoulder blade. Everything about it was strange. A blue smoky light drifted in the steam of its breath, and its body left the flash of a blue after-image behind it as it moved. It made it hard to focus, hard to keep your gaze locked on those dark eyes. When its grey fur caught the light, strange iridescent patterns glinted, then vanished. Jian fought creatures like that? And held them back? It took most of my courage to stand here and watch it while surrounded by warriors.

A strange voice echoed in my skull, and I realized it was communicating in the same way as Falada did. Only it could do so to everyone in the room without bonding, and even speak to people with no Old Blood in their veins. The voice was multi-layered and terrify-ing. Men and women and children speaking the same words at once, as if the beast was formed of a thousand trapped souls. The deepest voice was female and the loudest.

'*Prince Jian. It has been a while.*' I could feel tiny vibra-tions in the floor at her words, despite nothing being said aloud.

The Prince gave a short bow and displayed that both his hands were empty. "Tama'ha. Thank you for meeting me here. I understand the position it puts you in."

The wolf gave an audible, snarling chortle. The voice in my head spoke over the guttural sound. *'I haven't planned to see you dead, little general. Yet, anyway.'*

The Prince showed no alarm at the threat and his posture was smart but calm. "My brother has been killed with his men in the west of our lands. They killed even the horses. Do you know of this?"

Tama'ha's body twitched in what might have been a shrug. *'Perhaps the news has reached me. My condolences.'*

Jian's eyes hardened. "Who was it, Tama'ha?"

The wolf yawned, flashing large teeth and red gums. *'Not me, little general.'*

He folded his arms. "Tell me, and don't pretend something like this would escape your notice. We all know traces of the Old Blood run in most wolves in the Borderlands."

The wolf ignored the question and sniffed the air. Its ears pricked up. *'There is a new one here.'* It looked straight at me, pinning me with black eyes. *'You have never had one of her blood before. How exciting. Where did you find her?'* It eyed me with the same alert, excited expression a dog might make before it was given a new toy to play with.

I struggled to hold its gaze as it stepped towards me, lowering its nose so it was level with my face. Jian slipped his hand to his sword and rested it on the hilt. The room filled with the whispers of drawn swords. The wolf ignored them, its unnatural eyes boring into me. *'Tell me child, do you still yearn to fly? Pity your wings have been clipped.'*

"Tama'ha, you are dangerously close to breaking our

conditions." The Prince's words were cold and hard with warning.

The wolf didn't turn to him but let its tongue loll from its mouth as it loomed over me. *Your blood calls for the olden days, doesn't it, child? If you ever wish to fly again, come over the border. The Spirit-Birds would welcome you with joy.*

"Step away from her, Tama'ha, or I will be forced to act." I couldn't believe his audacity to threaten this beast with such confidence. He was so small in comparison. Tama'ha was a creature of myth, yet he acted as if they were equals.

It sniffed the air around me one last time, before turning back to Jian with an expression of sulky boredom. *You're rather protective of this one, general.* It stepped forward, then its ears pricked forward again as if it had caught an interesting scent. *Yes, you are very protective.*

Jian stiffened and his fingers tightened on his sword hilt, but his voice held no emotion. "Princess Elyanna is my betrothed. It is my duty to protect her."

The wolf's black lips peeled apart in a wild grin and my heart started to pound at the malice there. *You're betrothed? I suppose I should offer my congratulations. I never thought you would marry. I always thought you would live and die alone.* It tilted its head. *I can see your soul. Does she know what you're like inside? Does she know how broken you are? How dark and lost and guilty? Does she know about her and what you did?* It cocked its head.

Jian's face remained blank, but again I saw his fingers twitch. The corners of his eyes tightened, but his voice was calm. "Enough of your games, Tama'ha. I am tired of them. Who killed my brother?"

Tama'ha sighed and sat down, the movement causing its body to ripple with blue light. *'Not one of my tribe, little general. You have holes in your sight. You have grown complacent.'*

Jian took half a step forward. "Tell me. Whose tribe is responsible?"

It stretched out a paw and licked it, making us wait in breathless silence. Then its eyes turned to me and my heart froze. *'Ask her. She is the one who could tell you. I will not betray my kind, but she might.'*

Hundreds of eyes turned to me in surprise, and I listened to my pulse thud in my ears. What was it talking about? Sybera had nothing to do with Prince Han's death. Distrust and confusion glittered around me, and Tama'ha grinned again as it stood and strolled out from the hall without a farewell.

As the door clanged shut, I felt the tension leave my shoulders, but my heart didn't calm. What did it think I knew? What would Jian think of me now? And who was the *'her'* Tama'ha had asked if I knew about?

I dared a look at Jian, but his eyes were still on the door, his jaw tense. I couldn't let what the wolf had said hang over us. I needed to explain I knew nothing about what had happened to his brother. Ignoring the stares of soldiers, I wove my way towards him, conscious more than ever of how my pale hair and skin and fine cloak made me stand out.

Jian didn't turn at my approach, so I reached out and

touched his arm. He stiffened slightly beneath my touch.

"Jian, I..." I started. But he put one hand over mine and cut me off with the other. My breath caught.

"Not here. We can talk in private." He turned and strode to a back door, and I hitched my dress so I could match his pace. His voice echoed in the stone corridor. "Don't let what it said get to you. They like to weaken your resolve and play games of the mind. They detect weakness like a smell. Don't ever betray that they've won a victory."

I nodded, though his eyes were fixed ahead, and he seemed more rattled than he had let on. In some ways Tama'ha sounded like Elyanna. Once she found a subject upset you, she never let it go. She hunted for every weakness.

I followed the Prince into a simple study, glowing with firelight. It was sparse, but luxury compared to the dormitory. The heat of a fire felt like a wall as I entered from the bitter cold of the fortress, and I longed to warm my hands and feet.

The Prince poured two glasses of watery wine and motioned for me to sit in the larger chair. He didn't join me, but leant on the mantle of the fireplace, staring at the flames. I moistened my throat with the wine and hoped the alcohol might calm my nerves. It barely tasted alcoholic at all, however. As I waited for my heart to slow, I watched the way the firelight softened the lines of the Prince's face, making him younger and more vulnerable. But it couldn't hide the tension in his jaw or the way the tendons stood out in his strong neck. My eyes drifted to the shadow in the V of his throat, and I quickly looked down at my wine. It was still too hard to comprehend that he was to be my husband. I knew so little about him, yet felt drawn to him all the same, like a moth to a flame. Drawn by his strength and his confidence, just to be dismissed and belittled over and over.

He looked at me at last, and I sat a little straighter "Do you know who killed my brother, or how to find them?" His tone showed he already expected my answer.

"No. I can't understand what it said. Why would Sybera attack Borderlanders when they will do anything for peace? Even send me here."

He rubbed his chin. "I suspect it was not Syberans she was referring to. The Beasts care little for countries, only for blood, and you are of the Old Blood."

I frowned. "But you are too."

He gave a sharp nod. "But you are of the eagle Thrum'ban, and I am of the wolf Sal'hadar in their eyes. I suspect she meant the ones that killed my brother were Spirit-Birds."

I held my head in confusion, massaging my forehead. "But I've never even met a Spirit-Bird. The only Spirit-Beast I know is Falada, and he isn't a bit like... like that creature."

Jian's face softened, and he finally took a seat. "As I said, Elyanna, don't let its words trouble you. They sow discontent and hunt for weakness. We have a good lead now." He paused for a moment, swirling his wine and his eyes became dark. "I will avenge him. Even if it was

Jala'ban himself. They are foolish indeed to think they would get away with killing a Prince." There was a sorrow and a determination in his expression that put me at a loss of what to say. His hand was tight on the stem of his goblet.

"I'm sorry," I said, at last. "I know you cared for him."

He sighed and sat back, throwing one arm over the armrest. "Did you want to come here?"

For a moment I thought he was referring to the Border and frowned in confusion. I had begged him to take me here. Then I realized he meant the Borderlands as a whole. I opened and closed my mouth, caught off guard by the change in topic. I wasn't sure whether to be frank with the truth or dress it up. His eyes were studying me, and my heart clenched with resolve. If I wanted him to be honest with me, I needed to be as open to him as I could without betraying my secret.

I pulled off my gloves and looked at my hands, pale from cold, as I considered my words. "No. I didn't want to leave, and I didn't want to marry yet. I miss my family."

My breath hitched as I waited for his response to the admission, and the crackling of the fire filled the room. I lifted my fingers towards the heat.

"I'm sorry," he said, his voice ever so quiet. "Truly I am. It was not my intention to let this happen." He massaged his temple. "My world is cold and harsh and full of danger. You should have not been dragged into it."

My hands were unsteady, so I wrapped my fingers in my skirts instead and licked my lips, nerves drying my mouth. "I will try hard, though. Being your wife. Being your queen. Protecting the Borderlands. Even if it wasn't my choice." I met his eyes to show my sincerity.

He cocked his head slightly. "Being married to me is going to be hard, Elyanna. My life is difficult, and you will have a share in that. With Han's death, things will only be harder. And I understand that I'm not an easy man to love."

If only I could explain to him that my life had never been easy. I had always been afraid. I studied his dark eyes and saw traces of pain. "What happened?" I whispered. "Why did the wolf say you were broken? Who was the woman it spoke of?"

I regretted the words as soon as they left my mouth as his gaze dropped, and I saw his defenses rise. Then he sighed and the pain returned to his eyes, real and clear. One corner of his mouth twitched as if he were fighting an internal battle. My heart plummeted and soared at once as I realized he was going to answer me. "She was my sister, Feng."

I breathed out and lowered my gaze, relieved in part that I didn't have a lover to compete with. I remembered Ruo's tale about how the Princess had died so young when the Fort had been overrun. I should have guessed.

I expected Jian to stop talking, but to my surprise, he continued, turning a pendant on a chain around and around in his fingers. "She was almost two years younger than me, and my closest friend. We would play and learn together, and we were ferociously competitive in the sparring ring." He paused with a small smile.

"You two would have got along. You have a similar quiet strength." I licked my lips, but didn't respond, hoping he would continue, and I would finally understand. "Children are banned from the Border. It's too dangerous." He glanced at me sideways and pursed his lips. "I'm still not sure I should have brought you. But the law has always stated nobody under the age of fourteen may come within twenty miles of the Passes. When I turned fourteen, I was assigned to train here with the guards for six months, as is the tradition for royals. I missed her terribly, and of course she couldn't visit. I was very ignorant then. I thought the horrors of the world were exaggerated, and I thought youth and training made us invincible." His lips jerked in a humorless smile.

"After three months I returned to the castle for a fortnight with my family before I was due to be sent back. Feng had come up with a plan. She wanted to come too, disguised as a guard, and I would smuggle her into the fort. She was jealous that I was learning this whole brutal world without her. She dreamed of heroism and bravery. Feng was tall for her age and matched me in height, which annoyed me no end at the time. She also came close to matching me with a sword. She argued it was just as dangerous for me as it was for her." He paused to take a sip of wine and his lips twisted in self-loathing.

"So I let her come. It was fun, at first, exciting. So many little problems for us to solve together so she could go undetected. When we arrived her eyes glowed. However," his voice caught, and he seemed to almost stop breathing. I didn't move, dreading what he would say next. "The breakthrough happened. Spirit-Beasts and their crazed men overran the fort. It was much smaller then. They were everywhere." His jaw clenched and his eyes widened at the memories. "I had men specially assigned to protect me. I tried to reach Feng in time, but I wasn't quick enough. She was only thirteen, she didn't stand a chance. Nobody knew who she was. Nobody had been assigned to rally to her."

He gazed into the fire and the whites of his eyes were bloodshot. "She died alone and terrified because I was an idiot and took her to the most dangerous place on earth."

My heart hammered in my chest and I sought for words to say. "I'm so sorry, Jian." I met his eyes and swallowed at the pain there. "I'm so sorry. It must have been awful. But it was not your fault."

He shook his head sharply. "Oh it was. I knew the law. I knew the risks. I was the oldest. I cared for her more than I have ever cared for anyone else, and I still went ahead." He swirled his wine. "But I vowed I would never let an innocent like her be killed again. That's why I have spent so much time here. These Forts were neglected then. I've made them as strong as I can over the last decade. When Father dies, another will have to take my place as general, but until then, I can think of no better way to serve my kingdom than here at the Border." He looked at me with a vulnerability I had never seen before. "I need you to understand that my place is here."

I swallowed again, my mouth dry and covered his cool hand with mine. "I will help you however I can." I could accept always coming second to something so important as long as he didn't shut me out.

He didn't reply, but hesitantly turned his hand palm up and interlocked our fingers in a truce. I parted my lips, suddenly finding it hard to breathe in the smoky room, but not daring to move. As our eyes moved back to the fire, I started to feel a strange sense of peace and excitement tangled together in a way I didn't think was possible.

❄

THE NEXT DAY, Jian was a hive of activity. He seemed to have an endless list of things to inspect, people to meet, and training to review. His grief had transformed into a determined energy, and his confidence was back in full. The vulnerable man of last night was gone. In Stonekeep Jian had lurked in the shadows, often alone, leaking impatience. Here he was the center of every thing, and it seemed everyone wanted to talk to him, trusting him to solve every problem. It was like watching him wake from hibernation.

After an hour of following him around like a hound, I was bored, and it was clear I was just getting in the way. Thankfully, Jian said I could distribute the blankets without him, as long as all three of my guards were with me. His protectiveness was getting a bit annoying, but I couldn't really blame him when he had lost his sister in these very walls. I was on a war front after all and had no experience of battle.

I had twenty thick woolen blankets, though now I

was here, that didn't seem very many. Some had names attached but half were for whoever needed them the most. Hai Rong and Cai Hong knew most of the soldiers by name and pointed them out in the mess hall as they ate their grey porridge that tasted burnt. They received their blankets with heavy reverence, and I watched as notes were pocketed with care or kissed. I wondered how long it had been since these men and women had been home. Some asked if they could send letters in return, and I nodded to every request, hoping my bag would be big enough.

Chen, Ruo's son, loved his boots and assailed me with hundreds of questions about his mother, of which I could answer very few. He seemed young to be somewhere so harsh, though I guessed he was older than both me and Jian. The Prince was so serious and focused, it was easy to overlook his age.

There were badly repaired clothes everywhere. Cloaks with unravelling stitches, boots held together by string, poorly patched gloves. I collected what the men were happy to give me and wondered if Jian would let me use his study to sew. The fire there would help my numb fingers to work, and there was not enough light in my room from the single lamp to see well.

Cai Hong said Jian spent most of his time in his study when he wasn't inspecting the walls, so I went and knocked on the door. Jian seemed surprised when I entered, but happy enough to let me sit by the fire. The room was small, so my guard had to wait outside. Jeremiah and Hai Rong had been roped into unloading a cellar, and I hoped they were warmer down there. I felt mean making Cai Hong wait outside in the bitter cold, while I got to sit by the fire, but he didn't object. I heated some wine over the fire for him so he could warm his fingers on the goblet.

Jian was talking with two men sitting on the other side of his desk, and their discussion was hard for me to follow, mostly details of patrols and the number of men in rotations. There was a peace to concentrating on my stitching while I learnt about their world piece by piece. I wished I had brought some fur or lambs' wool with me so I could line the tattered shoes and coats.

I was coming to the last hole in a scarf when Jian laid his hand on my shoulder, making me jump. His lips twitched in amusement. "The meeting is over. I'm going to walk the wall to see if all is as it should be. Would you like to join me? Or Cai Hong can take you straight to the mess hall for dinner?"

I stood and picked up the last thing I had to give away; Jian's cloak. He was already leaving the room, so I hurried after him, eager for some fresh air and sunlight, even if it would be cold.

"You know, Princess, that you stick your tongue out when you concentrate on sewing?" He looked over his shoulder at me with a small smirk.

My mouth dried at the unexpected comment. Had he been watching me? I didn't know how to respond, so I changed the subject. "Your men have poor clothes for cold conditions."

Jian's face hardened. "We provide them with armor and weapons. It is their own responsibility to come with adequate clothes, just as it would be in any job.

The problem is many don't bother to maintain them properly. They learn eventually."

I shrugged. "They don't even have proper washing facilities. And there are bare nails and rough edges everywhere. No wonder they get torn."

Jian gave me an inscrutable look, and I met his eyes openly, showing I meant no offense. His expression lightened. "It is the same at the Western Fort. I prioritized the fortifications before the comfort of the men. The new money from Sybera will help us here. First, I hope to build more fireplaces and employ a large team of woodcutters to supply us. It would mean more people in immediate danger, however, if there was a breakthrough. I still believe the men should have the discipline to care for their own clothes. The commanders are not their mothers, and it's not your job either."

I bit back a retort and decided I would think of a solution rather than just pointing out problems. Maybe I could expand Ruo's knitting circle and fund more blankets and clothes to be made. I would ask Jian to send them on an extra packhorse whenever people traveled here.

The Prince strode through the maze of tunnels and staircases, and I felt more lost than ever. No enemy would have a chance attacking us in here. After our conversation yesterday, I felt more at ease around him and hoped he would remain more open with me. I still felt the weight of his presence, however, and the worry that one misspoken word could make him ignore me again forever. As we reached the end of a staircase, he unbolted a door and sunlight blinded my eyes as he led us onto the ramparts.

The wind was brutal but carried no snow. The walkway had been swept, but the stone was slick with ice. The view was the most incredible I'd ever seen. I looked out to the north and saw an unblemished land of mountains, lakes and forest stretching forever, blanketed in snow. This high above it all, I wanted to step off the ramparts and fly, sweeping down and becoming one with all the beauty.

I gripped the crenulations. "It's beautiful."

Jian nodded. "Every month this view holds a different attraction. In summer those valleys are so full of primroses and daffodils you can see the colors from here. In autumn there are floods and new lakes form that reflect the gold of the leaves. It is a more beautiful land than ours. It is unspoilt."

I could believe that. Even the air felt different. Cleaner and more delicate somehow. I leaned further over the rampart and thought I could hear faint voices in the wind. Hundreds and hundreds of voices, too faint to catch their words. "Falada says he can hear the Land's Song here."

Jian stood close to me and bent so I could hear his voice over the wind. I still wasn't used to his height. "I don't pretend to understand much of the Spirit-Beasts, but they say the Old Magic calls them here. It seeps naturally into all of us this far north, but if you try to draw on it yourself, it causes irrevocable harm. However, the land and animals flourish under its touch. You can have a closer look if you wish."

I looked at him in confusion and saw he was holding out a spyglass. I took it in excitement and scanned the gaps between the stretches of forest. Movement caught my eye and I darted the spyglass around until I found it again. I gasped. A stag was drinking from a hole in a frozen pond, but even from here, I could tell he was enormous. His antlers were as large as the surrounding bushes and branched into more tines than were possible. It was as if two trees grew from his skull, and vines dragged from them, green despite the snow. His brown coat was shaggy, and I glimpsed the same iridescent symbols across his body as I had seen on Tama'ha's, flashing in the light then vanishing. A white stork sat on his back, as still as marble. As the deer disappeared back into the trees, I felt a pang of loss.

I took the spyglass from my eye and looked at the Prince. "Why are we fighting them? They are so majestic, and this land was once all theirs. All we have done is damage it."

Jian took the spyglass back and gave me a knowing look. "Don't be fooled by their beauty. Every one of them would kill you if given the chance. They would kill as many men as they could. These are not the ancient Beasts of legend. These are half-crazed, drunk on the Old Magic and thirsty for revenge. They aren't Falada. They have no limits on what they will do to make themselves strong."

I frowned. "But in all the tales, Sal'hadar, Tamunden, Thrum'ban, and Bula were good and wise rulers. The new men came and caused all the divisions. We were the ones in the wrong. Is there no way back?"

Jian rubbed his chin. "Not all Spirit-Beasts chose this way. Not all decided to corrupt themselves. We can't change what happened in the past and those days where man and full Spirit-Beast lived in harmony are hundreds of years gone. We have to survive the present as best we can, and those Beasts have no goodness left in them."

He turned to resume his walk, his back straight despite the wind, and I caught him by the arm and passed him the cloak before I lost my nerve. It seemed silly now to have brought it all the way here when he had a perfectly decent one, but it would be even more silly to take it all the way back without handing it over. "I embroidered a cloak for you. I didn't expect to be here when you came to the Border, so I wanted to give you something so you wouldn't forget me."

I expected him to politely thank me, then dismiss it, but instead he turned his back to the wind, stretched the cloak out, and studied my needlework. "You are very talented. This must have taken you a long time."

I gave him a small smile. "I haven't had much else to do. I enjoy embroidery. I find it relaxing, and I like to make dull things beautiful."

His eyes moved from the large wolf head picked out with silver thread, to the small swan over the breast. I wished I was better at reading his expression. "What else do you enjoy?" His eyes flickered to mine with a hint of humor. "I'm guessing not board games."

I exhaled a sharp laugh. It warmed my heart to see him more relaxed. "I might like them if I'm given more of a chance next time." I gave him a meaningful look. "I'm not surprised Han had to resort to cheating."

Jian's lips formed a sad smile, softening his features. "He was always a terrible cheat. It had nothing to do with me." He looked up and the smile stayed, and I felt my stomach flutter. I was so unused to seeing him smile and having his attention. "What else," he said, snapping my thoughts back into the conversation.

"Erm, I enjoy sword play and reading and riding and walking in the Havan gardens."

"What do you read?"

I looked over the wall towards the mountains. "Usually books that take me far away." Ones that made me forget about Elyanna. Ones that took away the nagging sensation of being small and lost.

His eyes turned pensive. "You were unhappy in Sybera?"

I faltered, not wanting to be backed into a conversation where I would have to lie. "Sometimes. It was hard to have time to myself, and certain people were difficult. Falada was my true escape."

He followed my gaze out to the mountains. "You know, sometimes the way the two of you mirror each other and communicate, you look like a pair from the other side of the Border."

I blinked, not understanding what he meant. "We're bonded."

He nodded. "You are, but that doesn't always mean much. I can see what you mean to each other. Your souls have grown to fit around the other."

I gave him a strange look. "Now you sound like Falada himself."

He snorted. "There are men of the pure Old Blood out there who live and serve the Spirit-Beasts. Often they bond with one or two for life, and when you meet them, it's as if you are talking to a single person. You and Falada are the closest I've ever seen to that here, and you're not even from the same tribe."

I lowered my voice. "I will admit, I love him very much. I wasn't sure he would come with me. I don't know what I would have done without him here, or anywhere really. I've never been without him since I can remember."

He looked down at the Fort, and I watched the men patrolling on various walkways, wrapped up in furs, banners flapping above them in the harsh wind. "Often I see the Old Blood as only a negative thing. It is good to see a positive, untainted by magic."

I wondered how having Old Blood in his veins affected him. "Do you... sometimes hear voices?"

He tilted his head towards me. "Like your bird in the hunt? Yes. I hear fleeting words from the wolves and foxes, even as we must hunt them down to protect the livestock. Many of the forest animals with a trace of the Old Blood report what they see to Tama'ha. We can't let her be all seeing."

I thought about asking if he heard other voices, but I didn't want to raise his suspicions. I couldn't talk about the whisper I had heard in the garden without risking him knowing that it spoke my true name. How could anything know that? Maybe Falada was right, and I should just ignore it unless it posed more of a threat.

"What are the true Spirit-Birds like?" I asked instead.

"Huge. Deadly. Terrifying. Wild. We see mostly eagles here. Their leader is Jala'ban, and he has never really been up for negotiating. Tama'ha has sympathies towards us because we bear some of her bloodline. She and I have known each other ten years now."

"And you think Jala'ban is behind Han's death?"

He nodded. "From Tama'ha's words, yes, or at least one of his underlings. She said you might betray your own kind."

I looked out to the beautiful wilderness. "Does that mean I could find them more easily than you?"

He looked at me sharply, all softness from his features vanishing. "No. Don't take this the wrong way, Elyanna. I respect you. But Jala'ban is more dangerous than Tama'ha. He's a harpy eagle as large as a horse when his wings are folded. You are not strong enough to stand against him. If you ever see a full-blooded Spirit-Bird, you turn and run. Do you understand me?"

My chest clenched uncomfortably at his tone, and I laid a hand gently on his arm. "Jian, I understand the pain Feng's death brought you, and that you believe it was your fault. But it was her decision to come here in disguise." I hardened my voice. "I am not your servant or your prisoner. I will listen to your advice and respect your experience, but I won't let you control every aspect of my life because of what happened to Feng."

He looked away from me and there was pain in his eyes. I could see the walls forming behind his expression as it became cold and hard. "Highness." He gave a sharp bow and strode away across the wall.

I watched his retreating back and bit my lip. Maybe I should have held my tongue. His advice had been common sense after all. We had been doing so well, but his heart had been shredded so many times by those he had lost. Maybe there was not enough left of himself to love again. I sighed and edged my way after him, slipping on the icy walkway. I guessed he wouldn't be up for talking for the rest of the day. It was getting late, anyway.

One question niggled at me. If Jala'ban had really killed Han and his men and then disappeared back over the Border, was there anything we could do about it? If he could fly, this Fort meant little to him, other than protecting its inhabitants. We couldn't go into their land and seek him out or invade. What was to stop him periodically flying into the Borderlands and picking us off one by one? What revenge or retribution was even possible?

I shivered as I walked down the endless stairs, and Cai Hong, quiet and pensive as ever, led me to the mess hall. The room was half full with soldiers, and I sat alone on a bench while Cai Hong joined the queue for the disgusting broth.

"Princess, come join us?" I looked across and saw Chen waving me over with a grin. He was surrounded by four other soldiers, two men and two women. One elbowed Chen with embarrassment, but another was looking at me with a hopeful expression.

"It's alright," hissed Chen to the first. "My mother's

letter said she wouldn't mind. That she would like company."

I pretended I hadn't heard, smiled and sat down in the offered seat. "Thank you, Chen."

He grinned and I was surprised how much he looked like Ruo. "Don't hold your breath for the stew. I think it's made from drowned rats."

I looked at him in uncertain horror, and the woman beside Chen elbowed him. "Don't listen to him, Princess. It's chicken." She wore her hair in a high long ponytail, but it looked dull and fragile, without any of the shine of the ladies in Stonekeep.

Chen waved his spoon at her. "How do you know? Many animals taste like chicken when they're cooked."

She rolled her eyes. "If they all taste the same, why do you care?" She took a deep bite and rose her eyebrows provocatively.

Another man harrumphed. His voice was so deep I could feel vibrations through the table. He was large enough to have some Old Blood in him. "It all tastes gross, is what it is."

"Well what do you expect. It was fourth regiment's turn hunting. They're always the worst," said the second woman. Her hair was slashed unevenly at her shoulders with a fringe that covered her eyes.

"Hey, Princess," Chen turned to me. "Now that you're marrying our general and everything, maybe you could sort us out some better food? There's plenty of space in here for livestock."

The girl with the fringe gasped. "Chen! You can't speak to her like that."

I held up my hand. "No, it's quite alright." I turned to Chen. "I barely know him yet. I don't think he would appreciate my interference."

The first girl swished her ponytail. "Really. Because ever since he came into the room, Prince Jian has been looking at you. I don't think he's heard a word the Captain has said to him."

"Really?" I looked towards the front of the room and found Jian sitting with Captain Jun on the raised table. Our eyes met, making me miss a breath, and he looked away quickly as if it had been by chance.

I filled my lungs and let the air out slowly. "I upset him earlier, that's probably why."

The woman snorted.

"Or do you think he disapproves that I am sat with you instead of him? He wasn't here when I first came." It probably did come across as a slight.

Chen looked at me with wide eyes as he chewed the overcooked meat. "I think you're overthinking things. This isn't Stonekeep, where everything has to mean something. He just looked curious to me."

The woman snorted again and shook her head.

The other woman spoke as she stirred her stew and ran her hand through her short hair. "You know, you're a lucky one."

I stared at her a moment, trying to catch her meaning, but she didn't elaborate. I was feeling more and more lost in this conversation and was grateful when Cai Hong arrived with my stew. I busied myself with a mouthful so I didn't have to reply.

It definitely tasted like it could be drowned rat.

✳

"WE'RE LEAVING ALREADY? We only just got here."

Hai Rong raised his eyebrows and laughed, the sound reverberating down the stone corridor. "You want to stay here?" He looked over my shoulder into my room. "Are you hiding something in there? Like a fire and a bath?"

I suppressed a smile. "It's not that bad here. It's exciting and beautiful. It's only been three days since we arrived."

Hai Rong snorted. "Says the person who is allowed to sit in Prince Jian's office and sew in front of the fire."

I folded my arms and gave him an amused look. "I thought we'd be here a week at least."

Hai Rong sighed and his expression turned serious. "Prince Jian needs to report to Stonekeep, and it makes more sense to coordinate the patrols from there, considering Prince Han was attacked much further south. Whoever attacked him may still be on our side of the Border, so we're staying a much shorter time than usual. They're the priority." He looked me up and down. "I think he also worries about your safety."

I nodded but my mood fell. I feared Jian would stop being as open once we were back in Stonekeep. What if he became too busy to talk to me again? There was still so much I wanted to learn about this place.

I packed my few possessions and crammed all the letters and charms the soldiers had given me for their loved ones into my bag. For some reason, the sight of them all reminded me of my own parents and my throat constricted. I wasn't sure how I could write to them as Brianna without endangering myself. I was under no illusions as to the privacy of my letters, since they would be handled by a number of people on their journey.

Falada was happy to be leaving and would barely keep still as I saddled him in the wide hall linked to the stables.

'It's too cold up here, and dark. Horses shouldn't be kept in mountains. Tamunden always ran free across the plains.' His nose nuzzled its way under my arm playfully. When I pushed him away so I could tighten his bridle, he yanked the end of my braid.

"Stop that, you pest!" I pushed his head away roughly and chuckled. "Now I'm going to have yucky horse saliva turning to ice in my hair."

Falada shook out his mane in glee.

"Jian is speaking to me, Falada. He opened up a little, but I'm worried he'll stop once we're back in Stonekeep and he's occupied with his brother's death."

'Both your souls match when you talk.'

I gave him a strange look. "What does that mean?"

He pawed the ground in impatience to be under the open sky. *It means you could work together well as a team. You complement each other.'*

I snorted. "Sometimes I think you make all this soul stuff up."

He regarded me with a large dark eye.' *Even you can see the shadow of them in the Old Bloods using the deep magic.'*

I frowned. "The blue image around Tama'ha?"

The horse chewed on his bit, making it clink against his teeth. *'The deep magic is dangerous because it starts to separate the soul from the body. The Spirit can go mad, and to us, our Spirit is who we are far more than our body. But I think it is better to be a Spiritless dull beast, than have no soul.'*

I frowned as I led him out through the corridor to the mountain slope where the men were gathering in the snow. "You've never explained this to me before."

'You never asked. In Hava you couldn't care less about the Old Blood.'

"Do I have a Spirit then?"

'Yes. You have some Old Blood in you. You are part Spirit-Human.'

I laughed at the funny name. "Spirit-Human?"

He snorted and flicked his tail. *'But I have more Spirit than you. It's why you can't see souls.'*

I nudged him playfully and used a tree stump to pull myself into his saddle. Most of the men were already mounted, and there was something satisfying about being higher than them all.

Jian steered his black horse towards me. His face looked tired and his eyes had dark rims. I wondered when he had last slept.

"Are you ready, Elyanna?" His eyes were amused, and the question seemed directed at why I was sitting here laughing alone.

I giggled. "Falada just called me a Spirit-Human and then got offended when I laughed."

The horse snorted clouds of steam.

"Spirit-Human." Jian tasted the words. "Can't say I am an enthusiast of the term."

Falada yanked the reins. *'He's not an enthusiast of much, though, is he?'*

I tried to suppress a laugh which then came out as a snort.

Jian watched me strangely. "I suspect I don't want to know what he just said."

"Falada's in a grumpy mood after being kept inside for a few days." I leant forward and rubbed his neck.

"Hmm. Well he'll be glad of the rest between two hard rides by this evening." He eyed Falada's head as he chomped on the bit.

I shook my head. "He would never admit to needing rest. He's too stubborn."

Falada gave a little buck that only made me laugh harder.

Jian's lips twitched. "Come, we should ride."

There had been fresh snowfall overnight and the horses' hooves sank deep, even on the path. As much as Jian had talked about riding hard, the first hour was slow work until we reached higher ground where the snow was thinner, brushed from rocky ground by the wind, making strange patterns on its surface.

I glanced back at the Fort as it sank from view behind the rise and wondered if I would ever be back or see over the Border again. I wanted to see more of the Old Blood and that land of such beauty. Even the wind blew against us, as if tugging me back.

We reached a sheltered wooded valley, and I lowered

my hood so that it was easier to look around. Hai Rong was monologuing to Cai Hong and Jeremiah looked pensive. I was about to fall back to ride beside him while there was no wind to shout over when Jian held a fist in the air. The horses stopped at once and every conversation died. I searched the trees but could see nothing.

Jian turned to Captain Jun who rode beside him. "Do you hear that?"

The captain paused, then nodded. "It's coming nearer." He drew his sword and the hiss of the metal seemed amplified by the snowy sides of the valley. Every man around me freed their weapons, but I struggled to free mine from the scabbard, where ice had locked it shut.

Jian turned, his body animated. "It's a Nameless. Guard the Princess in the center. She is our priority." He pointed to Jeremiah with his sword. "Do not leave her side."

Before I could respond, men had surrounded me in a circle, and Jeremiah's horse was pressed against mine facing the other way. Cai Hong and Hai Rong positioned themselves at opposite angles on my other side.

Falada shifted beneath me and I tightened the reins, my sword finally coming free.

"What's a Nameless?" I whispered to him.

The horse shivered beneath me. *'I'm not familiar with the term, but Jian is right. Something comes. It doesn't feel right, though. It has no soul. I can hear its screams at the edge of my hearing. If Jian can hear it and you can't, it must be of Sal'hadar. The captain must have Old Blood in him too.'*

"A Spirit-Beast?"

'No. Something.'

I licked the ice from my lips and scanned the trees again. Silence coated the landscape and not even the caw of a bird could be heard. I fidgeted in the saddle and adjusted my grip on my sword. My gloves were thick, and I'd never fought while wearing them before. Nor had I ever fought from horseback. Suddenly all my sword practice felt like nothing more than a silly game. I was woefully unprepared.

"There," said Jian, his voice clear and steady.

I followed his arm and saw a black hulking shape creeping down the side of the valley through the trees. It was utterly silent. Jian barked more orders, but I was too transfixed by the creature to follow them. It was as tall as Falada and twice as wide. It was so black I couldn't make out a single feature, but it moved strangely, both elegant and erratic at once.

There was an ear-splitting crash, and the creature leapt towards us at a run, trees toppling and smashing in its path. It moved too fast for something that size and fear seized my heart. A multi-voiced scream echoed in my head, and I lifted my hands to my ears. It was a scream of terror and agony and madness.

"Concentrate, Princess," said Hai Rong calmly. "Don't fall for its tricks."

I lowered my hands and took a deep breath before the creature slammed into the spears of the front row of soldiers. Wood shattered and horses screamed. This close I could see the creature most resembled a bear, its fur matted and spiked with blood. Two old arrows stuck out from its flank but didn't seem to hinder it at all.

The men thrust spears towards its belly, and one was knocked from his horse by a blow from an enormous paw. A second row of soldiers charged between the gaps of the first line and shoved new spears and blades at the raging monster. The first line retreated behind them. The creature howled at the air and flailed around itself.

Jian had separated himself and circled the bear from behind. He slid from his horse and ran at its flank. His name caught in my throat as he ducked beneath its huge arm, and stuck his sword into the beast's chest, right up to the hilt. That horrible scream echoed in my head again, almost drowned out by an audible bellow. The bear knocked Jian with a paw, and he flew back into the snow. The other men used the distraction to thrust more of their spears into the creature.

The bear didn't retreat like any normal animal would, but its blows became weaker and it swayed on its feet. It let out one final, gurgling cry and collapsed onto the snow. The men surrounded it, swords and spears at the ready, as its eye rolled in its socket, watching them. Its chest heaved.

Jian stood up and spat blood into the snow. He seemed unhurt and waved the captain's offered arm away as he staggered to the bear. He watched with his men in a silent vigil as the snow stained red, and the creature's life faded away. The only thing I could hear was the pounding of my heart. My thoughts were erratic and startled.

The Prince mounted and shouted for us to ride. Everyone else seemed to know what to do. Injured horses were led on lead reins and two wounded men were lifted up to be held in front of riders. I followed, unable to think clearly or process what had just happened. Jian led us to a cave that was so shallow, it was more of a rocky alcove and ordered us to set up camp early. He doubled our usual guard but let us light two fires instead of one.

Six men and women were injured in varying degrees of severity, and I helped gather water and boil bandages, my feelings retreating to numbness.

I found Jian first. "Are you alright?"

He nodded. "I'm not injured."

"But there was blood?"

"I bit my tongue when I fell. Those other men need your help, not me. Have you ever stitched a wound before?"

I felt the blood drain from my face and shook my head.

"We're close enough to a village to just bandage the wounds for now, then. We'll make it there tomorrow. They should have a healer."

A sharp scream made me spin, and I saw one of the injured horses crumple to the ground. Its rider had slit its throat. I gaped in horror at the flood of blood, and my breaths came in unsteady gulps. Jian touched my arm. "Elyanna? You want to help? Then focus."

I nodded and shut out the image of the horse. Jian pointed at the pot of water full of strips of linen. It had been pulled from the fire and was cooling rapidly in the snow. Numbly, I picked it up, and Jian walked with me to the injured soldiers.

I tried not to see the injuries. One man had bone

sticking through his leg and it took ages to tourniquet, pad and immobilize. His fighting days would be over. A woman had gashes on her side from the bear's claws. The force had torn through chain mail, but thankfully had not broken her ribs. Last was a man slipping in and out of consciousness after a blow to his abdomen, but there were no external wounds that I could see. Jian had him lie completely still with his feet in the air as men forced him to drink. They were more concerned about him than the others, and one of his companions refused to let go of his hand.

As night fell, I sat by the fire and hugged my knees. Every sound in the wood made me jump, despite the men around me. My three guards sat next to me in silence staring into the flames.

A hand brushed my shoulder and I jumped and looked up. It was Jian, looking tired but alert. "You did well," he said softly, then disappeared to the other men. His praise washed away some of the numbness, and I watched as he spoke to the soldiers on duty, lifting each of their spirits so they stood a little taller. He was a good commander.

"What was that creature?" I asked Hai Rong when Jian was lost to the shadows.

"The Nameless? They're animals with a small amount of the Old Blood who try to saturate themselves with the deep magic. Only full Spirit-Beasts can use it without going completely mad. They're called Nameless because they're not often sentient enough to have a name before the madness takes them. That bear would have been little more than a normal animal a week or so ago."

I hugged myself harder. "Does that happen often? Jian said that there were many beasts here with traces of the Old Blood."

Hai Rong shook his head and his dark eyes met mine, reflected in the firelight. "No. Normally only a full Spirit-Beast tries to access the magic."

Cai Hong nodded. "These things don't just happen. Something forced it. Tempted it."

"What?" I whispered. "What would do that?"

Cai Hong picked up a stick and jabbed the fire, making embers swirl up in the smoke. "The true Spirit-Beasts used to do it often before attacks, back in the days when our defenses were weaker. They would create Nameless to wreak havoc and spread fear. They don't count them as lives lost."

My fingers stroked my sword hilt. "And this one?"

Hai Rong shrugged. "Something this side of the Border must have created it."

"A full Spirit-Beast?"

He nodded, and I stared back into the flames. The traditions and the cautions of the Borderlanders were starting to make a lot more sense.

FALADA'S SECRET

I was still in a daze when we arrived back in Stonekeep, and I had never been so grateful for those imposing walls. I couldn't imagine what it must be like for the villagers who had few defenses and knew things like that could prowl the night.

Jian dismounted from his horse and strode off into the castle without a glance at me. He had barely spoken to me since the Nameless, his persona becoming professional efficiency. He had a determined look on his face, and he didn't show the weariness he must have felt.

I stabled Falada, found him oats myself, and gave him a farewell kiss on his soft muzzle. I stumbled to my rooms, my legs struggling to walk normally after several days in the saddle. I clenched my fingers open and closed to get the circulation moving again.

Ruo appeared in the corridor ahead. "Princess Elyanna!" She hurried up to me and gave me a rough hug. I froze, not expecting the affection behind it. She'd never hugged me before, and I'd certainly never seen any maids hug the real Elyanna back at Hava. Ruo pushed me away from her and looked me up and down. "You look like death. I heard you were attacked on the way home. Let's get you warmed up."

She bustled around me, herding me to my rooms. I turned to my guards. "All of you, go and get cleaned up and rested. I'm sure I'll be fine with nobody at my door for the remainder of the day."

They looked at each other. Each had dark rims around their eyes, greasy hair and dirt ingrained on their hands, but their looks were stubborn.

"No offense, Princess, but Prince Jian would kill us if we left you unguarded. Especially at the moment."

Jeremiah stepped forward. "I don't mind staying."

I sighed. "Fine, one man only and take turns. You all need rest." I wrinkled my nose. "And a bath."

I closed the door on them and collapsed into a chair. Ruo had already started pouring buckets of heated water into the tub, but the idea of pulling off all my clothes felt like a lot of hard work. "I have a letter from Chen," I called to Ruo. "And letters from a dozen other men. Can you distribute them through your knitting circle?" I rummaged in my bag to free them.

"How was he?" she took his letter from my hand, the bath half filled.

"He seemed well. He was very excited to hear about you. He clearly loves you very much."

Ruo smiled a little sadly. "He's a good boy. Always has been."

"Were there any letters to me? I sent one to Queen Geraldina, my mother, before I left."

Ruo filled the rest of the bath with the letter safe in her pocket. "It's probably only recently arrived, dear, and I bet the Pass will be filled with snow within the fortnight."

She hesitated as if she had just remembered something but was wondering whether to say it. The bucket paused, dripping in her hands.

"What is it?"

"Well, you saying that reminded me of something. But I don't think it is at all connected to your letter, so I don't want you to worry. But they found a Syberan in the Pass a few days ago. A soldier. He was coming into the Borderlands. Only he wasn't equipped for the snow this time of year and had an accident. Broke his leg. It seems likely he traveled with others, but they must have left him to die. I assume they were in danger themselves. The men at the outpost there found him half frozen by a dying fire. He didn't seem like the sort of man to be carrying a message."

I frowned. "Who is he? What was he doing?"

Ruo placed the bucket down and stretched her back. "I don't know. It happens most years. A Syberan thinks he can brave Eagle's Pass in late Autumn and gets caught out by the weather. Normally they're criminals or poor folk. Maybe this soldier had done something wrong and was running away."

"Maybe. Could you keep me informed on who he is and his condition? A sketch of his features if possible?" I probably wouldn't recognize him, but if he was from Hava, I wanted to know.

I mustered the energy to strip off my sweaty clothes

and slipped into the bath. It was early afternoon, but I planned to go straight to bed afterwards. I had barely slept a wink in my tent since being at the Border, and I had been too cold to sleep there too. The hot water and the fire in my room now felt like a grand luxury, whereas previously I had always seen it as mean compared to Hava.

"If you wish." Ruo settled into a seat, smoothing out the letter from Chen. "I still can't believe you were set upon by a Nameless. They are rare enough at the Border, let alone a few miles south of it. I fear we're entering troubled times again."

"Any news on Prince Han's death?" I rubbed the cloth up and down my arms and felt the heat loosen my back.

"The King returned yesterday, but if they found anything, they've not made the information public. They've doubled the guards on the walls, and I've heard some of the smaller villages have been told to move to the towns for winter."

I moved to the edge of the barrel and rested my chin on my arms. "Do you think this is all the start of a big attack on the Border? A way of weakening us?"

Ruo met my eyes across the room. "By all that is good, I hope not."

❄

I SLEPT long and deeply and thankfully my dreams left me alone. When I woke, I stared up at the stone ceiling in thought. I should try and see Jian to help him in any way I could and call on Queen Fei to comfort her in her grief. Maybe afterwards I could persuade my guards to teach me combat from horseback and while wearing thick gloves. What use was dueling against a crazed bear, anyway? There had been no rules or grace in that battle. I'd only fought people. Everything I knew was probably useless. Maybe, if I was patient enough, I could get Jian to teach me again. Remembering how skillfully he moved, how clever his combinations, reawakened my joy for the sport. But seeing the Nameless and the men at the Border changed my desire to a frantic need. I never wanted to feel helpless in this new world of snow and ice.

Eventually, I felt I had been lazy enough lying around in bed, so I got up and dressed without summoning Ruo. It seemed wrong that Jian and the soldiers were so busy, yet I always had to look for something to do. Deciding on color schemes for the wedding didn't seem appropriate. And anyway, it was too hard to concentrate on that day, too hard to picture it. I should probably start working on the dress with Ruo in the evenings, however, or I would end up with nothing suitable to wear. How Elyanna would be furious if I turned up merely in one of her old ball gowns.

Ruo peeked around the door without knocking and seemed surprised to find me dressed. "You're awake. Why didn't you ring the bell?"

I rose and stretched. "I was fine getting dressed by myself. Cai Hong brought me some lunch. I was thinking we should start on my wedding dress today. And I also wanted to talk to you about sending more clothes and blankets up to the Border. The ones I took weren't nearly enough."

Ruo went to stoke the fire. "Well, you're certainly important enough to be able to make it happen. We would need more people to knit and sew though and more materials."

I nodded. "I will fund it as much as I can. Maybe I should talk to the Queen about it, too? Can you recruit more people? Many must be related to the men there."

Ruo gave me a restrained smile. "It is good to finally see you excited about something. The transport will be the tricky thing. Prince Jian has always prioritized the space on the packhorses for food, building materials and weapons."

"I'll speak to him too."

"There's something else you need to think about: the Winter Ball."

My heart sank. "When is that?"

Ruo chuckled. "A week before your wedding. Don't look so glum. I'm sure you will find it fun, and you have dresses aplenty for it already. We can still focus on your wedding dress. I have actually drawn some designs." She fished around in her belt pouch and pulled out some parchment. "Just rough sketches. I thought it might be fun to meld Borderlander and Syberan cultures together. You don't have to use these of course, but I thought it might give you ideas."

I looked through the drawings and a slither of excitement wound its way around my belly. "These look wonderful."

We discussed choices of cut and material, and I

traced Ruo's sketches but with added details of my own. Gradually the horrors of the Nameless melted away, and I felt myself relax.

There was a knock on the door, and Ruo rose to open it. I stood as Captain Jun entered. He gave a stiff bow and I resisted the urge to look over his shoulder to see if Jian was outside. "Princess, I was wondering if you could aid me?"

"Of course, come and take a seat by the fire." I indicated the seat that Ruo was vacating as she went to get wine. The Captain was clean shaven again, though his skin was pale and haggard. He looked like he needed a long night's sleep, and I felt a stab of guilt at my lazy morning.

"I won't be here long, I wanted you to look at some drawings for me of some Syberans. Tell me if you recognize them."

I frowned. "Who are they? Is one of them the man they found in Eagle's Pass with a broken leg?"

Captain Jun glanced at Ruo as if surprised I knew. "No. These three men were found yesterday south west of Stonekeep. I'm afraid they had been attacked either by Spirit-Birds or avian Nameless. All three were dead despite being well armed. There was a dead Spirit-Bird too. It's the quality of their weapons and chainmail which makes me wonder if you know them and the reason they have snuck past Eagle's Watch unannounced. We are seeing if their death was linked to Prince Han's."

My mouth dried. "It is only a day's ride between the Fever Mountain Range and Stonekeep. If they've come straight from Sybera, does that mean they were attacked only a few hours from here?"

Captain Jun nodded. "I'm afraid so. Spirit-Birds haven't attacked like this for years, but it's only been these two groups of people, miles apart. It's important we know who they were."

I nodded, my stomach clenching uneasily as he unrolled the parchment he carried. Sounded like we had been lucky just meeting a Nameless. But what had well-armed men been doing sneaking around the Borderlands?

My breath caught as I saw the three faces drawn before me. A few features were missing, I assumed from injury, but I recognized all three of them. Sir Hellard's stern face and strong jaw caught my attention first. He had worked for Queen Geraldina since before I could remember. The second was his younger squire, and the third was another soldier who had accompanied Elyanna to the Winter Palace.

I felt like a rabbit who had been caught at bow point by a hunter. I didn't think I would get away with pretending I didn't recognize them, but what were they doing? They should be with Elyanna.

"Were they the only people found? There was no sign of anyone who escaped?"

Captain Jun narrowed his eyes. "Should there be? The snow was trampled from the fight and there were signs it had been disturbed all around."

I looked back at the pictures, my mind racing. "That's Sir Hellard. He's often in Hava. I think that one is his squire. But I don't know what they were doing here. I wondered if they could be bringing a message from my parents. Perhaps they want to offer aid with finding Prince Han's killers?"

Jun looked skeptical and stroked his smooth cheeks. He gathered up the pictures and rolled them after his arm. "Thank you, Highness. Let me know if you think of anything else that might help."

As he closed the door, I stared into the flames, my heart pounding. My mind frantically pieced the information together. I had written home to tell of Han's death and that I had been treated well. That Jian was now the Crown Prince. Queen Geraldina had most likely informed her daughter, away at the Winter Palace. Elyanna would see I was going to become queen in her stead. She had always been so bitterly jealous. I guessed she had breathed no word to her mother and had come straight away with the soldiers before Eagle's Pass closed with snow. How had I not thought about this? I had been too caught up in the excitement of visiting the Border. I should have sent the letter in Spring when the snow had melted and Jian and I were wed.

Ruo touched my arm and I jumped. "Are you alright, dear?" She passed me the wine, taking the cup intended for the Captain for herself.

"Thank you. It's just a shock. I don't understand what they were doing here."

She sat down and leant towards me. "Do you want to talk about it?"

I shook my head and reached over to our designs for the dress and bolts of different shades of silk. My hands trembled. "No. Let's get back to where we were."

I would find her if she really was here and not eaten by a Spirit-Bird. Her height and features would make her stand out. I wouldn't give her the chance to ruin my life again.

I stabbed a scrap of silk with a needle and tried not to think about her coming closer and closer.

❋

THE NEXT MORNING, I got up early and felt refreshed. I dressed in fur-lined leggings and a tunic ready for Cai Hong and Hai Rong to teach me how to fight Nameless and Spirit-Beasts. Exercise often helped me focus. I hoped Ruo would find out more information about the injured Syberan from Eagle's Pass while we trained.

Ruo was fixing the final braid of my hair so it coiled around my scalp when there was a loud flurry of thuds on the door. She frowned and went to open it, one hand on the dagger she wore around her belt. I grabbed my sword.

Jeremiah stood alone in the doorway and I relaxed but froze when I saw his face. The guard's skin was pale, and he was panting for breath. His eyes were wide with horror. "Princess, you must come at once."

I opened my mouth to reply but he turned and ran ahead so fast, I had to pick up my skirts to follow him without tripping over. I had never seen him so distraught. My heart hammered in my ears and I felt dizzy. Pictures flashed of Nameless within the walls, or giant Spirit-Beasts, or Jian laid out on the stone plinth unmoving, just like Han had been.

As Jeremiah turned to the stables my sense of horror grew and I stopped following him. "Jeremiah, stop."

He skidded and came to take my hand. Distress was clear in his face. "Princess, you must see this straight away."

I pulled my hand from his grip. "What is it? Tell me now so I can prepare myself."

The guard looked at my face, then towards the stables and back again. He licked his lips and couldn't quite meet my eyes.

"Jeremiah!" I almost shouted at him.

"It's Falada. He's…" he took a deep breath. "He's dead."

It felt like all of my insides dropped at once, leaving my body behind as an empty, echoing shell. I whispered something but didn't register what. I walked to the stables as if in a trance. The world spun around me and I wasn't quite a part of it.

I opened the stable door and stepped inside. Even the geese next door were silent. I walked past the stalls to the one I had stabled Falada in yesterday.

My throat constricted and a strange moan escaped as I covered my mouth with my fingers. I felt my knees crumple as I knelt in the straw beside Falada's body. His pale fur was covered in sweeps of dried blood. I crossed my arms over his back and lowered my head into his fur to weep, but the tears didn't come. My body didn't work. All I could do was breathe in the cooling, musty smell of my best friend.

Falada was my everything. The only one who had always been there for me.

"Falada?" My voice sounded strangled. "Falada? Wake up. I'm here. I love you."

No words echoed in my brain, only a deep sense of wrongness.

"Falada? Please speak to me? Please? Tell me what to do. Tell me how to save you."

Nothing.

"Falada? I'll do anything. Just wake up. Please."

Heavy footfalls fell behind me, but I didn't turn, keeping my face buried in Falada's neck. They stopped abruptly and I jumped as a hand brushed my shoulder, then lingered on my back.

"I'm so sorry, Elyanna. I don't understand how this could have happened." Jian's voice sounded rough and disbelieving. I twisted my face to see him, my cheek prickled by Falada's hair, and found the Prince knelt beside me, his head bowed as if in respect. His fringe shielded his face and his hand stayed on my back.

I buried my face back in Falada, his fur becoming increasingly bristly, and his skin cold and hard. This wasn't him anymore. He was gone. Even his smell was changing. A few tears managed to leak from my eyes, and I wished they would come in floods and release me from this horrid numbness. I sat upright and rubbed the dust-filled wetness from my face with my sleeve. I stared, motionless, as horror started to creep into my awareness from every angle. My hands started to shake.

Jian moved closer and his hand brushed across my shoulder blades until it wrapped around me. "This was a human, not a beast. A clean strike with a dagger. I will find whoever did this."

I couldn't reply. All I could do was stare at the wrongness of Falada's unmoving body.

Jian cleared his throat as if struggling to know what to say. "I'm sorry this happened here on our soil. Some Borderlanders hate any trace of the Old Blood. People are scared in Stonekeep, though they might not show it. This could have been in revenge for Han, or out of fear that Falada could be turned into a Nameless, not under-standing how aware he was. Traditionally we don't let animals with Old Blood into Stonekeep." He hesitated, frowning as he searched for words. "I know you were very fond of him. I am sorry."

But I knew who had done this. Falada was strong and smart. He would only let somebody he trusted absolutely get close to him armed. There was no sign of a fight and I could only think of one person he trusted who would want him dead: Elyanna.

He was the only one here who knew what had truly happened. The only one who knew I had been ordered here by Elyanna and hadn't forcibly taken her place. They had been bonded, and still she had killed him.

Elyanna was here to take her place as the future queen, and she was out for blood. I thought of the drowned kittens bobbing in the water trough. The one she had missed hiding in the straw. The way I had whisked it away and hidden it with me inside an empty barrel. I hadn't realized she had seen me until she was sitting on top of the barrel nailing it shut. The way the kitten had cried as I had screamed.

Now the Queen wasn't here to hold Elyanna back. There was only me who could stop her.

I clenched my fists. She would want me dead too. But I wouldn't let her cause Falada to be buried and shut away in the dark like she had to me.

I waited until I had caught my breath. "May I... make a strange request?" I whispered.

I felt more than saw Jian nod, his full attention on me.

"Falada was so special, and I want him remembered. In some way, I would like to feel like he is still here, with me. I don't want him shut away in the dark. I don't want him to be trapped."

Jian's voice was soft. "What do you have in mind?"

"I would like to have his head preserved and hung from the South Gate where he can look over the river and fields and mountains of Sybera's border. Then I could go and talk to him sometimes." And Elyanna would see his eyes watching her.

His fingers brushed my shoulder. "I'll arrange it. I'm sure many would go to pay their respects."

"Thank you," I murmured, suddenly exhausted. I felt so alone. I had lost my one true friend. Tentatively, I leaned closer to the Prince, letting his arm wrap around me. I expected him to push me away or awkwardly stand up, but he didn't. I leaned further, nestling into the firmness of his chest, his arm now circling me fully. He froze and I couldn't even feel him breathe. I waited, my mouth dry and my limbs tense. His thumb twitched, then stroked my upper arm. I melted into him and he took a deep breath. As much as it scared me, I needed him right now. I was too scared to do this alone.

In his embrace, my numbness crumbled and pain

stabbed through my stomach into my heart. Agony, shock, and horror encircled me tighter and tighter until I could barely breathe. Tears soaked his shirt and I let myself be weak, trusting he would keep away all the darkness around us.

I cried until the numbness returned to my heart and my legs cramped. Jian disentangled himself from me and stood. "Elyanna, let me take you away from here. If you've finished saying your goodbyes, that is. I'm sure you would like happier memories of Falada."

I nodded and took his hand so he could help me stand. When I was steady, he let go and folded his arms behind his back in a formal posture. "Shall I take you to your rooms?"

I nodded and gave one last look to Falada as he slowly became overrun with flies. The warmth I had felt from Jian's embrace twisted and heated to a deep hatred. I took a shaking breath and tried to cool the bubbling rage. I had nothing left for Elyanna to take from me, but I couldn't let her hurt anyone else.

But where was she?

❆

THERE WAS a knock on my door, and I washed my face in the bowl of water before pulling on my fur robe and opening it. I'd been crying all night, sinking deeper and deeper into an endless black hole, and knew I must look a mess. I took a step back in surprise when I saw it was Jian. I should have at least brushed my hair, but it was so hard to care. Normally when I felt this bad, I could go and hide with Falada. The one person I needed the most right now, was the one person I couldn't have. I didn't have the energy to try to impress Jian anymore.

The Prince was standing with his side to the door, dressed smartly as always, and looked like he might have been pacing.

He didn't meet my eyes but held out a wooden box. "I wasn't completely sure what was appropriate to give you, but I have this as a sign of my condolences. If it is not right, say, and I will get you something else. I've never been good at these things. I've heard in Hava it is customary to give flowers, but they're all dead this time of the year, so..." He shrugged and finally met my eyes. They were full of guilt, and I realized he blamed himself for Falada's death. I'd never seen him off-kilter before.

"Thank you," I managed. He scratched his neck awkwardly as I took the box and looked like he would rather be anywhere else.

I opened it and pressure built behind my eyes as I looked at a bracelet made of Falada's mane woven with silver wire. A small silver pendant dangled from one side. I held it up to the light and made out an intricate galloping horse.

A tear escaped down my cheek and Jian fidgeted, his hand freeing the pendant he wore around his neck from under his tunic. "I'm sorry if..."

I held up my hand. "No. It's very kind and means more to me than you know. Thank you." I slipped it onto my wrist and smiled through my tears. Part of Falada could always be with me.

Jian's eyes met mine. "He runs in the wind with Tamunden now."

I nodded and felt the silkiness of the strands of mane, so different from any other horse I'd ridden.

"And the tanners are doing as you asked and preparing his head. He will watch over the South Gate by the end of the week."

"Thank you, Highness." I gave a small bow before retreating into my room to cry in private.

IDLE CONVERSATION

*R*uo threw open the curtains and I groaned. She stood over the bed with her hands on her hips.

"Do you know how long it is until your wedding day?" she asked.

I sat up and shook my head. The days had lost any pattern since I had arrived here. My eyes were grainy from another night spent crying. When I drifted asleep, nightmares haunted every moment. Nameless, and dead soldiers, and Elyanna hammering me inside a barrel. There was nobody left who understood.

"Two weeks. And one week until the Winter Ball."

Two weeks. That was very soon. A week ago, that would have terrified me, but since losing Falada, it was hard to feel anything. I couldn't imagine dressing up and having a hundred eyes on me while I felt like this. And knowing one pair could be Elyanna's.

Two days had passed since his death, and there had been no sign of her. How could she possibly hide with her height and Syberan features? It made no sense. Back in Hava I had always believed she was stronger than me. Perhaps I had been right. I felt like I was merely being pulled along by her little game. If I put one foot wrong, I would give away that I was looking for the real princess and everything would be over. Guilt at my deceit sat heavily in my stomach.

Ruo seemed to have been expecting more of a reaction from me. She sat on the bed and took my hands. "I know you're grieving, child, but grief is part of what it means to be a Borderlander. You are to be our queen and have much to prove. You have no time for tears and shutting yourself away. Jian has lost his brother. The King and Queen their son. But they are still there every day serving our country and keeping us safe. Grief doesn't destroy us. It keeps us focused on what is important."

I nodded, but her words did little to stir emotion in the empty cavity of my chest.

She pulled the covers from my body. "You are going to get up, do your normal exercises, eat a proper breakfast and then dress for lunch with Queen Fei and Prince Jian. The King is away again as of this morning seeing to the security of the villagers. Half the guard are out hunting for any signs that a Spirit-Beast is still this side of the Border and warning any small groups of travelers."

I nodded and did as she said, not having the will to fight. The familiar movements of my stretches and the flow of sword positions cleared my mind. If I stayed hidden away for much longer, Elyanna would be able to take advantage. I had nobody to help me in this. I needed to focus.

"Ruo?" I asked as she braided my hair.

"Hmm?" She coiled a group of plaits into a snake at the back of my head.

"You remember how you said I would never be able to pass as a normal townswoman in your knitting circle?"

"Yes. You look completely different than a Borderlander."

"Well, have you seen anyone suspicious the last few days? Anyone who looks like they could be from Sybera?"

She frowned at my reflection in the mirror. "Not that I have heard. Why? What are you worried about?"

I hesitated. "There was somebody in the palace back in Hava who hated Falada. A young woman. I was wondering…" I turned to face her. "Just keep a close look out, will you? You and your friends? Especially for a girl who looks like she may have Old Blood in her veins. Tall with white hair."

Ruo gave me a strange look. "You think a Havan noble is here and killed Falada?"

I held my face in my hands. "I don't know. I don't know what to think. Please don't tell Jian or anyone. They'll think I'm mad." I rubbed my eyes and looked back at my maid. "But watch out for me? It will put my mind at ease."

She nodded, but I could see she wasn't at all convinced. She reached over and lowered my hands.

"Now, see here. I'm going to have to redo that kohl now." Her scolding was gentle.

I straightened and let her redo my makeup. Despite the practical nature of their clothes and speech, the Borderlander makeup tended towards bright and bold. Red lips and pale eyelids. With my fair skin and hair, such colors made me look drained, and Ruo was struggling to find tones that truly suited my skin. Still, I was pleased with the natural look she was creating and explained how in Hava we darkened our eyelids instead of dusting them silver.

Ruo finished the outfit with two large disks of bronze earrings. I smiled at my reflection, liking the way our cultures merged.

Ruo helped me stand. "Talk about the wedding. It will be a welcome distraction for the Queen, and a helpful reminder for Jian. The wedding is a sign of hope and stability for Stonekeep. Remember it is about more than just the two of you."

I nodded and slipped the bracelet of horsehair on my wrist before leaving.

Cai Hong and Hai Rong stood either side of my door and both eyed me wearily as if certain I was about to burst into tears. To be fair, they were probably right. I was too fragile to deal with much today. Still, I felt better with them by my side. But if Elyanna attacked me and told them who she was, surely they would take her side as the real Princess? I was a nobody.

I took a deep breath and closed my eyes.

"Princess?" asked Hai Rong.

I opened my eyes and set my jaw in determination.

"Lead the way to the Queen and Prince. Ruo says we're lunching together."

My guards gave short bows and Hai Rong took the lead while Cai Hong fell behind. I thought about Jian and the familiar nerves prickled my stomach. It was so hard to work out what I felt about him. Two weeks. Two weeks before he was my husband. If Elyanna came after that, it would be too late. We would already be married. And being married to Jian no longer seemed like such a bad thing. He'd shown he had a heart, and I believed he was a good man despite his aloofness. Maybe we would be able to become friends.

Hai Rong led the way to the Queen's private dining chamber. It was high in one of the towers and was a large round room with windows in every wall showing the view for miles. Over the last few days, the snow had fallen in earnest and blanketed the world in white. The dark smudges of the trunks of the pine forests, and the muddy sludge of the roads were the only features I could see until the mountains.

Queen Fei was wearing a scarlet robe that dragged along the floor behind her and was lined with brown fur. A blue sash tightened it around her slim waist, and from it hung a gently curving sword. Her black hair fell loose like a sparkling waterfall to below her waist. It was hard to remember how old she was when she still seemed so strong and elegant. A woman old enough to have three adult children, and to have lost two of them. Her head was held high as if nothing in the world could stop her. This was who I was expected to be like. How was I to replace somebody who was so perfect in her

215

role as the Borderland queen? I didn't have the blood of Sal'hadar in my veins. I wasn't even the princess they thought I was. Guilt stirred in my stomach.

Queen Fei smiled and took my hands. "Thank you for joining us. I know how hard the last few days have been for you. I thought we could all do with some healthy distraction."

I forced a smile. "Thank you."

The door creaked and I turned to see my guards opening the door for Jian to enter. His eyes went straight to mine, then to my wrist. He seemed to relax a little when he saw the bracelet there, and I was glad I hadn't forgotten to wear it. I slept with it by my bed and only took it off in the day to bathe. Nobody had ever given me something so thoughtful before.

"Elyanna, how are you?" His posture was less formal than normal, though his uniform was as immaculate as ever. His eyes seemed earnest, as intense as ever. As I held his stare I felt drawn in, yet pushed back simultaneously.

The question made me waiver, and I struggled to control my emotions. "Delicate."

The Queen placed her hand on my shoulder. "Then let us stay away from delicate conversation. Nothing serious." She smiled at her son. "Pour some wine, Jian, if you would."

He turned to do her bidding, and I sat next to the Queen on the couch. The way she glanced at the two of us made me suspect she was trying to encourage our friendship.

"How is your wedding dress coming along?" She asked with a bright smile.

"Slowly." Very slowly. I wondered if Ruo had told her we hadn't even finalized the design. Though I had ordered the material.

She took her wine from Jian, and he handed me mine. For some reason I couldn't meet his eyes as I thanked him. He felt… different.

"Well, you don't have to make it all by yourself with Ruo. There are many people who would be eager to help. We might be a practical people who value self-reliance, but we work together more often than we work apart."

I thought about how the Borderlanders valued fore-sight and preparation, and I wondered if I was being subtly scolded for being underprepared. If so, she didn't realize how woefully underprepared I was for every aspect of this wedding. Especially the part where it made me the future queen. The dress should be the least of her worries.

I caught Jian studying me out of the corner of his eye and wondered if my expression had betrayed my thoughts.

"I wouldn't worry, Mother. I have never seen needle-work so fine as Elyanna's. She has spent her time making me a cloak, and I am honored she put that before her own needs. I have no doubt her dress will be ready and beautiful." He took a nonchalant sip of his wine.

I looked up at Jian in surprise. I had not been

expecting him to say that. He'd never spoken up for me before.

Queen Fei seemed equally surprised and beamed. "Jian, I didn't know this! Why haven't you shown it to me?"

He cleared his throat. "I will wear it next week at the ball."

I fidgeted. "I'm afraid it's not very grand. I made it more for riding. If you wish, I can line it with silk to make it finer so it would be more worthy of a ball?"

Queen Fei gave a very unladylike snort. "He will only be wearing the same uniform he always does, dear."

Jian shrugged. "It helps me remember my duty and who I am." He looked at me. "Your cloak also helps me remember that." Our gazes locked again and this time it was him who looked away first.

I licked my lips, not sure what to make of this new Jian. Queen Fei seemed taken aback by it too, though it only made her quicker to smile.

I listened to her talk of her own wedding and she described her dress of silver and gold. Then she spoke of Jian, Han and Feng's childhood antics. She required little response from me, so I just smiled and nodded, and stole looks at Jian who had seemed to draw more in on himself, his eyes staring at the fire. How I wished I could read his mind.

Servants brought food and we ate fried fish, potatoes and a boiled green leafy plant I couldn't identify. It started to snow, and white flakes swirled around and around the tower windows on all sides.

As we finished, Queen Fei stood. "I have asked for some milk cakes for dessert, but first I must excuse myself. I won't be long."

She glided from the room, and I assumed she was going to relieve herself. Or pretend to, so Jian and I were left alone. Why else mention the desserts so that it would be rude if either of us left now.

Jian was rotating his wine cup in long careful fingers as he stared into the fire. I had drunk more than my normal one or two glasses. I thought this was possibly my fourth, but I couldn't be sure. I pushed it away from myself before I could be tempted to drink any more and lose my wits. The warm fuzziness cushioning my brain was a welcome relief from the hollow pain, however.

"You're very secretive, you know?" said Jian as he stared into the fire. I jumped. He looked at me with an amused twitch to his lips, and the wine sat like warm honey in my stomach.

I frowned. "*I'm* the secretive one? I talk a lot more than you! You keep on walking off in the middle of conversations."

The corners of his lips sagged. "I do not. I only leave when the conversation has ended." He flicked his fingers up into the air.

I snorted. "Well you can't continue a conversation on your own, can you?"

He rolled his shoulders. "I become tired of idle chatter in this place. Everything is inefficient compared to the Border."

I folded my arms. "You think I speak idle chatter?"

"No, I just walk off when what needs to be said has been said."

I raised an eyebrow at him. "Who made you the judge of that?"

He batted my words from the air. "Stop being difficult and ignoring my question." His tone was teasing more than accusatory. "I know next to nothing about you. You don't talk about Hava at all. Or your family."

I shrugged, hoping he didn't see the unease he'd awoken in my stomach. I didn't want to lie to him. "I miss them but they're not part of my new life now."

He frowned and twisted his goblet. "Elyanna, why were you sent here with only one permanent guard and no maids?"

I sighed, but my throat tightened. "Both the maids went with my lady-in-waiting." I attempted a smile at him. "They were scared of you all."

He snorted. "Flighty Syberans."

"And Jeremiah is fiercely loyal. In fact, he is the most loyal person I've ever known. You have done him a disservice with the way you talk to him."

He raised one eyebrow. "And they did you a dishonor by letting a child guard you. He's not even a knight. Do your parents not realize the danger they could have put you in? Mother has spent days wondering if some slight was intended towards us, or if there was some disagreement between you and Queen Geraldina."

I licked my lips, not liking where this was heading and tried to change direction. "Jeremiah's station is not his fault. He is a good guard and serves me well."

Jian tilted his head and ran his fingers through his fringe, studying me. There was a gentleness in his eyes that I'd not seen before, and it made my stomach twist in a delightful yet unnerving way. The sensation was unexpected, and I felt warmth sweep through my body.

"I will apologize, Princess. I'm very glad you have a loyal guard."

I smiled. "Thank you."

His eyes didn't leave my face, and I struggled for something more to say. In the end I just looked back at him. There was a softness around his mouth and an openness in his eyes that didn't belong on the face of the General of the East Fort. It suited him. My eyes fell naturally to his lips.

Words tumbled brainlessly onto my tongue. "Well are you not going to leave now, for fear of idle chatter?"

He half smiled and dropped his eyes. "Quite right. I will see you tomorrow." He stood up.

I stood too. "That's not what I meant. What about dessert?"

He suppressed a laugh. "I'm sure you and Mother can enjoy it without me. You're quite right, I should be working instead of talking."

He bowed his head and strode to the door and I wanted to kick myself. He didn't look back as he left. I put my head into my hands. I'd not meant the words as a dismissal. I hugged myself, feeling colder and a little sad. I shook my head. What was wrong with my emotions today?

I reimagined the glance he had given me from the shadows of his hair and the gentle look in his eyes. My stomach twisted again, and I sat down. I hadn't expected any pull of attraction and a thrill of nervous excitement tingled down my limbs. I reached for my wine to calm myself down. I still barely knew him. It would not be sensible to get carried away.

HUNTER OR HUNTED

*T*he next morning, I wandered through the town with Ruo, Jeremiah trailing behind. I had said I needed some fresh air and a change of scenery to prepare myself to see Falada's head, but in reality I was looking for any sign of Elyanna or her maids or soldiers. Every single person I passed looked like a Borderlander, and her height and green eyes would make her stand out even if she covered her hair.

Maybe I was worrying for nothing and Falada's death had nothing to do with her?

Jian had posted a permanent guard by Falada's head, on top of the two usual guards of the South Gate who kept an eye on who was passing in and out. I asked them if anyone suspicious had been seen, or anyone they didn't recognize had been looking at Falada's head. They all replied they hadn't. With the attack on Han and the Syberan soldiers, and the appearance of the Nameless, they were even more observant than normal. I couldn't believe Elyanna would have got past them.

What if she was still out there and she had some-body on the inside kill Falada to prepare for her arrival? The only person from Hava was Jeremiah. I glanced back at my guard who was staring up at Falada, his face lined with sadness. Could it really be all an act? I felt guilty for even doubting him. But still...

I tried to force Elyanna from my mind and looked up to Falada's beautiful head fixed above the gate, his glass eyes staring over the snowy plains. The tanners had done a wonderful job and I could almost believe him alive. His mane streamed in the wind as if he were galloping.

"Oh Falada," I whispered past the lump in my throat. "What am I to do? How am I going to be happy without you here to guide me? Who do I trust?"

I listened for his familiar voice in my brain, but it didn't come. I strained all my mental senses towards him, begging for there to be part of him left and that he hadn't left me alone.

'Briaaaanna...'

That voice again. That child's voice. I looked around, but there was nobody. No bird or beast that I could see either.

'You're not alone. Don't be sad. I am here.'

The tone was comforting, but a shiver ran up my spine.

"Who are you?" I whispered.

Jeremiah touched my shoulder. "Princess? Are you alright?"

I shook myself and gave him a smile. "Sometimes I hear things. Don't worry. I'm told it's quite normal for people with some Old Blood up here. Jian said to ignore it."

But he hadn't spoken of something that would know my true name. Only snippets of conversation from passing birds or beasts. And why did I only hear it here in the castle?

Ruo looked out over the fields. "That's good advice, Princess. Nothing good comes from listening to the wild ones."

I gave one last look up at Falada and wished I could bury my face into his warm fur and hear his calm words. He had always been right, and he had told me to give Jian every chance I could, so that was what I would do.

I wandered back through the streets, peering at every face I passed.

Ruo grabbed my arm and pulled me towards a low house. "Look, Changying is here. You should meet her."

I followed her gaze to where a woman was cracking ice over a private well. She looked up as we approached, and her eyes widened when she saw me.

"Princess Elyanna," said Ruo grandly. "Meet my dear friend Changying. She is one of my knitters. Her son is on the Border."

Changying curtsied to me and looked at Ruo with uncertain eyes. I smiled warmly to ease her nerves. "It's nice to finally meet one of Ruo's friends, Changying. The soldiers at the Border were so happy when they received the blankets when I visited. I wish you could have seen their faces after all your hard work making them. Your group deserved all the praise, not me. I am hoping we can send even more there next time. I'm sure we can work out an efficient way."

The woman smiled and tilted her head as she studied me. Her face had rounded with age, and her lips were chapped from the cold, but there was no grey in her hair. She was still beautiful. "You delivered my letters to my son and brought back his reply. That meant a lot to me. Thank you. It's the sort of thing I never feel I can request from the Prince himself."

I smiled. "I'm happy I could help. I hope he rotates out soon and you can speak to each other in person."

She stood a little taller. "I miss him, but I am so proud of what he is doing there. If only they worked out how to properly heat such a big place."

Ruo gave her friend a sideways hug. "They'll look after him, Changying. There is no use in all this fretting. Chen said they're both doing well."

I looked around at the low water-reed-thatched houses with walls insulated by a thick layer of smeared clay over the bricks. From her door I could smell chicken stew and wet leather, and I wished it was easier for me to be part of this world.

I snapped my attention back to Ruo's friend. "Changying, have you noticed any suspicious behavior around the village? Any strangers?"

Ruo gave me a patient look and folded her arms. "Her Spirit-Horse was killed last week," she explained to Changying.

The woman shook her head. "There aren't many strangers at this time of year. The snows make travel hard. It is just the farmers and their families who come within the walls for the winter, now they don't have crops to protect."

I let my gaze keep wandering around, looking for clues. It was such a tight-knit community here, how would Elyanna hide to be close enough to kill Falada? Even if she dyed her white hair, her features were Syberan, not Borderlander. She would stand out.

"Are there many people here with Syberan blood?"

Changying pouted in thought. "Only a few families. None I know well. They're all farmers or herdsmen."

"Any with white hair?" I pushed.

Changying snorted. "By the Spirits, no. None with Old Blood. No offense, Highness, but any Syberan with money or title wants to stay far away from here. They are too soft."

I nodded, feeling a little foolish. "Could you do something for me? Could you find out more about the Syberan families and tell Ruo your findings? I especially want to know of any newcomers. A girl in her late teenage years."

Ruo was looking at me oddly, but Changying bowed. "Of course, Highness. I would be happy to assist you since you have helped us."

I thanked her and Ruo led me away. She looked concerned. "This white-haired girl you keep worrying about." She frowned. "If you are as suspicious about her as you sound, you should tell Prince Jian. He could organize a thorough search for her at once and see if she is really here. Did she know Sir Hellard?"

I shook my head. "Please, Ruo. I know this all sounds odd, but it is probably just a flight of fancy. I don't want to bother him with it. But I feel safer knowing that somebody has their eye out, even if the whole thing is foolish. Besides I should know which families of Syberan descent are here. I feel like I have a duty of care to them. I don't want any more to die."

She raised an eyebrow. "You don't want to tell the Prince?"

"No," I said firmly. "He has far more important things on his mind."

I was going to have to be more careful with my questions, or I would catch myself out.

Ruo gave me a bright smile to cheer me up. "Well, if you are finished out here, I think it is time for lunch."

❄

THE AFTERNOON LOOMED, and I didn't want to fall back into grief and self-pity. I missed Falada terribly, finding myself naturally turning to the stables for comfort, only to remember he was gone. I needed distraction. After eating lunch, I decided to go for a walk around the castle. Well, that was what I told the guards and Ruo. I was actually hoping to catch a glimpse of Jian training his men. I wanted to spend more time with him but wasn't sure how to make that happen without the Queen's intervention. He was busy with the Spirit-Beast attacks, and I knew he needed to concentrate on that, but I had started to enjoy our conversations. I could spare an hour or two before working on my dress again, even if it was just watching him from afar.

The wedding dress was starting to take shape and

Ruo had helped me design a wonderful mix between Borderlander and Havan fashion. I sketched and designed my embroidery, while she cut each panel down to size ready to stitch together. I couldn't help but wonder what Jian would think when he saw me in it.

I wandered through the higher floors of the castle, guessing the best direction until I found a window that looked over the parade ground, three floors below. The parade ground was a frozen field that only soldiers and guards were allowed to enter. About thirty spearmen were standing in rows, assembling into different formations at barked commands from Captain Jun. I watched them, mesmerized, as the lines rippled and bled into each other, each spear held at the same angle.

Jian strode in front of them, his eyes on each man and woman. Now and again he would hold up his hand to freeze the soldiers in place so he could talk to an individual or adjust a hold on a spear. His posture was one of pride and devotion, and I felt a flicker of admiration.

I wished he would fight with Jun again. I wanted to watch the graceful way he moved, the precision and skill, but I supposed all his focus would be on training the men.

A man I vaguely recognized appeared at the corner of the field and called to Jian. The Prince clapped Jun on the shoulder and hurried over. The two disappeared back into the castle.

I sighed and pulled myself back from the window. Jeremiah gave me a questioning raised eyebrow and seemed a little annoyed for some reason. I pointed down at the field. "They're much better than Syberan troops, aren't they?"

He nodded. "Sybera's strength has never been military." He sighed and kicked his boot against the wall. "You shouldn't have to resort to spying to see your betrothed, Princess. His lack of regard for you borders on insult."

I gave Jeremiah a warning look, a strange surge of protectiveness warming my stomach. "He is very busy, and he's becoming much better at talking to me, actually."

The guard shrugged and looked down at the floor, still unhappy.

I turned and made my way down the stairs, curling around and around, my fingers brushing against the cold stone. I could live like this, I decided. I could live second place to a man's duty. For surely that was the role of a married queen? The country always had to come first, whatever the sacrifice. It just seemed such an odd idea that the queen would be me. And Jian was not cruel. He was a good man. Maybe even one of the best.

I rounded the corner of the cloister and heard the echo of a familiar voice, and my chest tightened with excitement. Jian. I hurried forward whilst still trying to look elegant and saw him walking away from me. He was talking to two men dressed like soldiers and their tone was serious. My heart became heavy with disappointment. It looked like they were discussing important matters, probably Han's death, and idle talk with me was hardly worth distracting him for.

He was responsible for so much, and now his

brother was gone, I could see the weight of it on his shoulders. He wasn't just a general anymore, responsible for protecting the lives of his people, he was now the future king, overseeing everything in this kingdom. I needed to help him other than simply making clothes. He was strong, capable and devoted, but nobody could bear that alone. He pushed too many people away in Stonekeep.

Jian must have heard my faltering footsteps because he turned. His expression was serious, but when he saw me, the heaviness fell away from him. He stopped walking, stood straighter and a smile flirted on his lips. There was a bright eagerness in his eyes that took me aback. He studied me, taking in my clothes, my hair, my features, and my skin flushed as I closed the distance between us. The other two men had stopped as well and stood awkwardly behind the Prince, their sentences hanging in the air.

I inclined my head respectfully. "I'm sorry, I didn't mean to interrupt. You're all clearly busy. Please continue."

The Prince's eyes didn't stray from my face. "You're not interrupting, Elyanna." As he said the name, it jarred with me, and I wished for all the world he had called me Brianna. I wished he didn't see the fake vizard of the princess but saw me truly as I was. For the first time it felt like a tangible wall between us that I would never be able to remove.

The Prince turned to the men. "Thank you for your advice. I'll heed your words and continue these discussions this afternoon when I've had time to think."

One of the men frowned and took a step towards us. His hair was in waist length braids and I remembered him as a friend of Prince Han. "But, your Highness, we haven't…"

"Thank you, Shunzi, that is all for now."

My heart thudded in disbelief as the two men bowed and left, leaving me alone with Jian. "You didn't need to do that, Highness. I told you I wouldn't get in the way of important business."

He waved his hand in the air and sighed. "It is nothing that can't wait a few hours. We seem to be going around in circles with no clear way forward. And call me Jian, please. I thought we were past using titles." His smile broadened. "In truth I could do with a change in conversation. Something light for once. Something happy."

I opened my mouth in mock surprise. "You can't mean you want *idle chatter*?"

He chuckled. "Spirits, no. Anything but that."

The silence stretched, and I searched for something to say. Neither of us seemed to know how to breach the space between us. I started a sentence at the exact same time as him, and we both stopped with open mouths before smiling.

He spread out his hands. "Apologies. What were you saying?"

"I was going to suggest we go to the garden, if you could spare the time? You could show me around the parts I haven't yet explored." Their garden was small compared to Hava, and I wondered if he would find my words ridiculous, since you could see all of it in under an hour.

He nodded and held out his arm. I looped mine through his, and he rested his hand on top. I was aware of the pressure of each of his fingers, the calluses on his palm, the rigid strength of his arm, and the closeness of his body looming beside me. My heart pounded despite the lazy pace. Please don't let me mess this up.

"It is only two weeks to the wedding," said Jian.

"Thirteen days." I looked down, wishing he had brought up a different topic. "It is unfortunate timing with your brother and the... attacks. If you wish to delay, I'm sure Sybera would understand."

My stomach twisted. I both wanted more time to get to know him, and feared that if the wedding was delayed, that would also give Elyanna more time to plot against me. If it was indeed her. She wouldn't be able to touch me once I was Jian's wife in truth.

He shook his head and his fingers tightened over my hand. "No. It is good to show a united front at times like this. We offer stability and a tangible future." Silence hung in the air for a few moments as we climbed down a flight of stairs into the garden. The cold wind froze my ears, so I pulled up my fur hood. The snow creaked under our footsteps and small pyramids of white slid from the branches of bushes as we passed. "And I want to marry you."

I looked at him in surprise at the sudden words. "You do?" I tried not to assume his meaning. After all, I knew he was eager for this to be over and done with so he could return to the Border.

He attempted a smile, but it fell away into an earnest expression. "Very much so."

"Oh," was all I could manage. It felt like all the breath had been pushed out of me at once.

His eyes flicked between mine and then he glanced away, suddenly awkward, and I realized how my response might be coming across.

I gave him a teasing smile. "It might mean you have to stand dancing with me."

"I wasn't that bad, was I?"

"And your comment on how much you dislike my idle chatter."

He breathed a short laugh. "You're always going to hold that against me, aren't you?"

"I will until you stop walking off abruptly."

He smirked. "Today I will be your prisoner then in every conversation until you release me."

I huffed a laugh and my breath misted between us. "I'm not a cruel master. You'll survive."

He stopped by a frozen fountain, and I pretended to study the statue of Bula the whale coated in ice. I couldn't concentrate on anything but him, however.

He took a sharp intake of breath as if preparing to force words out and I tensed. "Elyanna, I am sorry you were forced into this marriage. If you are still truly set against it, I promise I will try everything in my power to release you from the arrangement and send you home safe. You never agreed to take on the role of queen." He paused, his whole body tense. I couldn't believe what I was hearing. "But, if you were still will-ing…" he paused again and looked into the frozen waters to collect himself. "If you are willing, I promise to try to be a good husband. Just as you said you would try hard to be a good wife and queen and Borderlander."

I realized I was gaping at him and tried to swallow, but my mouth was too dry.

His eyes rose to mine and pinned me in place. "I didn't expect you to understand, but I think you do. My first duty will always be to my men. To this country. I have to keep us all safe. We will never have much time for our marriage. But, if you can accept that, I would welcome your help beside me. I am so tired of doing this alone." His mask was cracking, his eyes tight.

I licked my lips and struggled to find words. This was Jian, the real Jian, finally.

He gave me a sheepish smile and shifted his feet. "I'm not doing a very good job of this, am I?"

I laughed, despite myself and it came out high-pitched and strained. "No, no, I just didn't expect you to say that."

He was still looking at me expectantly, seeking a reply. My heart thudded harder. This was his proposal. This was *him* asking me to be his wife, not our parents, not our nations. Jian. And I believed him. I believed he would let me go if I wanted.

Jian couldn't bear my hesitation and looked away. "I know it's not an ideal life. I'm not an easy man to like, let alone marry, but…"

I touched his arm to stop him. "Jian, I will marry you."

His shoulders relaxed and he looked down to his

polished boots. He attempted a laugh. "Well I am glad I didn't have to break that one to Mother. She likes you."

I pushed a stray strand of hair behind my ear. "She has always been very kind to me."

He stepped towards me, his hand on his sword hilt. "Hai Rong said you have been jumpy recently as if expecting somebody to attack you. I can understand that after what happened to Falada and seeing the Nameless." His gaze was fierce and gentle at the same time. "I want you to know you can tell me anything, and I will always do everything in my power to protect you. I have been neglectful of your welfare in the past, but I don't intend to be in the future." His gaze was so intensely earnest, it drew me in completely.

"Thank you," I managed.

He took my arm again and seemed more relaxed as we wandered through the frozen labyrinth of the garden, most of the paths hidden by snow. He talked about his plans for the Western Fort, and I nodded along as I watched his features move with excitement at his ideas coming to life. I realized for the first time how handsome he was. The elegant curve of his jaw. The strength in his neck and broadness of his shoulders. How had I never seen it clearly before?

"Jian," I started. He had been brave in saying what he had, and I had given him little in return.

"Yes."

"I am happy to marry you, too. I want to help."

He grinned and the light behind his eyes caught my heart. I had a sudden terrifying urge to touch his face, stroke his hair, trace his lips.

I looked away hurriedly and tried to calm my heartbeat. We had reached an agreement and an expectation of the future, that was all. We were an alliance. A friendship. But these new emotions were so unexpected, I didn't know how to act.

A man waved at us from across the garden. It was the stocky figure of Captain Jun. He held a scroll of paper in his hand.

Jian stopped and turned to me. "I should go. Will you release me? Or blame me for running off again?"

I didn't want this walk to end. I wanted to hear him say nice things and examine the strange feelings in my chest and stomach. But he was the Crown Prince, and no one person could ever have a prince all to themselves. That was our understanding after all. "Will I be able to see you tomorrow?"

He smiled. "I have an early morning meeting with the Farmer's Guild, but then only drill training until eleventh bell. I'm sure Jun could lead the warmup alone tomorrow. The afternoon meetings with the scouts are more important, I'm afraid."

"If you're sure I wouldn't be in the way. I would like you to show me how I can be useful."

He nodded, making his fringe fall across his face. "Come to my reception room at the ninth bell."

I smiled. "Then I release you."

He laughed softly then turned to hurry to the captain. I watched his back straighten as he adopted his normal military mannerisms, but he looked over his shoulder at me before disappearing inside.

Jeremiah appeared by my side and I jumped. "I didn't

hear what you were saying, but it appears to me that man has finally come to his senses."

I elbowed him. "Or lost them. I fear I am becoming an unhelpful distraction from everything he needs to do.

Jeremiah adjusted his sword. "He should never have been so rude to you in the first place."

I ignored him and glanced at the sun. It was further in its arc than I was expecting. Well, I wasn't in the mood for walking further, anyway. I turned to head back to my rooms to sew and chat with Ruo. I had a wedding dress to work on.

Maybe everything was going to work out after all.

✳

Ruo had done even more drawings of additions for the dress, and I was happy to follow them all. She had found some exquisite silver thread for the embroidery, and I could only gape at it and hug her. It shimmered even in the dimmest light. Who knew what she had had to do to find something so fine? It looked like it could be all the way from the deserts of Kilamore.

I hemmed the sleeves as the light faded and pictured what embroidery I would put around the edges. I had drawn a dozen images, and I knew I could go on and on designing more and more. Maybe the galloping white horses in Falada's memory on the sleeves. Then wolves around the neckline to represent Jian, and swans in the skirts to represent me. Or who I was supposed to be anyway. I clicked the needle against my teeth. This was *my* wedding dress, not Elyanna's. I would fill it with things I loved. I would sew flowers and mountains and swords and glittering stars. Maybe even a heron to represent Gilava. I had come here for the good of my people and to protect my parents after all. The heron should feature.

Ruo chuckled beside me. "You've been getting such a look in your eyes recently, like your imagination has been freed. You are finally thinking about the future." She reached over and brushed her hand over mine. "You look happy and I'm glad. I trust things between you and Jian are going well?"

I nodded. "We've... reached an understanding. He's been much more attentive recently."

She gave me a knowing smile. "It was a good idea, going with him to the Border. It showed him you cared and could love what he loves."

I shrugged. "It was exciting. Until that Nameless, anyway. I still see Tama'ha in my dreams. She was so beautiful, but nothing like Falada." I trailed off and the sudden sadness caught me unawares.

Ruo shifted in her seat. "Of course she was nothing like Falada. Your Spirit-Horse was pure and noble. Tama'ha is corrupted by forbidden magic. They pretty much all are up there."

I touched Falada's silvery mane on my wrist and bit my cheek. I would never see him again, and that felt so wrong. He had always been there for me when my own family had been many miles away. He had been all that had kept me going when I had been young.

Ruo sensed my tone and gentled her voice. "Changying sent me a message just before you arrived."

I raised my eyebrows. "That was quick. I only spoke to her yesterday."

Ruo shrugged. "With things like this, you need to know who to talk to. Stonekeep is not that large, and some people specialize in things that aren't their business. We have more than enough gossips." She passed me a list. "These are all the families in the city with Syberan blood."

I frowned at the messy writing, holding it closer to the candle in the dying light. "There are more than I thought." There were about twenty families in total, some with six or seven members. Most didn't have a name attached, just 'man', 'woman', 'boy', 'girl', 'child' or 'unknown.'

Ruo nodded. "As I said, many of them are farmers or herdsmen, and many of them come to the city to over-winter with their animals. It can be brutal out there for a few months, and the wild animals get bolder as they start to starve."

"She didn't say any were newly arrived from Sybera?"

Ruo shook her head. "These families are integrated, with homes and livestock. The maid you fear isn't here. If newcomers arrived from Sybera, the guards would have taken them in for questioning on the spot. Captain Jun is eager to find out what those dead soldiers were doing. It is almost impossible to communicate with Hava this late in the year."

I put the list to one side, wondering if I was being

foolish. But somebody had killed Falada, and Elyanna had always wanted to be a queen.

"Tell Changying to find out more, can you? If she doesn't mind?"

Ruo sighed but nodded. "If it puts your mind at rest, child."

I smiled at her. "Thank you. I really do appreciate it."

We sewed until it became too dark and Ruo stretched to pop her back. "You should get an early night, Princess. There are still bags under your eyes. It would be good for you to see the Queen again tomorrow. If you are going to one day take her place, she will be an invaluable teacher."

"I'm seeing Jian at ninth bell."

Ruo gave me a knowing smile. "I'll tell the Queen you'll join her for breakfast at eight then. She exercises before then, and believe me, you wouldn't be able to keep up with her."

I nodded, even though I wished I could concentrate on seeing Jian. Ruo was right. I had a lot of things to learn.

✳

I KNOCKED on the Queen's door and waited to be let in. A maid opened it from the inside, and I smiled to her in thanks. Queen Fei looked like she had just washed. The fire was blazing, and her hair was wrapped up in a towel. She wore a simple navy woolen dress with a wide leather belt and sleeves that whispered along the floor. Leaning against the wall, as if it had not yet been put away, was an ornate spear with engraved metal all the way down the shaft. It looked heavy, and I wondered if it was hers or the King's.

"Come, Elyanna, sit." She patted the space on the couch next to her.

I walked over to the fire and sat down next to the Queen. She looked at the large silver disks in my ears.

"They suit you. It's nice to see you enjoying some of the Borderlander customs."

I smiled and touched the smooth cool surface of one of the disks. "I love them. They're so simple yet elegant."

The Queen folded her legs and leaned back. "Do you know where they originate from?"

I shook my head. I hadn't realized they had any symbolism or history.

Queen Fei looked into a fire. "There is a myth amongst our people of the Old Days when the Old Blood was at war with the newcomers from across the sea. It is set at the climax of the war when the Old Blood accepted they would have to change their way of life and live alongside their enemies in order for there to be peace. Too many on both sides had died, even though the newcomers only became more numerous. But some of the Old Blood didn't see this as an option. They found us too destructive and believed too much that is important in the world would be lost. So they turned to the old forbidden magic in the earth and became monsters." Her eyes met mine. "You know all this already, I assume?"

I nodded, eager to hear more.

"Well, some Spirit-Beasts were torn and sought out a

middle way. They wanted to dabble in the magic enough for it to make them strong, but not enough for it to corrupt their bodies. They wished to still live among us and rule both Old Blood and new. They wanted power without the sacrifice all power requires. But that in itself is the mark of a monster."

I shifted in my seat trying to glean the meanings behind her words.

"The Borderland women started to wear mirrors dangling from their ears. You see no beast is interested in its own reflection. They only care if they think it is another animal, so they never see themselves. The Old Magic changes the user physically. They become stronger, larger, more terrifying, but it starts to prize away the soul. Beasts can see souls in ways none of us humans can. Beasts who had been tempted to dabble would look in the mirrors and see their souls trying to flee and would be too scared to ever use it again. Either that or they would flee north to hide what they were becoming." The Queen reached over to a low table and took a sip of wine. "Or so the legend says. So all the corrupted Spirit-Beasts hide beyond the mountains, where they can forget what they once were."

I tapped one of my earrings again. "I like that story. I suppose it applies to humans too."

The Queen raised a perfectly sculpted eyebrow.

"Nothing reminds us who we are and what we're willing to go through more than looking in a mirror. These earrings are a reminder to take care of what you are becoming."

The Queen gave me a pleased smile. "And the danger

of seeking power. All of us have a monster within. We must never let it out."

I looked down at my hands on my lap thinking of Elyanna. Was that what she was? A human monster? Just with none of the outward signs that Tama'ha had borne. And she had never fled from her reflection.

There was a clink as the Queen put down her wine, and I looked up. She pulled the towel from her head and shook out her hair in front of the fire. It was impossibly long and thick for a woman of her age. "That is enough of serious talk. I wish to talk to you about Jian."

My mouth dried. "Jian?"

The Queen reached over and took both my hands in hers with a warm smile. "I don't know how you managed to gain his approval, but I've not seen my son so peaceful in years as he was last night. Thank you, from the bottom of my heart, for being patient with him and seeing past his mask." Her eyes creased with emotion. "After Feng, his sister, died, I thought he'd always do everything alone. Never let himself get attached to any individual. He was in such a bad place for months afterwards. Nobody could reason with him, and he destroyed his living quarters. He slept on the cold stone floor of his room, surrounded by the splinters of his bed, but wouldn't let us repair it. I think he encased his heart and emotions with metal so he could never feel such pain again."

I squeezed her hands. "I'm so sorry for your loss. Of both Feng and Han. I can't imagine what you've been through as a mother."

She released her grip and sat back, a shadow over

her face. Then the sorrow passed from her eyes and she smiled again. "I am happy that the two of you will respect each other, and I am proud to have you as my daughter-in-law."

I licked my lips, unaccustomed to so much praise. "Thank you. But it's me who is grateful for how I've been received here and for the attention Jian is showing me. He is being kind even though he's stressed. I'm happy to call Stonekeep my home."

The Queen leaned forward and kissed my forehead. "The two of you will lead this country to greatness. My son's mind always turns to war and tragedy and fearing the worse. Your compassion, steadiness and empathy will complement his strengths. You can give him hope of a stable future."

I looked back at my hands. "I hope so, but I feel so out of my depth knowing I am meant to become queen."

She hummed in agreement. "I'm afraid, my dear, that feeling will never go away. But you have years to learn, and I will show you everything I know. The first lesson is always to be proud of what you are becoming when you see your reflection."

I nodded. "I will remember that."

The Queen stood. "Now we should eat. It's only bread and honey I am afraid, but it is nice to have company while my husband is away. His scouts said he will arrive this evening if the weather holds."

I sat up. "Have they found anything?"

Her face became hard. "Not much. We already knew their wounds were a mixture of human and Spirit-Beast. Whoever it was knew how to cover their tracks and create false trails. Tama'ha hinted it was Jala'ban's work to you and Jian. I could believe that, but there is no trace of him anywhere. I wondered if they returned back over the wall long ago, but then those dead Syberans make me worry. They were very close to Stonekeep."

"What motive could he have?"

The Queen sighed. "I don't know. Jala'ban is not careless, but maybe he never expected to run into Han and it was an unfortunate skirmish. Or maybe it is meant to unsettle and disorganize us before they plan a mass assault on the Border." She picked up her wine and swirled it around in the exact same way I had seen Jian do. "We have so little intelligence from across the Border, we must simply be prepared for anything. The fact that you met with a Nameless only makes me more concerned."

I suppressed a shiver. "The East and West Passes are better defended than ever. I'm sure Jian will hold them back."

She gave a firm nod. "And your family's gold and trade will ensure that even more in the years ahead." She gave me a smile that was surprisingly sad. "Even so, best to always sleep with your sword beside you and never go out alone in the dark." She reached across the table and cut a slice of bread. "Honey?"

※

I REACHED Jian's door and felt nervous butterflies battering their wings as they tried to escape my stomach. I took a deep breath, but it didn't help. Part of me wanted to skip this stage, where everything was so uncertain, to when I felt secure with Jian. But I also didn't want to miss a single moment. There was always the fear I would mess this up and it wouldn't last. I could almost hear Elyanna's voice telling me I was too plain, too boring, too fat for Jian to have any prolonged interest in me.

I stood with my hand on the door handle until Hai Rong leaned over. "Want me to open that for you. Princess?" He was grinning from ear to ear. "It's quite simple really, you just push the handle down."

I glared at him and he laughed. There were hurried movements from behind the door. Jian must have heard I was here. I licked my lips and checked for any stray hairs, tucking them behind my ears, before opening the door.

Jian was standing right behind it, his arm outstretched to push the door handle. I stumbled backwards and let out an awkward laugh. Hai Rong looked away and snorted. I hurried in, away from Hai Rong's amusement, and Jian left the door ajar for propriety's sake, since I'd not brought Ruo with me. I didn't want to imagine my guards all huddled by the door, trying to listen, so moved to the other side of the room.

I'd never been in Jian's reception room before, or any of his quarters. It looked like a place of long meetings and boring conversations. Everything was practical and impersonal. There were no pictures on the plastered walls, and the rugs on the floor were too worn to see their patterns.

I raised an eyebrow. "Is this where you invite people to impress them?"

He looked around the room in amusement. "No, this is where I take people so they listen to me instead of being distracted by their surroundings."

I leant on the back of a dark wooden chair, though didn't sit. "I would like to come to some of your meetings. Just to listen. I have much to learn."

Jian barked a laugh. "You don't want to sit in on my meeting with the farmers. Seriously, it's just a checklist of making sure the right proportion of food or hay is going to the right places. My mother's meetings would be more appropriate. I can do military, commerce and business. I struggle with politics. Mother has a way of charming people and persuading them. She creates unity and solidarity. I think you may have a gift for that too, Elyanna. We can work to our strengths, together."

I looked down. "I'm not sure I do have a gift for that. Certainly not like your mother."

Jian tilted his head. "You've been here a month, and half the people of Stonekeep love you."

I took a step back. "I haven't interacted with many people."

He smirked. "Even the men on the Border seemed sad to see you go."

I waved my hand. "That was because Ruo sent me with the blankets and letters. That was her doing, not mine."

Jian was giving me a strange, knowing smile.

"What?" I smoothed down my dress.

"You're just very different from what we expected.

I'm afraid Syberan royalty don't have a favorable reputation here. Most thought you would hide in your rooms and spend a fortune importing silk and complaining about the cold."

To be fair, that probably was a good prediction of how Elyanna would have acted. Jian took a step closer and my thoughts slowed. "It is very cold," I admitted. That look had returned in his eyes. The one that made me feel weightless and caused my toes to curl. "And you were the coldest thing of them all."

He didn't reply but stepped right in front of me, reached out and brushed a stray curl behind my ear. His finger brushed my neck as he placed it on my shoulder. I stared forward in shock, taking in how each coat button was polished, then slowly, I reached out and touched his chest, my palm tingling. It felt like it should be forbidden to ever touch a man so intimately, let alone a prince. The boldness of it only heightened my emotions. My mouth went dry and I couldn't swallow. I could feel my blood rushing around my body, my chest constricting. I froze, marveling at the new sensations and the way my body responded to him. I had never felt like this before, so alive. Every nerve in my body had become sensitized towards him, my stomach knotted uncomfortably yet wonderfully. His breaths deepened and came quicker beneath my fingers. I moved my hand to the center of his chest and felt his heart pounding, echoing mine. I withdrew my hand in surprise.

He leant forward and for a terrifying, exhilarating moment, I thought he was going to kiss me, but instead he rested his forehead against mine. His lips were parted. I closed my eyes. The warmth of his breath tickled my cheeks.

I didn't dare move, not wanting to break the feelings I was experiencing. I wanted this to go on forever.

Slowly, he raised his hand to cup my cheek. His skin was hot, his fingers gentle. He traced his fingertips lightly across my jawline before brushing them over my throat. The emotions became too intense, and I needed space to breathe.

I took a step back and looked down, my breaths ragged. I glanced up to gauge the Prince's reaction, hoping I hadn't offended him. Jian was staring at me, his cheeks flushed and his lips still parted. His hand remained outstretched where my face had been, and he lowered it slowly.

He tried to collect himself and gave a stiff bow. "Forgive my forwardness, Elyanna."

I shook my head, my mouth too dry to form words, and my mind spinning and unable to focus. I kept my eyes fixed on his face: the straight nose, the high cheekbones and the delicate set of his jaw. The way his hair rebelled against the neat way he dressed and those eyes which were normally so cold, now so open and vulnerable. I drank in how he moved, always so careful, yet strong and purposeful. I felt a gentle yet powerful warmth flood me, starting from my stomach and reaching all the way to my fingertips. A warmth that pooled behind my eyes and made me want to cry, to laugh, to dance, to bask. I wondered if this was what love felt like. If so, it was glorious, and he was mine. My betrothed. Soon to be my husband forever.

I couldn't help but smile, and the action broke the intensity of our shared gaze. He returned my smile and it was warm and tender. Then he grinned widely and looked down, rubbing his chin. I desperately wanted to know what he was thinking, experiencing, but wasn't sure how to ask.

"I thought you were going to kiss me then." My heart dropped as if it couldn't believe I'd said something so bold.

He brought his eyes back up and they flicked to my lips. "Would you like me too?"

A jolt both hot and cold shot down my spine. "I… I don't know."

He raised an eyebrow and took a step forward taking my hands and enveloping them in his. My heart thudded so hard I was sure he would hear it. The corner of his lip twisted up. "That's a strange answer."

"It's an honest answer." I couldn't look him in the eyes. His whole presence bordered on too much.

He bent his head down. "I would like to kiss you. But only with your permission."

I forced my eyes up and met his gaze but still couldn't reply. I focused on breathing and trying to keep the giddiness at bay. His face was already so close.

I realized with sudden panic, that I didn't know how lovers kissed. What if I didn't do it right? I wasn't sure I could do anything right when I felt like this; it was hard enough to form a sentence. What if I was a disappointment and it broke the spell?

His face leaned closer and I panicked and blurted, "I don't know how."

He gave a breathy laugh. "Well, we have a lifetime to practice."

The warm sensation flooded me again, melting me from the inside out, causing me to lean on him, nestling myself in his arms as he embraced me. I tipped my head up and his lips found mine, soft and smooth and warm. The kiss was brief, tender, gentle. He moved his face away and I frowned up at him. "That's it?" I spoke before I could think.

He barked a breathy laugh. "I'll try not to be offended by that comment." He shook his hair from his forehead. "You are making no sense. You didn't even know if you wanted to be kissed."

I backtracked in panic. "No, no, it was wonderful. I just thought it was more complicated than that."

His lips twisted into a smirk. "I've never heard anyone describe a kiss as complicated before."

I looked down and felt my cheeks heat. His arms hadn't released me and kept me firmly against his chest as if now that he had me, he was never going to let me go. He was so strong it was like he shut the entire world away.

"You're very beautiful, Elyanna." The words exhilarated and shamed me. He found me beautiful. *Me*, not Elyanna. This was between us and had nothing to do with her. He had never even met her. I wasn't lying to him, not really. Nobody here would ever know, and Elyanna was just my new name. This was between him and the real me. My mask didn't come into it.

Still, I wished he would use my real name. I looked down, inwardly cursing that my secret was spoiling something so perfect. Something I wanted more than anything I'd ever wanted before: an honest marriage with him.

His fingers found my chin and lifted it. "What's wrong?"

I forced a smile and took his wrist. "I'm happy to be marrying you, Prince Jian."

He grinned. "Well, you've certainly caught me off guard."

"In a good way, I hope?"

His smile softened, and he placed a second kiss on my forehead.

My heart raced harder than ever, and I felt like I was going to start crying with joy. I opened my mouth but no words came. He relaxed his arms and turned so I stood beside him. "Come, we should find some food before I go to the parade ground."

I nodded and had to concentrate on walking properly Everything was perfect, I wasn't going to let my secret corrupt this. I didn't want to ruin the best thing I'd been given in my life.

I pretended not to notice Hai Rong's hasty step back from the door as we passed through. I didn't even want to contemplate what he might have heard.

THE WINTER BALL

I decided to wear Elyanna's gold dress to the ball. The one she adored. I'd never felt the urge to wear it before, but after Jian had kissed me, I wanted to be extravagant, eye catching, glorious. I didn't want his eyes to leave me the whole night.

Ruo was looking at me with an amused expression as she laced up the dress. "Are you thinking about Jian?"

"Hmm?" I asked, trying to catch her meaning.

"You're smiling to yourself again. You've barely stopped talking all day, and now you're suddenly quiet. You're imagining his reaction to you in this dress, aren't you?"

I felt the heat rise up my neck. "Sorry, I've been so distracted. It must be irritating for you."

She chuckled as she wove sapphires into my hair. I had never seen them before. "He's to be your husband next week, dear. You can daydream about him as much as you like. It's quite allowed."

I shifted at her boldness. "Does it last, these feelings?

254

Is this excitement and..." I waved my hand in a circle, unable to describe how I felt when I saw him. "Is this what love is?"

Ruo grinned. "Do you mean, will your heart leap every time you see him? I doubt it. But I never stopped feeling warm and safe and strong with my husband. Like being with him empowered me and made me capable of achieving anything I set my mind to. Love is something that grows with time if you nurture it well. You find your attraction moves deeper and deeper beyond the physical, until you love each other's very souls. But a healthy marriage takes work. A lot more work than falling in love."

I snorted. "Well, that wasn't exactly easy either. If I am in love, I mean. I'm pretty sure he's not, but I don't know how I'm supposed to tell."

Ruo chuckled. "Give it time, dear. The two of you have spent very little time together. You will learn to read his feelings soon enough."

I spun Falada's mane around my wrist. "I mean he wants to spend time with me and er... embrace me. But I know that is not always love. I just hope the feelings he has don't fade as quickly as they came."

Ruo fastened a sapphire necklace around my throat. "Prince Jian didn't want to like you, Elyanna. In fact, he was determined not to. His decision to be open with you isn't a flight of fancy. He is careful and deliberate. He thinks through everything deeply. I don't think you have anything to fear."

Only Elyanna. And what if Jian found out the truth after we were married? Would he still like me then?

Surely he would see my old name and title were irrelevant?

Ruo smiled at my reflection in the mirror. "These jewels were the Queen's. They were part of her dowry and she wore them to the ball where she met the King. She asked me to give them to you, and I thought it apt for you to wear them tonight.

I touched the silver and blue at my throat and hair and grinned. They highlighted my eyes and the silver in my hair. "They're beautiful."

"Now remember not to drink too much wine. And that Jian does not like to dance. Don't be hurt if he doesn't want to dance the night away with you. He's never liked to be the center of attention. He can still greatly admire you while you're sat down."

I nodded, though I hoped I wouldn't have to be the one to ask him, this time.

I helped Ruo get dressed in her own gown, and insisted she wear some of my diamonds in her greying hair. I even attempted her makeup, but her skin tone was different from mine and her almond eyes a different shape. In the end she battered my hands away with a laugh, cleaned her face, and merely reddened her lips.

Jeremiah, Cai Hong and Hai Rong had dressed up too, though they were still armed. I complimented each of them and told them all to have a good time.

Jeremiah grinned at me.

"What?" I asked him, as we walked down the bare corridor.

"I've never seen you this happy. It's like it's bubbling out of you. It suits you."

I elbowed him. "You've only known me two months, and they've hardly been my finest. I'm starting to believe things will get better."

Jeremiah nodded. "I think that's what everyone here needs to believe."

His words dampened my mood a little. Was it right for me to be happy after what had happened to Han and Falada?

Ruo seemed to catch the change in my mood and hooked her arm through mine. "Don't overthink things, dear. Tonight is a time for joy and feasting when we shut the dark thoughts of winter away. It is a time to focus on what we have, and not what we must overcome before the days lengthen again."

We reached the stairs to the great hall, and thoughts of my reply were lost in the pull of the music and of the man who I knew waited within. I clenched Ruo's arm, and she chuckled as she escorted me inside.

The room had been transformed. The fires made it as smoky as ever, but torches and candles lit the dark corners and bright red and white berries had been hung from the roof beams. There was no feast, like there had been to welcome me, but instead guests grazed from tables against the walls. The women wore bright colors, silk or velvet with long sleeves that pooled on the floor. Tight waists were created by broad sashes of painted silk. The men wore dark traditional robes with wide shoulders, and panels that fell to the knees. I had never seen such a show of finery here. A nod to grander times long past. However, there were still a few men who wore the military uniform. And one was looking straight at me.

I met Jian's eyes as he stood by himself in the far corner, and I attempted to smile as the nerves twisted my stomach again. He started towards me, and I relaxed a little in relief. At least this time he wouldn't ignore me in front of everyone.

Ruo patted my arm. "Oh look, there's Changying. I need to talk to her about her son. I shall see you later." She unhooked her arm, winked, and disappeared into the crowd. My guards had made themselves scarce too by the time Jian reached me, and we were surrounded by a halo of space.

Jian gave me a small, sharp bow and offered his arm. I took it, my heart pounding and my mouth dry, and he led me deeper into the room. He was wearing the cloak I had embroidered for him and the swan fell directly over his heart. The sound of fiddles intensified, and I had to lean into him to catch his words. "You're looking very beautiful tonight, Elyanna."

I smiled at him, enjoying the rush of emotions caused by his words. Nobody had ever called me beautiful before him, and I wasn't quite sure how to respond so I turned to humor. "And you look exactly the same as always." I laughed to show I meant no offense.

He straightened. "I spent an extra hour shining my buttons."

I gave him a sideways look and gathered from his expression that he wasn't being serious. I grinned.

A new voice distracted me. "Did Jian really just

attempt a joke? Spirits, what have you done to him, Elyanna?"

I turned to see Captain Jun had approached. I wished he'd left us alone like everyone else, but still appreciated he was Jian's closest friend here. I needed to befriend him too. His hair had been cropped even shorter than Jian's, and I thought it only drew attention to his scar.

He passed me a glass of wine, and I smiled my thanks. "I hope you're not here to steal Jian away from me like you normally do."

He spread his arms. "It's the Winter Ball, Princess. Tonight is the one night all work is forbidden for everyone. It is why even the servants are dressed to dance and everyone helps themselves." He leaned in and gave me a secretive grin. "This evening he's all yours."

I shifted my feet as heat prickled my cheeks and Jian cleared his throat. "Elyanna, would you like to dance?"

I suppressed a smile and gave him a mock frown along with my best impression of his voice. "Do you know this one? No? I suggest, then, that this is not the first one you attempt." I dismissed him with my hand. "You can ask me again later. I may possibly deign to dance with you then." I shrugged. "If it's a short one."

He laughled and slipped his arm around my waist, pulling me in. His voice was lowered and playful, but sincere. "I know all the dances, Elyanna. I will dance every single one with you, if you wish."

I frowned at him, trying to not let him know how breathless he was making me. "But you hate dancing."

"Not with you."

My reply fled.

It was Jun's turn to clear his throat. "By the beasts, I think I may need some more wine."

A hand touched my arm, and I turned to see who the owner was. I was surprised to see Changying dressed in a traditional dress, if a lot less grand than those of the nobility. Her expression was concerned, and I took her hand, turning to Jian. "Excuse me a moment."

The joy faded a little from his eyes, but he nodded, his face becoming stony. The warmth from his arm disappeared as it left my waist and the cool air of the castle replaced it. I took a deep breath to clear my mind and let Changying lead me away from the noise of the fiddles to where she could easily talk.

"I'm sorry to disturb you, Highness, but something happened this morning I think you should know about." Her eyes seemed troubled.

I leant closer to her. "Go on."

"Well you know you were asking about the families in Stonekeep with Syberan blood? Well… three Syberans were found dead this morning. It looks like they hung themselves. Nobody knows why."

All the warmth and joy felt sucked out of me in one cold blow. "Who?"

"The couple were cowherds. The son was a goose boy."

My mind raced. "Did any of the family remain?"

"A daughter. A goose girl as well. She has disappeared."

My heart sank, "Tell me about her."

Changying spread her hands helplessly. "I know

very little. They were a private family. The boy was called Conrad. I never met the girl. She and her brother were in charge of the care of the geese all year around. They took them out to the fields and marshland when there was no snow and brought food to them in winter months. It's lonely work and they had few friends."

"Did she have white hair?"

Changying shook her head. "There has never been anyone in Stonekeep with white hair except you."

I took both of Changying's hands. "Thank you for telling me this. But please think carefully. When was the first time you heard about the daughter?"

She shrugged. "I only learnt about the family when you started asking questions. I've seen the couple around for years of course. And I knew it was Syberan children who cared for the geese. But I must be honest, I'd never taken much notice before, Highness."

I forced a smile. "Thank you, Changying. Please let me know if you learn anything else or if the girl is found."

The lady bowed and left me. I walked to the wall to steady myself. If Elyanna was in Stonekeep, there were few places she could hide when her face shape and features looked different to the Borderlanders'. Getting a family to quietly take her in made sense. Maybe in return for money. But when she was ready to make herself known, she wouldn't want them there in case they knew too much. Maybe she had let something slip. Could she have staged their suicides? If so, that meant she was ready to move tonight.

That meant she was here, in the castle. Maybe in this room.

I scanned the faces around me for any Syberan features. Any hint of pale hair. But there were too many people in the smoky room. I should have taken more precautions and been more prepared. But it had been so easy to be distracted by Jian. Even now, all I wanted to do was forget about Elyanna and dance with the Prince until dawn.

I wrung my hands as I kept examining each face, focusing on those with taller stature. I couldn't tell anyone else without risking my identity. I couldn't explain to Jian without bringing everything crashing down.

My fingers twitched for my sword hilt, but it wasn't there. It was too big to look good over a ball gown with wide skirts, and so I'd left it in my room. That seemed foolish now. Elyanna had turned into a murderer, she had always had it in her. She would be out for my blood too.

I could go back to my rooms and get my sword before anyone noticed. It would be good to have space to think.

I slipped through a servants' door and took swift steps to the nearest staircase. I hurried up and turned into an empty corridor.

"Hello, Brianna."

I whirled, my heart in my mouth. *That voice*. That awful voice.

"Elyanna." The word came out as a whisper. I realized I'd made a terrible mistake leaving the ballroom alone. I'd been so eager to not let anybody find out what was going on, I hadn't been thinking straight.

The Princess grinned. Her hair was bound in a ragged, faded turban and a thick fur coat hid her slender frame, but I would recognize her anywhere. All at once, I was a small girl living in fear of her every whim.

"Do you have any idea how stupid you look in that dress?" She let out a stifled giggle. "I've come for what is mine. You can't imagine what I have had to endure to be here." She swept her hands over her dull coat in disgust. "What I have suffered and how I have waited. But, did you really think you would steal the title of queen from me? *You*?"

I gaped at her, trying to think ahead. There had to be a way I could avoid this looming disaster. "Steal? You forced me here because you didn't want to come. You wanted to stay in Sybera in your life of luxury."

She shrugged. "I changed my mind." She unwrapped her faded turban and let her long white hair cascade to her waist. A bird sitting above our heads flapped its wings at the movement, and I glanced up to see it watching us from the shadowy rafters. Elyanna's voice regained my attention. "You have not been treated badly here. I can see that being Jian's wife is safe enough. He seems rather preoccupied by the Border, so I will be able to do what I wish. And I wish to be queen."

I took a step forward. "You can't change your mind about something like this. If they found out the truth, it would be war. Does your mother even know you're here?"

She sniggered and shook her head. "Oh, Bria. They're not going to find out the truth. We're going to tell them you took the role by force and left me alone to starve on the way here. The guards were in on it too, you see."

Cold shot through my body. "They will kill me."

Elyanna stepped forward with a twisted smile. "It's crazy enough that you could have the chance to be a princess. But a queen? Don't be ridiculous, Bria. You're a lady from a remote province that farms potatoes. People like you never become queen." She stepped even closer to me, until her breath tickled my skin. "You don't belong here. But I will give you one chance to save yourself." She dropped her voice to a gleeful whisper. "Run."

My heart was tearing itself to pieces, terror freezing my stomach. Then one thought condensed in my mind. "You killed Falada, even though he trusted you. Even though you were bonded."

She tilted her head. "I will kill whoever I need to, to get what I want. It's really not that hard. So I would advise you to run, Brianna." Her hand dug into her skirts and pulled out a long thin knife. I stepped back and cursed again that I didn't have my sword. The ball gown would significantly hamper my movements as well.

"One," smiled Elyanna.

I dug in my feet and took a deep breath. How could I leave Jian? And Jeremiah, Cai Hong and Hai Rong?

"Two."

But she was right. I had no right to be here. My relationship with all of them was built on lies. My relationship with Jian was fake. He had no idea who I really was, and I wasn't sure I could bear lying to him any longer. I had nothing to recommend myself.

"Three. That's the end of the warning." She launched at me, slashing the air.

Part of me wanted to attack her with the full force of my fury and grief over Falada. Using my nails if I had to. But I needed to stay calm if I was to work a way out of this. Or as calm as I possibly could with panic threatening to build up inside. I dodged the blade and aimed a blow for her arm. It hit in the fold of her elbow, but somehow she managed to maintain her grip on the hilt. She was stronger than I remembered, and faster.

She turned again and slashed at my face. I ducked and kicked out at her legs, sending her falling. She cried out as she fell, but she rolled back to her feet at once. My skirts were tangled from the attack, and I had to stagger back to upright, dangerously close to falling myself. Now she was determined, she was a much better fighter than in our training sessions back in Hava. And she had a knife.

She ran at me with a screech, and I knocked her knife hand up and over my shoulder. I turned and twisted her arm, disarming her. The knife clattered to the floor. Elyanna grabbed my hair and yanked it back, pulling the braids free. The Queen's sapphires sparkled in the torchlight as they flew to the floor. She yanked harder, until my body threatened to collapse backwards. Her other hand grasped for my neck. I hit her full in the face with the heel of my hand, the angle awkward. She didn't let go, and I elbowed her in the throat.

She crumpled, gasping for air, making a horrible rasping sound. Her nose was bleeding, vibrant red across her snow-pale skin. Her fingers fumbled towards the knife. I took two swift steps and prized it from her grasp. I stood over her, panting, and for the first time in my life she was at my mercy.

She glared up at me with real hatred, and I gripped the knife harder. What should I do with her? She was a monster. She had killed Falada. She enjoyed the pain of others. She had locked me in a barrel and left me for hours when I had tried to save a kitten. I should kill her. It was the right thing to do. The logical thing. Then she wouldn't be able to ruin my life any longer. Elyanna spat at my feet and I took a step back. She croaked a laugh.

Could I do it?

I stared at her pathetic form and leveled the blade at my former mistress. I needed to think. I needed time to think. Queen Geraldina would find out she had come here eventually. I didn't want the alliance to be broken, let alone war. But I couldn't let her live. She would never stop trying to kill me and become queen.

As a collected calm settled over me, I noticed a flicker of fear in Elyanna's eyes. For the first time in my life I had the power to make my own decision.

A door opened behind me and I heard heavy boots approach, but I didn't dare take my eyes off Elyanna. They must have heard her scream. She smiled at me, but when she saw my confidence was unwavering, she glared at me, uncertain.

A hand grabbed my arm and I looked to see Jian, sword drawn. His face was a strange mixture of alarm and relief and his eyes sought mine, even as he leveled his sword at the real Princess. Despite everything, I felt a warmth stir in my stomach. "Elyanna, are you all right?"

I had a fierce desire to kiss him, to drink in his strength and get lost in his arms so everything else melted away. I wanted his touch to erase Elyanna's, his words to drown hers. But my world was crashing down around us and I needed to think straight. I nodded and didn't meet his eyes. My deceit was staring him straight in the face.

Captain Jun and Cai Hong ran between me and Elyanna, and studied her with cold eyes. The Princess staggered to her feet, wiping her bloody nose on her sleeve.

Her earlier amusement was gone. "I am the real Princess Elyanna. You have all been tricked. Put your swords away."

None of the men hesitated. They must trust me so deeply, they never even questioned whether she was telling the truth. Guilt twisted my insides as Jian's grip on my arm tightened protectively. Elyanna stared at me with such hatred, I looked away.

Maybe I should tell them to lock her up, so I could have space to think. She had the white hair of the Old Blood. They were bound to become curious about her identity eventually. I would have to come up with more lies. I bet nobody in all of Hava knew where she was. Queen Geralidina would never have allowed her to come in this reckless fashion. It could be months until she found out she was missing. Eagle's Pass was closed, Sybera couldn't interfere. I could tell Jian she had murdered Falada and have her executed. Maybe write to Queen Geraldina to say she had perished in the snow with her men. I had the power to defeat her forever.

But that meant more lies. Lies that would confuse the Borderlanders.

Elyanna staggered forward. "I said, put your swords away! Arrest her before her schemes can do any more damage. She is my maid. She usurped me on the journey here and left me alone to die. I only survived by getting a job as a goose girl."

I turned my back on her.

"Don't let her escape," Jian ordered and pulled me away into another empty corridor. I looked back and saw Cai Hong clamp his hands down on Elyanna's arms while Jun checked her for weapons. Her eyes flashed pure fury. She seemed so small now. The smallest she had been in her life.

Jian closed the door behind us and sheathed his sword. His presence was so strong and comforting, but he wasn't meant to be mine. Our relationship was built on lies. Every emotion I had was twisted with guilt. "Elyanna, do you know what's going on?"

I stepped away from him and opened the window shutters into the dark night. Cold wind buffeted my face, clearing my mind. I gasped as snow hit my cheeks, but I didn't step back. This was my decision, and I chose not to live a lie anymore. I wanted my relationship with Jian to be genuine. I didn't want to get caught in layers of lies about how Elyanna had died or ended up locked away, when Queen Geraldina found out.

A lump formed in my throat as I realized I had to tell Jian. This was an impossible situation and it affected him most of all. This was his wife, his alliance, his resources for the Border. His marriage. He shouldn't be forced by lies. He deserved to know the truth and make his own decision. It was the right thing to do. And maybe there was the chance he would still choose me when he realized Elyanna had fooled him in the first place.

I closed the window and took a deep breath, turning to the Prince who was standing patiently. I couldn't meet his eyes, my insides squirming. Jian's warm hand cupped my chin to lift it, and his breath heated my face. He was so close, like he was trying to shield me from the world. I so badly wanted him to be mine, but he never truly would be until he knew the truth.

"Elyanna, don't worry," he breathed. "Nobody will believe her. She is clearly lying. I'll have her removed at once."

I removed his hand and took a step back, ice running through my body.

"Jian, I need to tell you something. She's not lying. She really is Princess Elyanna, not me."

His lips turned from scoff to laugh, then the expression froze as he saw my face. The smile twisted into a confused frown and he shook his head. He seemed to struggle to speak. "I'm sorry?"

I just looked at him. The hurt in his eyes ripped through my heart like a physical blow. I reached out to take his hands, but he jerked them away and took a step back. "Who are you?" His voice was terribly cold.

I took a deep breath and looked at the buttons on his coat. "You know who I am, Jian. The only thing that is different is my name."

His coldness was replaced by anger, he took a step forward and raised his voice. "I asked you, who you are!"

I felt a stab of fear down my spine, not because of his anger, but because I might lose him. Lose the last thing I had left. My chest tightened, making it hard to breathe. "Lady Brianna Silver of Gilava. I am… was Princess Elyanna's lady-in-waiting."

He stared at me for an eternity, then turned his dear face away from me in disgust. "So what she is saying is true? You stole her place and left her to tend geese."

"No! No, Jian, you must believe me." Tears were threatening to break now, and I tried to push them back so I could explain everything. I needed him to look at me, that raging coldness to soften.

He angled his whole body away from me and faced the wall. "When addressing nobility, you should always use a title." He bit off each word, and now he was making my anger flare at his pettiness.

I almost shouted at his back. "Queen Geraldina made me take her place. She was scared you would murder her daughter, and Elyanna refused to wed you. They dressed me up as her, threatened to kill my parents, and sent me instead. I had no choice. They hoped you would be none the wiser. Now Eylanna realizes she could be queen and has changed her mind. I suspect her mother thinks she's still safe in the Winter Palace."

Jian swung around and flung up his hands, his chest heaving, but his voice was dangerously quiet. "You have lied to me about everything. Why should I believe you now?"

I held his gaze and didn't flinch. "Because deep down you know I'm telling the truth. You know me, Jian, the real me. I am unchanged."

Jian sagged, breathing heavily. "Do you have any idea what you have done?" He looked at me, defeated. "I have been a fool. I fell for your every trick like an idiot. I let you in when I promised myself I would keep you at arm's length! How could you play with me like that? Play with two whole kingdoms and risk a war that could claim thousands of lives? You have caused so much pain with your stupid game."

I shook my head, torment exploding in my chest. I tried to step close to him again so he could see the sincerity in my face. "This is not my fault. I care about you, Jian. It was never a game. All I ever wanted was for everyone to be happy."

He gazed at me for a moment, his eyes drinking in every detail. "Then you're an idiot," he spat. He turned and swiped a vase off the nearest table before striding from the hall. The sound of breaking china accosted me as it bounced from the empty stone walls.

I collapsed to my knees, surrounded by silken skirts and shards of pottery, and wept.

THE PRICE OF FREEDOM

My wrists were tied with coarse rope, and two guards I didn't recognize escorted me to the hall through back passages to hear what the King and Queen would do with me. The castle was silent, everyone asleep after last night festivities, despite it being hours past dawn. I was dressed in a simple brown dress and hadn't seen Ruo or my usual guards since coming to the ball. The same two guards had collected me from the corridor where Jian had left me last night and had shut me in a small room with a pallet bed until the sounds of the festivities had long died. I was cold, tired and very alone.

I had hoped Jian would return to the room once his head had cooled and talk things through. I had been wrong. Maybe I had misread his feelings towards me completely. But at least my conscience was clear now.

The guards prodded me into the shadows in the corner of the hall, the tallest one laying a heavy hand on my shoulder. They had taken the royal signet ring from my finger, and a female soldier had searched me thoroughly and even removed the bracelet of Falada's hair, despite my protests. I imagined the King and Queen had been discussing my fate with Elyanna and listening to her lies. And Jian would just let it all happen.

I had told him the whole truth and it was as if I meant nothing to him.

I watched the people bathed in sunlight in the center of the hall and felt as if I'd been thrown into a different world. Jian stood stiffly, his face completely blank, but distracted from the others. His skin was pale, his cheeks gaunter than before. I could tell he was hurting, and my heart nudged me to run to him and comfort him, but that wasn't my role anymore. I had deceived him, and now he didn't want me.

And I had let her win. I could have lied, and he would have believed me. He had trusted me completely. They had all been in my power and I had chosen to give it all away.

"We're just glad you're here and safe," the Queen was saying to Elyanna, who was now clean and well dressed. A falcon sat on my former mistress's shoulder and spread its wings as Fei grasped the Princess's hands.

The Princess's face was a mask of long-suffering innocence, though she kept glancing at Jian, annoyed that he ignored her, instead of fawning like everyone else. For the first time in my life I felt a stab of jealousy towards my former mistress. She was going to marry him, have him, have everything. His joy was so precious because he had had so little of it, and she would ruin his life. She was the last person in the world I wanted him to marry. But he was choosing her and that was his decision. I clenched my fists in my skirts.

"Your maid must be severely punished to make sure this never happens again," said the King. "Her actions amount to treason towards two countries." My mind snapped back to their conversation. Spirits, Elyanna would kill me just for fun, especially after I had bloodied her nose. Now she saw that Jian was distant to her when he hadn't been with me, she was going to be angry and spiteful as well.

Elyanna turned to me with bright eyes and a triumphant posture. There was no sign of our fight now. "Indeed. We need to make an example of her. She left me to die in the wilderness so she could take my place. She even killed my Spirit-Horse so it wouldn't tell the truth." She cocked her head and pursed her lips, enjoying the suspense. "She should be placed inside a barrel of nails and dragged through the streets by a horse until she's dead."

Cold terror tore through my numbness and up my spine. The barrel was forming around me, my legs screaming from cramp. Splinters under my nails. Blood in my mouth. Too hot, hard to breathe. Only now I could also feel the nails stabbing, biting, tearing in the thunderous half-dark.

I took my habitual deep breaths. Not again, not again, not again…

The King's voice echoed from far away. "If that is…"

"No." Jian's voice was forceful, and he was suddenly very much present in the room. The barrel was gone, and I sagged against the guard, waiting for my strength to return. Jian still refused to look at me. My stomach twisted in agony at the coldness in his voice. "That is too public," he said stiffly. "We don't want this talked about any more than it already is. The maid will be disposed of quietly."

Elyanna frowned and opened her mouth to object, but Jian held out his hand to stop her.

"This means that the wedding can go ahead as planned. No one needs to know that the bride has changed, and nothing needs to be delayed. All the arrangements will remain, and it can happen in six days."

His words hit me like a blow to the chest, and I struggled to keep my breathing calm. Jian's words pleased Elyanna and she nodded with a sweet smile. "Yes, let's not cause a fuss. Though we'll have to have a new dress made. I'm much slimmer than Brianna, and knowing her, she'll have ordered something too frilly and tasteless. I will need to see the meal and decoration plans too, as I can't imagine she would have known what is appropriate."

She continued on, having already forgotten me, and the King waved a hand for the guards to remove me. As I was pushed from the room, Jian gave me one cold, angry glance that rocked my whole body, before turning back to his new bride.

❄

I HADN'T REALIZED there were dungeons below the castle. There were no fires here, only the occasional torch, and the sound of the wind howled outside the walls. A tiny window high on the wall let in occasional flurries of snow. It was barely bigger than my hand. Thankfully I'd been given my fur cloak and a woolen blanket, but none of my other possessions. I wondered what would happen to them now. I supposed they always had been Elyanna's, except for my sword. I would miss that sword. It represented the few times in my life when I had felt strong.

I cradled my knees and tried to prepare for what would come next, but Jian invaded my every thought. Jian and Elyanna. She would be queen and her cruelty would have no bounds. She would get away with everything. He wouldn't prioritize her and that would only make things worse. She would punish and hurt him every way she could to get her revenge.

And he had just given up on me. That hurt most of all.

I had been so stupid. Perhaps I could have stopped all this from happening. I had always sought to placate those stronger than me rather than follow my instincts. I had done everything Elyanna and Queen Geraldina had desired. I had fought to make Queen Fei and Jian like me and please them. I had done it to keep myself safe, but it hadn't worked. Falada was dead and I was utterly alone. I should have done what was right and told Jian the truth in the first place rather than trick him.

The door at the top of the stairs creaked open and quick steps pattered towards me. I looked up and was surprised to see Jian heading to my cell alone. A burst of hope rippled through me and I rushed to the bars, then I saw his expression. I bit my lip to hide my emotions and gripped the bars. He still wouldn't look at me. Did he really hate me that much?

I forced myself to stand taller. "Why are you here?" I asked.

He held up a leather pack. "I've packed food, water, money and clothes for you. Your sword is there too. A guard will escort you out of the city, then you are not to turn back. I suggest you ride far away."

I pressed my forehead to the bars. "Jian, you can't marry her. She's a murderer."

The Prince held up his hand. "I don't want to hear it," he snapped.

"Is that really the woman you want as queen of the Borderlands? She could do so much damage."

His eyes remained stubbornly on the wall, his features set in a restrained mask. "Our marriage is a political arrangement and no more. I long accepted I could do my role alone."

"I'm sorry," I whispered.

He looked down at the floor, pursing his lips. "Why did you tell me the truth? You could have told me she was anyone, and I would have believed you."

I hugged myself. "I didn't want to lie to you anymore. I hoped you would understand."

He sighed and gripped one of the prison bars with white knuckles. "I do understand, Ely… Lady Brianna. I believe you. Mother does too. Though we no longer trust you." He spoke through gritted teeth. "But you must understand. The Border has to take priority. I can't sacrifice the money from Sybera so I can marry you. I must marry the true Princess or risk losing it all."

I nodded through tears and pushed one hand through the bars to touch his arm. "Be careful," I whispered.

He didn't reply but unlocked the gate and shoved the pack into my hands.

"Don't come back." He muttered the words as if they were nothing, and they tore apart my soul.

I couldn't reply. Anger, hopelessness, shame, and confusion made a bitter tonic in my stomach. He turned and ran back up the stairs and was gone. I kicked the gate of my cell and let it clatter against the wall, then I clenched my fists. He had made his choice. So be it. I couldn't blame him. He had always told me I would come second to his country.

I didn't need him. The pain in my heart cried out for comfort, but now I didn't have Falada either. I had nobody.

"This way," came a male voice to my left.

I jumped and squinted into the shadows, seeing the taller of my guards by an open door. His posture was formal and stiff and didn't betray what he thought about Jian letting me sneak from the palace.

He turned as I approached and led me down a narrow corridor without a word. The air grew even colder, until the floor and walls were slick with ice. I slipped and stumbled against the wall, but the guard didn't slow or hold out a hand to steady me. What did he think of me? What did they all think of me?

He led me to a small, empty room and gestured

inside. I frowned in confusion. Wasn't he supposed to be leading me out of Stonekeep?

"Wait here," he said gruffly and pushed something in my palm. I looked down as he shut the door behind him. I didn't hear the click of a lock. Tears pricked my eyes. In my hand was Falada's bracelet. I slipped it back onto my wrist.

The room was empty except for an unlit metal stove built into the wall and a second door which was locked. Sunlight peeked around the edges, and I guessed it led to the outside. Maybe this was some sort of respite room for the guards to make warm drinks when on long shifts. There was a pile of wood in the corner, but it was covered in dust and cobwebs. I dropped my pack and sank to the floor, tears wracking my body as I thought of the way Jian had looked at me. I had nowhere to go. Nobody to turn to.

The strength left my legs as soon as they didn't have to bear my weight, and I rested my face in my knees, letting my skirts soak up my tears. I'd been playing an imaginary game. Of course it would go wrong. Girls like me weren't meant to marry princes. I was lucky to be alive and not being tortured to death as part of Elyanna's sadistic revenge. But it hurt so much. A great emptiness stretched in front of me and ate its way to my center. How was I going to form a life, a future, for myself from the dust of ashes?

There was a strange clanking noise inside the oven, distracting me from my self-pity. I brushed the tears from my face with my sleeve and frowned at the closed black metal door. The banging and scraping happened again, and I crawled over and opened the door.

The stove was deep, built right into the wall, and I realized the other side had a second door so that one person could place food or wood into the oven, and a second could take it out in another room. That door was open merely a sliver, letting in golden light. The oven itself was empty, traces of ash streaking its gridded floor.

"Brianna? That is your name, is it not?" I froze and leaned into the oven. That was the Queen's voice. How was she there in the other room? Her voice was far colder than she'd ever spoken to me before.

"Yes, Your Majesty."

"Forgive me for the strangeness of the situation, but I promised Princess Elyanna I would not see you. This way I can honestly say I have not laid eyes on you and not spoken to you directly, merely to an oven."

I shifted, not sure how to reply to such a strange admission.

"Tell me the whole truth as clearly as you can. Leave nothing out and do not lie to me. If you do, you will not leave this room alive, whatever Jian has arranged."

I let it all come tumbling out, trying not to let the words catch in my raw throat. As I progressed through the story, the more stupid I felt at ever believing this could have worked out in my favor. How could have I upheld a lie for the rest of my life to those I cared about most?

There was silence on the other side of the oven, and for a moment, I was worried she had gone. Then she said, "Just because you didn't come up with the initial idea, does not free you from blame. You still came here and willfully deceived us all. I wish you had told us."

I bit my lip and cradled my head in my hands. "I couldn't risk damaging the relationship between our two countries. I thought you might kill me and declare war on Sybera for trying to deceive you."

"We are used to managing complex political situations. Did you really think this beyond us?"

"I was scared, your Majesty. Queen Geraldina threatened to kill my parents. She was going to blame them for the flooding and loss of life on their lands."

A heavy sigh echoed through the stove. "Your feelings for my son are real?"

"I admire him very much. I swear I never meant to hurt him."

She paused. "You have sent him to a dark place, Brianna. It is dangerous to give a man hope and then take it away."

The cold was eating through my limbs into my chest. "I... I am so sorry."

"Your place isn't here, girl. But I realize this has caused you pain too. Perhaps in a different life we could have been true friends. Go now. Watch your back but be free of this mess. If you want to stop causing pain and trouble, stay far away and let Elyanna think you're dead. Don't try to contact my son. Go and do good in the world."

I gripped the sides of the oven. "But what about her? She is dangerous and deceitful and cruel. Not to mention a murderer. I'm sure she killed the Syberan family in Stonekeep as well as Falada. You must stop her from killing anyone else. What if she tries to kill Jian?"

Another pause. "We have prepared for the likes of her. She was closer to what we were expecting. It was you, in fact, who was the surprise. Spoilt younger daughters who have always learnt to have their way rarely make good queens. But they can be managed. We must pretend to accept her story as true, because to do otherwise would start a war. And Jian wants the money to protect his soldiers."

I nodded and wiped the tears from my face, forgetting the ash on my hands. Their affairs had nothing to do with me now. "I… I hope he can find happiness."

"So do I. He will find his first love embraces him again: the love of the battlefield. The admiration of his men. The thrill of escaping death. He will find his place again."

I nodded, imagining him fighting alone, reckless, surrounded by monsters. I shook my head. He wasn't mine to comfort or protect anymore. I had to let him go.

"Goodbye, your Majesty."

"I have a parting gift for you." There was a soft thud inside the oven. "Next time when you see your reflection, be proud of what you are becoming. Don't let lies determine your future."

"Thank you. Farewell," I whispered, and reached into the oven.

The far door of the stove clanged shut, and I saw a large key resting on the metal grid. Beside it was a velvet pouch. I pulled on the draw strings and fished out two silver disk earrings, polished to a high shine. The reflection caught one of my eyes, red and smeared with tear-stained kohl. I sighed and placed them into my belt pouch. I took the key and forced my frozen legs to walk to the outside door.

People got their hearts broken all the time. It was part of growing up. I had to move past this, beat it. But I'd never imagined it would hurt so much. I clenched my fists. Pain became numb with time, and until then I would distract myself. This wouldn't break me, just become part of who I was. Like Elyanna's barrel. The pieces of me would just fit together differently afterwards.

But how I wished I could turn back time.

I turned the key with numb fingers and stumbled out into the snow. The door led straight out into the fields that hugged the town wall in the shadow of the rising slopes of forest. I turned to close the door and saw a silent figure detach himself from the side of the wall closer to the town gate.

I squinted but would recognize those brown curls anywhere. My heart warmed.

"Jeremiah, you shouldn't be here. You should stay with *her*." I couldn't bring myself to say Elyanna's name.

He scratched the back of his head as he stopped in front of me. "I'm pretty sure she wants me dead, actually. Thinks I understand too much of the truth. Prince Jian hinted you would be here."

I squeezed his arm. "I'm sorry I never told you who I was."

He shrugged. "Queen Geraldina sent me to guard

you without question, so I shall. It was you she said was her daughter, not the other Elyanna."

I smiled warmly at him and a pressure built behind my eyes. "Thank you. I don't want to face this alone."

He adjusted his sword hilt and shifted his feet. "Well, I never thought Prince Jian was right for you, anyway. He was rude and arrogant."

I held up the palm of my hand. "I know you're trying to make me feel better, Jeremiah, but can we not talk about him? Not at all?"

He grinned. "Every memory of him has gone from my mind." He turned in the snow. "But you might struggle to erase him from theirs." He nodded back towards the castle. Two men dressed in black were riding through the snow towards us, each leading a second horse. Cai Hong and Hai Rong.

"What are you doing here?" I gasped as they approached.

Hai Rong shrugged. "Prince Jian didn't relieve us of our guard duty. We're still under your command."

Well, he had promised always to protect me. I decided not to overthink the words with my emotional mindset. "Thank you. I'm grateful for your company." I could have hugged them both.

Cai Hong passed his spare horse to Jeremiah. It had two loaded saddle bags and a bow and arrows on its side. "Lady Brianna, I don't know what your plans are, or where you are headed, but I must beg your leave. This is not a time to leave my wife alone with her baby, and I suspect you do not plan to return anytime soon."

I nodded to him. "Of course, Cai Hong. Thank you

for guarding me. I wouldn't want to take any of you away from here against your will, no matter what Jian says."

The guard smiled, nodded in his quiet way, and headed back to Stonekeep. I was amazed his loyalty to Jian ran so deep, he would have abandoned his family to come Spirits-know-where with me.

Hai Rong adjusted his grip on the reins, looking around. "So, where to, Lady Brianna?"

I mounted the unfamiliar horse and gazed at the endless forests of pine, the snow dusting their branches. I took a deep breath of fresh, chill air. This was what I had always wanted, wasn't it? True freedom. I had always tried to please others, going along with their goals. Elyanna, Queen Geraldina, Jian. I had bowed to their wishes in everything against all of my instincts. And still they hadn't protected me. That ended today. I would choose my own goals and learn to protect myself.

I focused on the positive train of thought, longing to suffocate the pain and emptiness inside me. Shoving down my fear and hopelessness was something I had years of training in after all. But now there would be no more scraping and bowing. I would even be able to write openly to my parents. I placed the Queen's earrings in my ears. I would be as strong as the women of Stonekeep. Able to scare away monsters merely by showing them their own reflections.

Shame it didn't work on Elyanna.

I forced a smile but couldn't resist a glance back at the castle and the bitter ache in my heart at the sight of it. I bit the inside of my cheek hard enough to taste blood. That future had never been mine. Jian had been Elyanna's, not Brianna's. Our love had been a fantasy built on deceit. It was never going to last.

Now I was nobody but me. Completely and openly me. I would find my way.

'Briaaaana...' called the child's voice, faint on the wind. *'Come, daughter of Thrum'ban."*

I turned to face it, surprised by how familiar the voice had become. I had nowhere else I could go. It would be death to show my face in Sybera. I wanted answers, and I wanted to understand. Maybe I could be the one to find out what had happened to Prince Han after all. Tama'ha had said I would be the one to know. It would be dangerous, but I badly needed a distraction right now. So much about the Spirit-Beasts was unknown.

I tied my pack to the saddle, nodded to my guards, and rode off in the direction of the call.

FEATHERS OF BLOOD

Brianna and Jian's adventure continues in 'Feathers of Blood.'

OTHER BOOKS BY ALICE IVINYA

ACKNOWLEDGMENTS

Thank you to my fantastic editor, Claire Staley, and my proofreader, Carolyn Gent. I couldn't do this without you.

Thank you so much to all the authors who have supported me while writing this. Astrid V.J, Sky Sommers, Elena Shelest, Sarah Hill, Jennifer Kropf, Lyndsey Hall, Sydney Winward, Nicolina Diana, and Jenni Sauer. I love you guys!

Special thanks also to my husband, Sam, for freeing me up to write and beta reading for me. I am one lucky chicken.

Elena Lawson, your covers are incredible! I love them so much!

Finally, thank you reader. I am so happy that you are coming on all these adventures with me.

ABOUT THE AUTHOR

Alice lives in Bristol, UK, and has loved fantasy all her life. Her favourite author is Brandon Sanderson. When she's not off gallivanting in other worlds, you can find her looking after her young son, working as a small animal vet, hanging out with her church family, or walking the best dog in the world with her husband.

www.alicegent.com

FOLLOW ME ON FACEBOOK

https://www.facebook.com/sarahsfootsteps/
https://www.facebook.com/groups/AliceIvinya/

Printed in Great Britain
by Amazon